SAVING MY ANCIENT LIFE

PALMETTO
PUBLISHING

Charleston, SC
www.PalmettoPublishing.com

Copyright © 2024 by Ken Luber

All rights reserved

Hardcover ISBN: 979-8-8229-3947-9
Paperback ISBN: 979-8-8229-3948-6
eBook ISBN: 979-8-8229-3949-3

Copyright Registration Number: TXu 2-414-091

Saving My
ANCIENT
LIFE

KEN LUBER

Chapter 1

June's early evening light still warmed the field. El rocked the baby back and forth in her arms. He made no sound. He, too, was waiting it seemed for his father to return. El's lover had left, even before the baby Bran was taken from her womb by her own mother's hands, more than two months ago.

There were no tears in the young girl's eyes, as she turned away from the field and followed the path back to the stone cottage she shared with her father and brother. The tears were buried in the meadow's earth many visits ago, tears for her mother, too, who had died shortly after Bran was born. Her seventeen-year-old brother, Ciaran, her twin, would be working on a farm throughout the weekend, but her father was home in the cottage to keep her company and help her watch over Bran. He was a carpenter, working at nearby farms and in the village an hour by horse away.

She reached for the cottage door and heard hoofbeats pounding up the trail. A dread raced through her as she turned to face two soldiers calling out her name as they dismounted their horses. She knew by their uniforms they were soldiers of the Abbot's Guard, and she knew why they were there.

"Faither," she cried out. "Faither!" By the time her father threw open the door, the soldiers were struggling with El, trying to wrest the child from her arms.

"Na," she screamed. "Ye cannae tak' mah baby!"

The helmeted soldier sneered, shoved her father back into the cottage and threw him against a chair.

"Leave mah faither," she cried out. "Take me if yi'll want, bit let me keep mah baby!"

The soldier with the yellow beard dragged her to the stone floor, ripped her dress and forced himself into her. When he got up, the other soldier handed him the wailing baby and he took his savage turn, raping her before her father's eyes.

The soldier got up, belted his pants, and looked over to El's father. "Ye see, yer daughter is a whore! Always she has bin a whore! Her baby wis ne'er christened in the kirk. He belongs tae the Abbot!" The old man struggled to stand up, but the soldier's knife was already at his throat. In three slashes, each one, accompanied by El's anguished screams, the carpenter's head fell to the floor.

Her baby was gone, her father beheaded. She struggled to her feet, wiped the blood from her face where the soldier had cut her, and wailed in the house of death. "Whaur haes mah baby gaen?"

Five hundred years ahead, in the present, snow was coming down hard on the small central Illinois town of Cederburgh.

No one inside the four walls of the packed Lincoln High School gym heard El's screams, amidst their own cacophonous sound, or seemed to care about the blizzard snow, as they watched the two combatants in the center of the roped wrestling ring. The boy with the slim, muscled body topped by brown, buzz-cut hair had just taken down his opponent. His arms straight out flattened the kid in the green wrestling tights. Billy leaned his weight and strength against his opponent's chest. The crowd on the right side of the gym started to hoot and holler "Lincoln High!" They stamped their feet, chanting "Billy, Billy!"

Half-way up the stands a woman, with short blond hair, was raising her arms. Amidst the bedlam of victory, the woman, who looked more likely to have the nine-year old daughter next to her than a sixteen-year-old son, smiled proudly and clutched Kaylee to her side.

Billy looked up towards the stands and caught his mother's eye.

"I know I always loved him. That it didn't matter what he said or how he said it." LuAnn shut the glass pastry case and stood up, five foot-six, in flats, with blue eyes that saw a lot more than people gave her credit for. Her pink bakery blouse, ruffled down the front, and tall legs in tight blue jeans gave her more the look of a rodeo queen than a bakery clerk. She glanced at the clock above the bread rack. "That's how I loved him, Isabel, not the other way around. It didn't come back the same way."

"Didn't come back the same way." Isabel, the Latina bakery clerk, softly breathed the lyric. "Sounds like a country song."

"Well, yea, that's why his mom named him Cash." She looked over to the college girl in the berry-stained apron, hoping she got the joke. "Look, you're young. You never met Cash. I'm making him sound like one big jerk. But love hugs a lot more jerks than saints."

"Love hugs a lot more jerks than saints." Isabel smiled. "Another country song."

"He gave me two beautiful kids; that was the tradeoff." LuAnn set glazed and sprinkle donuts aside. "These are for Billy and Kaylee." She snapped the vinyl gloves off her hands. Everything she did had a quickness to it, as if she were burdened with impatience and a secret agenda. She looked out the front window. Steinfeldt Bakery was lettered in a pink arc across the glass. "I think it's going to start snowing again."

"When I came in to work yesterday, Max told me the Cambodians got a lock on donuts." Isabel's dark eyes sparkled, as if she were sharing the owner's dream. "'But Cederburgh,'" he said, "'will be the home of streusel and strudel'."

"Exactly why I got knocked up at sixteen. Who wants to be homecoming queen at a streusel town dance?" LuAnn turned a wry smile to Isabel. "But we went to the dance, although honestly, Iz, I wasn't showing then." She threw away the last line, as if it was meant for someone long ago.

A "DIVISION FINALS" banner hung from the locker room ceiling. Billy stuffed keys into his jeans' pocket and buttoned up his shirt. He reached for a necklace inside his locker. The chain was silver with a flat metal tag hanging from it. The name "Cash Blackwell" with his Army service number were etched in the metal. Billy had worn his father's dog tag ever since LuAnn had given him the necklace when he was ten years old. He never took it off except for wrestling practice or a match. Quickly he clasped the silver chain and threw on his khaki-green parka.

"Melanie, hi honey." LuAnn leaned her ear against the cell phone. "Traffic is miserable, all snarled up. Everybody's last minute Christmas shopping. What's Kaylee doing?"

"Homework and watching TV." Melanie, the thirteen-year-old babysitter conveniently lived next door. She was usually at the Blackwell house after school.

"I'm not getting back by seven, but Billy should be home by then and you can scoot. If Kaylee gets hungry, there's some tuna salad in the fridge."

LuAnn said goodbye and gazed past the wipers, fanning the white lace of snowflakes on her windshield. *Do I really have to get Billy skateboard shoes? He doesn't even skateboard that much, afraid he's going to sprain an ankle.* The light blinked green. She followed a line of cars into the Cederburgh Plaza Shopping Mall, the one Mall in the small, midwest town a hundred and fifty miles south of Chicago.

She snapped off the local news station predicting a foot and a half of snow by morning.

White puffs of air jumped from Billy's lips as he biked between cars in the steady snowfall and rolled into his part- time job at Steve's Tire World driveway. "I'm closing up in fifteen minutes," Steve barked, huffing out of a red brick warehouse adjacent to the store showroom. "Stack them against the wall next to the work bench."

Billy looked over to the short, heavyset man pointing to a pile of truck tires in front of the rolled-up warehouse door. "They're super, friggin' heavy. Don't hurt yourself stacking'em up. Roll'em, don't lift'em. I don't want Coach Anderson comin' down on me 'cause you screwed up your back two days before the Riverside match." He pulled a cigarette from his mouth and flicked it into a patch of snow. "Go Lions." He punched the frigid air with his fist. "Lock the garage up when you leave. You know the drill. Leave one fluorescent on."

The warehouse was filled with stacks of new and used tires. Panels of fluorescent lights hung from chains bolted to a maze of rafters. Wire glass, grated windows ran along the alley wall.

Billy turned off one section of lights and stared at the ceiling, pitted with darkness. There were times in the summer, at the fall of dusk, when the warehouse glowed with a soft, hazy light. Often, he would imagine the tall, black columns of tires, some that nearly reached the ceiling, as forts or castles. There, on the plain of rubber towers, he would meet his imagined enemy, the men who killed his father, the dragon in his heart he was determined to slay.

Billy pushed up the last truck tire, unzipped his parka and leaned against the workbench. He could see the showroom lights go off and Steve's gold Cadillac leave the driveway. He checked the time on his iPhone and walked over to one of the tall columns. He had done this many times before, wedging his fingers between two tires and shimming his body up. His left hand grasped the wall of the top tire.

He lifted himself, twenty feet above the floor, and straddled the summit. "Go Lions!" he shouted into the silence.

He jumped up and down on the tire, springing towards the ceiling, strengthening his legs and enhancing his balance and agility. His head grazed a darkened, fluorescent fixture.

Instinctively he ducked and reached out. But only air was there, nothing to stop his momentum. His left foot slid off the tire wall. His body fell forward, tumbling down into the tunnel of used tires, landing hard on the cold circle of cement. He was scrunched up in a cramped, dark space. His left foot was caught between the sidewall of the bottom tire. Gingerly, he wiggled his hiking boot out. His ankle throbbed. "Damn… It can't be broken, it can't be fractured, Coach is going to kill me. I can tape it. I can fight with a taped ankle. I've done it before, Oh, shit."

His hand pressed against his chest. "My dog tag's gone." Frantically he padded the cold cement, most of which was covered by his own body. *Coach rushed me out of there. I didn't set the clasp tight enough!* Billy angled his back up and slid his hand under his rump. "Maybe I landed on it. That's it! That's it! Jesus, thank God." But as he gripped the tag, his fingers started to tingle. The dog tag felt colder than the cement. A numbing feeling spread through his arm. He kicked at the tire wall with his good foot, as if his boot could knock a hole through the rubber.

He felt a dryness in his throat. His lungs were collapsing. His mind blurred. With each kick the darkness grew heavier, wiping out the slimmest ray of warehouse light. He was frantic and miserably cold.

He walked slowly, stiffly in his hiking boots. Wind howled through barren trees. The clouds looked like gray wolves racing through the sky. Jagged snowdrifts covered the hills. No houses were on either side of him. No wires strung between poles. No roads shooting off in any direction or signage helping the traveler find his way.

He jerked his head from side to side. He saw nothing ahead but the desolate, dirt road, scarred with ice. He stopped abruptly in his tracks trying to orient himself to this strange place. *Where the fuck am I?* With hands trembling he touched his head to make sure he wasn't bleeding. He held two fingers up to his eyes, relieved he only saw two fingers and not three. He was all too familiar with, as an athlete, being susceptible to concussions. If it wasn't a concussion: *Am I hallucinating?* He reached inside his parka. His iPhone was still in his chest pocket. His woolen gloves were in his side pockets. Under one of his gloves he could feel his father's dog tag.

I've got to call mom. Maybe she'll pick me up if I can figure out where I am.

She pushed and sweated her way through the crowded aisles of last-minute Christmas shoppers.

"Excuse me." LuAnn tapped the shoulder of a young Sears clerk bent on a knee, as he fitted a boot on a customer. "Can you just point me in the direction of the skateboard shoes? For my son."

"LuAnn?"

Her blue eyes shifted to the voice of a stranger seated across from the shoe clerk.

"You don't recognize me, huh?" The man with the gray beard lifted his shaggy brows. He was outfitted in bib over-alls over the hefty bump of a tummy hidden by a flannel shirt, like a weekend farmer or a woodsman. "I married you and Cash Blackwell."

"Pastor Pauly?" LuAnn's face teetered between a smile and disbelief.

"Must be fifteen years ago, or so." He patted his substantial girth. "And fifty pounds lighter. I blame it on the church bake sales." He smiled and handed the shoe clerk a Sears card. "Wrap 'em up and I'll take them."

"You've got to take that boot off before I can wrap it."

"Of course. They do things different in Chicago," he chuckled. "I'd still be in the boot when they put a box around it."

As he leaned forward, LuAnn noticed a balding crown where once waves of sandy brown hair had been.

He stood up in his stocking feet. "I'm sorry about Cash's passing. I shook my head when I first heard about it. I was sad. Sad for you and your kids. Who would have a thought a hell-raiser like that boy could have done such a heroic deed. Jesus must have been with him."

"Jesus didn't stop the grenade from going off."

"We don't always understand the Lord's plan."

"Well, this wasn't planned either, running into you." LuAnn was getting restless and feeling a slow anger crawl up her back. She didn't want to say anything wrong or get in a fight a week before Christmas with a Pastor her parents adored, even though he had blatantly chastised Cash and LuAnn for their foolishness and sins against church teaching. But that was years ago, long before he moved up to a Chicago congregation. "I'll be sure to tell my mom I saw you."

"You were the first and only marriage I've ever done with a pregnant bride, LuAnn." His words stopped her from moving, as if he wanted to idle a few more minutes in a chat.

"Your mom and dad begged me to marry you two in the Church, even though you were in sin and they weren't crazy about Cash. I guess I can say that now that he's passed."

"Now that he's passed, maybe we should forget what my parents thought."

Pastor Pauly smiled. "You never could bite your tongue to save a word."

LuAnn managed a pointless smile. "Merry Christmas."

She felt anxious to finish her shopping and get back to the comfort of her home before the snowstorm slammed through the town. His voice caught her as she walked away. "The boy must be about sixteen now. Just about how old you were when I married you. You ever get married again?"

"No." She pursed her lips, took a deep breath and kept on walking. *He didn't know what love was about then and probably still doesn't, no matter how many people he's married. All he could do was rip me.*

Chapter 2

Billy looked up and saw a lone figure about a hundred yards up the road. He wasn't sure if he was imagining it, or if it was a straight-up animal, or a boy wrapped in a blanket.

"Hey! Hey!" Billy waved his arms and limped forward. The wind stripped light from his eyes and made him forget the nagging pain in his ankle.

When the stranger stepped into the road, Billy could see it was a boy about his age, with long, dark brown hair.

"Hi. My name's Billy." What he thought was a blanket wrapped around the boy was a large, gray, woolen coat. Billy made an effort through his wind-stiffened face to smile. "I'm kinda lost. Where am I?"

The boy didn't open his mouth, nod, or even move his eyes.

"I'm a friend. I'm not asking for anything. All I want to do is have my mom pick me up. I lost my bike somewhere. But I have no fucking idea how I got here and can't call anyone until I know where I am."

The boy reached out and placed a hand on Billy's shoulder. "Caraidean sinn. Mise Ciaran."

Billy didn't know what to make of his language. The last word he heard sounded like Korian. "Korian," Billy repeated.

"Billy Blackwell. I go to Lincoln High in Cederburgh. This wind is killing me. Do you know anyone at Lincoln?"

The boy's answer masked an intense, silent stare.

"I don't want anything from you, Korian. My ankle's really hurting me. Are you listening to me?"

Korian started walking. He hardly spoke at all, and what he did say sounded like gibberish to Billy. They were both limping, which gave Billy a sense of camaraderie with his new- found acquaintance. At the same time, looking down at Ciaran's feet, he had no idea why the boy was wearing brown leather wrappings instead of lace-up boots.

"Where are the houses, Korian? Where's a store, a Seven/Eleven, or someplace I can talk to someone?" Korian's silence was unnerving Billy. "Look, I take second year high school Spanish. I don't know a lot of words, but I can probably figure out a sentence. If you know another language beside the language you're talking, like Spanish, we can communicate."

Ciaran bent his head back as if he were catching snowflakes in his mouth.

"How far before we get to a town, Korian? I think I need a doctor. It's my ankle." Billy hoped the boy wasn't homeless. He felt a pinch of guilt at having his own hands in warm, woolen gloves.

He looked over to a grove of snow-packed trees that followed a curve in the road. A few steps past the trees, the ground banked steeply to the sound of a river. Beyond the river were the white hills woven together in a silent, untold story, much like the boy whose steps he followed.

Billy marked off in his mind the Fox River, the Norris River, the White River. They all flowed within ten miles of Cederburgh. But they weren't surrounded by nothing, not like this. "Is this river close to your home? Is there a town on the river? Do you live in a town?"

Spreading his arms, a big clownish smile creased Ciaran's lips.

He's having fun with me because I don't know where I am.

They left the road, trudging deeper into the woods. The boughs of the trees, bent low with the weight of a winter storm, made their advance even more onerous. Billy was getting nervous and anxious. *I'm following a kid I don't know to a place I've never been! What kind of bullshit is that?*

The stranger raised his arm. Billy looked over and saw what Ciaran was pointing at: a cottage, half-hidden by over-hanging branches and nearly dwarfed by a huge boulder on one side. Smoke rose from the thatched roof, mostly covered with snow. The winter grey sky was darkening.

Ciaran pushed the plank door open with one hand. With the other, he grabbed Billy's arm, pulling him in.

"Take it easy," Billy scowled. "I told you my ankle hurts!"

They entered a small, low ceiling room. A candle-lit lantern and fireplace flames were the only light. Billy didn't notice another doorway until a girl stepped out of the darkness. She stepped further into the room and talked to Ciaran in the same language as he was speaking. Then she turned from him and addressed Billy in the same strange language.

"I don't understand anything you guys are saying. I'm from Cederburgh."

"Cederburgh?" she sputtered, raising her auburn brows.

Billy explained that all he wanted to do was make a phone call.

"Ah un'erstan ," she said. "'Nae everything ye say, bit some."

We're even, Billy thought, threading through her accent. He held up his cell phone. "I'm just calling my mother. I'm not trying to get anyone in trouble." A moment later he stared at the "Service Unavailable" post on the screen. He looked up again. "Where am I?"

The girl, as old, he thought, as one of his high school classmates, was quick to answer his question. "Scotland. Ye're in Scotland."

"Scotland?" A wary smile lit Billy's eye. "I don't know it."

"Th' kingdom above Englain."

Billy stared at her incredulously. "Scotland above England?"

"Aye. Oor king is James the fifth."

Chapter 3

"He never called." Melanie threw on her striped, purple and white parka.

LuAnn stared back, biting her lower lip and thinking of some other way to restate the question.

"Is something wrong?" Nine-year-old Kaylee was standing in the kitchen doorway.

"No." LuAnn answered quickly. "Give mama a kiss." Kaylee skipped over and threw her arms around LuAnn. Her glasses squished to the side of her face in the bosom of her mother's coat. LuAnn kissed her daughter's silky black hair. "Did you eat?"

"Yes."

"And finish your homework?"

"Ditto."

LuAnn smothered her with another kiss. "I've got your favorite donut. Leave one for Billy."

Kaylee pulled one out of the white bag on the table. "Sprinkles! Love you, Mom," she yelled, on her race back to the living room TV.

Her swift exit ushered in LuAnn's growing concern. "Where could he be?" She glanced up at the wall clock. "He never works this late on a school night."

"He probably stopped at a friend's house and got hung up in a video game. The games really get in your head."

LuAnn could see that Melanie was throwing out the first idea she plucked from the ether. The babysitter was reliable, even though, with her nails painted gold, her legs often wrapped in ripped, mesh stockings and a silver star at the corner of her eye, one's initial impression might challenge the range of her reliability. "Was Jimi Hendrix any different?" she was fond of saying in a nasal French accent. Still, the wannabe artist had a warm heart, and Kaylee loved her. Besides, LuAnn, having had her own crash and burn tour through adolescence, wasn't too quick to throw stones.

Melanie grabbed her book bag off the kitchen chair. "Oh yeah, you got another phone call from a man. I wrote down his number." She handed LuAnn a scrap of blue paper. "He said his name was Steve." LuAnn stared at the blue paper and didn't look up until Melanie was saying, "Bye, Mrs. Blackwell," halfway out the kitchen door.

LuAnn's gaze drifted back to the scribbled number, just as the phone rang in the kitchen. In two steps she had the receiver in her hand. "Hello.... I don't know, Steve. I just walked in the house. I was going to call you?"

"The police called me. My warehouse door was left open. Billy's bike is here, but he ain't around. That's not like him."

"He didn't leave a note?"

"Nothing. He didn't call you?"

"No. I couldn't even reach his voicemail."

"Did you talk to the police?"

"Yeah, they stayed till I got here. They know Billy from his old man and Billy's wrestling wins, but they don't know nothing." The tire boss told LuAnn to have Billy call him when he got home. His voice grew more agitated. "It's like something his old man would pull when he was working here. I'm locking the place up and going back home. He's got my cell."

LuAnn hung up. She didn't appreciate the slam on her deceased husband. She glanced at the wall clock again. It was after nine. "Billy isn't Cash," she mumbled and slowly unbuttoned her coat.

"Kaylee, darling, turn off the TV, wash up and get ready for bed."

She heard her daughter's voice, "Ten more minutes. The show's almost over," as LuAnn walked down a dark hallway.

She flicked on a light in the master bedroom and walked over to her computer on a small table beneath a gold framed picture of Jesus that her mother had insisted she hang somewhere in the house. She scrolled down her emails, hoping there would be a message from Billy, but in the back of her mind, she knew he would have texted.

"Mom, Mom!" She heard Kaylee's voice down the hall. "TV's off. I'm going to bed."

She didn't want Kaylee to see the tears in her eyes. In her heart she knew that somehow Billy would have gotten in touch with her. That was the difference between father and son, and that's what frightened her, what made her think something was terribly wrong.

She thought of calling Billy's wrestling pal, Justin, but she knew that calling around would only heighten her own anxiety. *Jesus, all he's doing is getting home late. Get a grip. Okay, it's a snowstorm but he's not ten or twelve. Like Melanie said, he's probably hung-up playing War Games at Justin's house.*

But she had no way of resolving Steve's concern and statement that Billy's bike was still there and the warehouse door had been left open.

"Justin," she said, hearing his voice on the second ring, "It's Billy's mother. I hope I'm not disturbing you. Just wondering, is Billy there." ... "Oh. You don't, by any chance, know if he mentioned something about going someplace after work and maybe getting caught in the snowstorm?" ... "No, no worries. Sorry to bother. Good night."

She started down the hallway to Kaylee's bedroom. *At what point do I call the police? But the police already know something isn't right and Billy is somehow involved. Steve said that.*

LuAnn kneeled beside her daughter's bed and snuggled her with kisses. "How's my Pumpkin? Did you have a good school day?"

Kaylee giggled between saying "Yes, yes" and wrapping her thin arms around her mother with an affection and easy laughter that Billy rarely showed.

"You're gonna be my party girl," LuAnn said, nuzzling her cheek. "Sweet dreams, honey. I love you."

"Mom?" LuAnn stopped at the door. "Did Billy call?"

"No, not yet, but I'll bet he beats you to the breakfast table tomorrow morning." She closed the door halfway, like the halfway truth in her heart, and walked across the hall.

She stood at her bedroom window watching starry flakes of snow fall through the streetlamp lights. *It's going to snow all night. He's gotta be somewhere.*

She turned on the bedside lamp and slipped her feet into a pair of fluffy pink slippers. She grabbed the phone on the first ring. "Hello." ... "Hi, Ron. What's happening? Is everything alright?" ... She stood up and walked back to the windows, feeling her heartbeat ten times as fast as the steps she was taking. "Of course, but Billy isn't here. He hasn't come home" … "This isn't like him, Ron. The snow hasn't let up and I'm a little worried." She hesitated, "Would it be crazy to file a Missing Person Report?"

Ron Wisnefski, a Lieutenant with the Cederburgh Police Department, had been Cash's high school buddy. He had read Steve's Tire World police report and told LuAnn that she would have to wait another twelve hours to file an MPR, but in the meantime to email him a photo of Billy. "We'll blow it up, make copies and I'll alert the guys in his precinct. He's probably just doing some crazy stuff," he reassured her, adding in a tone she didn't appreciate. "Like Cash. You know how it is with kids, LuAnn. The apple doesn't fall far from the tree."

It was nice of him to call, but he doesn't know Billy.

LuAnn walked back to the kitchen, letting her anger sweep her worry aside. *He was just as big a dick in high school as Cash.* She poured a glass of wine, thinking over the fate of different lives. *They did all the same shit. The cards just didn't fall the same way.*

He got out of the army and became a cop. Cash got out of the army with his body in pieces. So much for being a hero.

She took a sip of wine. Then she picked up her cell and clicked a dial code.

"Maddy. Too late?" … "I've got a problem." Her voice crumbled into a broken whisper. "Billy's not home. Nobody knows where he is." … "That would be so good. I've got the wine poured." She laughed, but the stab at humor tumbled into a quick gasp of air as she clicked off the phone.

Chapter 4

Billy looked over to the boy with tangled hair, sitting on a bed, set in what looked like a large, open cabinet abutting the wall near the door. "Well, that's really wild," he nodded. "That's a lot to take in. You're telling me I'm in Scotland, the country above England."

"Aye."

"But I live in Cederburgh, Illinois. That's my home. I was working there, maybe an hour or two ago."

The girl gave him a wary look. "How old are ye?"

"Sixteen."

She moved closer to the fire. Shadows had left her face.

Still, she looked drawn, as if something was wrong, some kind of stress, a worry or misfortune was in her head or heart. A thin, gray scar ran just below her left eye down her cheek, heightening her troubled appearance.

"What's your name?" "Elspeth."

"Like Elizabeth?"

"Like Elspeth." She spoke with a soft lilt Billy had only heard before in a few movies his mother had watched. "Folk ca' me El."

Billy shifted his look between Ciaran and El. "Are you sister and brother or...."

"Ciaran an' ah are brither 'n' sester. We were born the identical year, an the identical day, only a wee time apart."

"Twins." Billy shifted his look between the gangly boy with the grin and El, who didn't seem capable of a smile. "That's really interesting. You don't look anything like twins. I have a pair of twins in my biol...." His voice drifted. He stopped. He had fallen between the cracks of his own reality and was flailing with hopeless thoughts. He took a deep breath. "So tell me, really, where am I? Don't goof on me, please."

"Scotland," she repeated. She took a step towards the table. "Ah believe ye are here fur a reason. Ah don't know whit that reason is."

"The reason is simple. I'm lost. I need directions on how to get back to Cederburgh, that's all. Nothing mysterious."

"In yer eyes yer lost."

"Yes, I suppose that's true." He was managing his voice, trying not to be insistent but pleasantly social. "Your brother, Mr. Korian, brought me here. Don't get me wrong, I'm glad. I was freezing, and my ankle's killing me. It's nice meeting you."

"Ciaran. His name is Ciaran. Yer are mispronouncing it."

"Kiran."

"Ciaran," she repeated.

"I'll get it." His competitive instinct fired up. He dropped his jaw and rolled the "r" as best he could. "Ciaran."

She nodded. "Close."

"In Spanish, you roll the *r* the same way." His minor linguistic victory made him feel a little more comfortable. He glanced over to her brother but turned his gaze back to her. "Your pronunciation of Cederburgh needs a little work, too." For the briefest moment he thought he glimpsed a gentle, welcoming ray, like a visible whisper, cross her face. "Can I sit down? My ankle hurts."

She pointed to a wooden chair beside the table.

He sat down and stared at the slate floor. His gaze wandered over the bare stone and timber walls. He extended his right leg straight out. *What a mess I'm in. I've got a wrestling match in two days and then Christmas.* "Is there a doctor in town? Maybe if I rest my ankle for a while, I can walk there."

"Nae. It is too dangerous."

"Dangerous? Gangs?"

"Ah dinna know that word, Billy."

He looked up. "I didn't tell you my name, did I?"

"Ciaran told me. I'm off tae make some food. Ciaran is hungry. Did ye want me to make some fur ye too?"

"What kind of food? No." He winced at the thought that these two strangers might try to poison him.

She looked over to Ciaran and addressed him in their same shared language. He immediately charged out of the cottage.

Billy watched El take stuff that looked like dry leaves and a vegetable that resembled a potato or a turnip from a hanging woven basket.

"How did ye hurt yer foot?"

He told her about his part-time job at Steve's and how he was jumping on tires and then he slipped and fell into the tire hole and then, "Suddenly, I'm walking down this strange road and I meet Ciaran and he takes me here. Do you understand anything of what I just told you?"

"Ah un'erstan' everything." She paused. "An' naething."

"So that's about fifty percent." He enjoyed watching the slim teenager with gray eyes and reddish blond hair, in a white shapeless gown that reached her knees and a scar down her cheek that stirred a mystery. For the moment, he forgot he was lost. He was willing to hear more of her irony.

"I don't think Ciaran understands anything I say."

"We dinnae know. He suffers from some kind o' condition. Sometimes he answers me, Sometimes not." She turned away from the fire toward Billy. "Ah shouldn't be tellin' ye any o' this. Bit ah have a feeling ye should be here."

"You said before you didn't know why I was here, and honestly I shouldn't be here. I've got a wrestling match in two days, for the conference championship. I really want to get back home, even though I'm beginning to feel we're friends but...."

"Whit?"

"Isn't there someone around here who can help me get back to Cederburgh? I won't tell anyone about where you live, nothing about you, really."

"Then ye dinnae want to hear aboot Ciaran?"

"Yes, of course, I want to hear about him." Billy didn't want to upset the only person with whom he could carry on a conversation and his only hope for getting to a town that was on the grid. "I'm open to any conversation about your brother."

"Ciaran is very smart, he's very tough 'n' he's loyal tae me." She looked towards the front door. "Like jis now. Ah asked him to fetch me some water. He should be back, bit maybe he's jumping in the snow, or tracing the flight of a cloud. Sometimes, he'll rock back an' forth fur hours."

"Sounds like he's au—." Billy stopped. He thought better of calling her brother "autistic" when he didn't know anything about her family or the disability. He watched Elspeth dump the food she had taken from the basket into a large black pot. "Do your parents live here, too?"

"Ma mother died after the baby was born. Ma faither â..»

Billy watched her shoulders draw up. Her head bent towards the fire. He had seen the same pose before when he was a kid, after his father was killed and he would walk into his parents' bedroom and see his mother facing the windows with her head bent and her shoulders hunched up just like El's were now.

When she finally turned to face him, there were no tears in her eyes, but it looked like she had been crying for centuries, and all the lines of age from all of her misfortunes had gathered in the narrows of her face. He couldn't even see her scar.

"Ma faither wis murdered by soldiers. They took ma son, who wis hardly two months auld."

"I'm sorry." He took another deep breath. "And your son's father? Is he here?"

"He ran awa' afore the' baby was born."

The front door flung open. Ciaran walked in talking and carrying a pot heaped with snow. El turned to Billy.

"Ciaran says he took a branch an' brushed yer footprints from the snow leading` to our house."

"Nobody will know I'm here." Alarm set in the wrestler's eyes. "Someone might be looking for me. My mom or my buddy, Justin."

"It's best that way, Billy."

"Best? Are you joking me?" Images of Freddy Kreuger horror films flashed through Billy's mind. His eyes darted back to the door. "I don't know who you guys are or what you're after, but all I want is to get back to my home.

My mom's probably going out of her mind wondering where I am." He braced himself with the edge of the table, stood up and looked over to the darkness that shaded the small window near the door. Daylight was gone. He knew that leaving the cottage and moving ahead on a dark, desolate road offered no promise of reaching a town. "I've got some really important things I've got to get done."

El turned to face him. "Billy, this isn't aboot ye. Some things are mair important. Aye," she exclaimed, "mair important! An' yer life will become mair important to everybody ye love because o' what ye find here! From the fire," she said, pointing to the hearth, "ah heard ma mither's voice."

Billy couldn't believe he'd been in the house less than an hour and the golden-haired girl was judging his life and talking about a voice from the fire.

"She wis sighted, Billy. It's given to some who see ahead. Thay call it sighted in the Highlands."

Billy had heard of psychics and had passed fortune tellers' tents at the county fairs. There was always someone foretelling the future in the sci-fi and adventure-quest books he read and video games he played.

"What's mair important than findin' ma son?"

"I'm in high school. A junior in high school. I'm not a detective, El. I don't even know where I am or how I got here!"

"Ciaran found ye. He's a guid judge o' men." She turned back to the fire, as if the discussion was over.

Billy's gaze fell to the slate floor, to the lanterns, the pots hanging over the fire, and El's ancient clothes.

Whatever she was cooking, was starting to smell good. "Yes," he announced, "I'll have some, whatever you're making. I haven't eaten since lunch. I'm starving. But you've got to please help me find a way back to Cederburgh."

He looked over to Ciaran rocking back and forth, hugging his pillow. Her story was unbelievable. *Why would she lie to me? I've got six bucks in my pocket and an iPhone I can't get a signal with. Nobody's happy when your mother's dead, soldiers cut off your father's head, and your kid's lost.* He stared at the flaming reddish gold hair falling against the back of her white shift. "I'd love to stay, but I've got to get back."

Chapter 5

Madeline Lorene Gipson stomped into LuAnn's living room in a rush of cold air and snow flying off her high leather boots. "This is going to cost you, honey. I'm thinking shrimp fajitas at The Wagon." She did a kind of 50's Twist, shaking more snowflakes from her leather coat. "Has he called?"

"No." LuAnn took her friend's fleece-lined coat and laid it on the couch.

"I had to park a block away and high-step like a majorette through the snow." The tall Black woman followed LuAnn past the Christmas tree lights into the kitchen. "They haven't plowed the street yet. I was swerving side to side in a fishtail conga line."

Before LuAnn had finished pouring the wine, Maddy was sitting at the table, lighting a cigarette. She and LuAnn had been best friends almost from the time of Cash's death. LuAnn had gone to Social Services for grief counseling. She always considered it a blessing that Ms. Madeline Gipson was assigned her case.

"You called that friend he hangs out with?"

"Justin didn't know anything." LuAnn was used to her friend's no-nonsense, cut-to-the- chase approach. She told Maddy how Steve had called.

Billy had left the warehouse open. His bike was still there, and the police were investigating.

"No note?"

LuAnn shook her head, reached over for a cigarette from Maddy's pack.

"You quit smoking three years ago."

"No one quits smoking, Maddy. You just don't light up again until the worries outweigh the wins." LuAnn flicked Maddy's jeweled lighter and lit her cigarette. "Once he walks through the living room door, I'm done with ash-trays." She didn't know if Billy had any new friends. "I've told you enough times, Billy isn't a talker. He holds a secret better than a dead man under water."

"Girlfriend?"

LuAnn shrugged. "No one steady. Between wrestling and homework, he's dead set on getting an athletic scholar-ship." She took a sip of wine. "He still doesn't know anything about the money I've got set aside for him and Kaylee from Cash's death benefit. Not that a scholarship wouldn't help."

Maddy moved the ashtray closer to her. She was only a few years older than LuAnn, but sometimes it seemed like she could be her mother. "This is all about Billy, not Cash."

"I just mentioned his name. Jesus, Maddy, cut me some slack. I'm ten feet from a nervous breakdown." She took a puff of her cigarette. "And he's two days from a wrestling championship."

Maddy pushed a smile across her red lips. Her eyes spar-kled, as much with fun as with wisdom.

"Maybe he just has a hot chick who's pulling his chain." She raised her amber, threaded brows. "And much as you don't want to hear it, it's prime adolescence, 'screw mother' time."

LuAnn got to her feet. "Don't tell me it's dump mother time in the middle of a snowstorm. Plus, his scholarship rides on winning, plus Christmas is a week away." She walked over to the sink. "He's got better timing than that."

Maddy smiled. "It's about teenage boys living in the real world."

"You don't have boys; you don't have children. How would you know?"

"Wow, come on; I didn't tackle two feet of snow to hear this, LuAnn." Maddy's dark eyes checked her friend. "I know you're upset, but I don't have your son, and I don't know where he is any more than you do." She stubbed out her cigarette. "And you snapping at me is going to give you one less person to help you find him."

"I'm sorry." LuAnn felt the sting in her friend's voice. "I'm being a jerk. I'm just nervous, Maddy… I just want him home."

"He's got to eat, doesn't he?" Maddy glanced at her watch. "He's only four plus hours late for dinner." She stood up.

She was a few inches taller than LuAnn and broader in the hips and chest, but she kept a workout-smart figure and dressed with a color and flair that always drew a jealous eye from coworkers. "Now, let's see his bedroom."

"Why" LuAnn's face squished up, as if Maddy had asked her how many cavities Billy had.

"Clues, honey, clues. I don't have kids, but I grew up with a brother who thought he was in the C.I.A. when he turned eleven."

LuAnn sat down in front of Billy's computer monitor and fiddled with the keyboard. "He's not logged in, and I don't know his password."

"Try the Lions or Roaringlions. One word." Maddy settled down at the edge of Billy's bed, turned on a lamp, and started shuffling through Billy's bedside table drawer.

A large color poster "Summer Olympics – 2008" with the bronze and silver winners on either side of the US gold medal wrestling champion hung above Billy's bed. A skateboard stood upright below the bedroom window and a slant board for sit- ups next to it. A rack with various size weights took up one corner, and a framed picture of Cash in his Army uniform sat on top of a chest-high dresser.

Maddy held up a thin pamphlet. "I found this old Greyhound bus schedule. Is he planning on going someplace?"

LuAnn shook her head. "Nothing's working, sweetie."

"Holy bjeebees." Maddy smiled. "Look, a condom."

"He's had the same one for three years. I need a password."

Maddy tilted her head back, as if in great thought. "Try wrestle, lower case."

Seconds later, LuAnn's arms poked the air. "Bingo! It works. Upper case W." She scrolled through junk mail and read Justin's emails. "I'll be damned. Two from my mom. I didn't know she sent him emails."

"What's she got to say?"

"She wants Billy to come to church with her. 'If you tell your mom you want to go, she'll come along, too.' Can you believe that? I'm only thirty-three, haven't committed any major crimes, not on anyone's 'wanted' list, and she's using her grandson as a shill to get me saved."

Maddy laughed. "Speaking of grandmas," she held up an envelope and read the return address. "Mrs. Jean Blackwell, Pleasant Valley Trailer Park, #12, Cederburgh, Illinois."

LuAnn bounced out of her chair. "Cash's mom! I was just thinking about her before I left work!" She slipped a single blue page from the envelope. "I didn't know Billy was talking to her, either." She read down to the last line, her mouth half open as if she were breathing in each word. "'With all my heart and love, Grandma Jean.'" LuAnn looked up in disbelief.

"What's the letter say, honey?"

"She's talking about Cash's name. Billy must have written her wanting to know. I could have told him. It's really dumb." LuAnn sat down at the foot of the bed. She told Maddy that when Jean was pregnant, she listened to 'Ring of Fire' over and over. So when the baby was born, she named him Cash after the guy who sang it, Johnny Cash. Why didn't she name him Johnny? That's a real, recognizable name." She got up and walked over to the window. "All the time we were married, she'd be calling him for money. He half-supported her. That's the only cash she cared about. She never asked about Billy."

Maddy glanced towards the door. "If you keep raising your voice, you're going to wake Kaylee."

LuAnn dropped her voice to a whisper. "When Kaylee was born, she sent her a dress the baby couldn't wear till she was five! You know why?" LuAnn crossed back to the bed. "Because she was either drunk or so high it's lucky she even remembered it was a girl and didn't buy her khaki briefs!"

Maddy took the letter back and put in the drawer. "Don't let her get you upset again. Names don't determine your destiny." She raised her brows and looked towards the window. "That's a snowplow I hear. The first good sign of the night."

LuAnn wasn't listening. "Maybe he's with his grandma. That's why he has the bus schedule." She theorized that Jean might have picked up Billy and driven him back to her house in the trailer park, promising him some of Cash's stuff. "She'd do something like that. She's sneaky."

"Do I check your temperature now or later? You're saying a sixty-year-old grandma kidnapped a high school wrestling champion in the middle of a snowstorm. Do you know how crazy that sounds?" She picked up a thumb-worn paperback. "Check this out. It fell between the table and the bed." She handed LuAnn the book. "I had to read that same book for a Comparative Lit class in college."

LuAnn stared at the cover. "The Hero with a Thousand Faces", Joseph Campbell. I never heard of him."

"He's famous. The guy who wrote Star Wars read that same book."

"Billy wrote something." LuAnn folded back the cover page. "'A hero ventures forth from the world of common day into a region of supernatural wonder.'"

"That's straight from the book, sweetie." Maddy got up from the bed. "Remember the psychic you went to after Cash died. Maybe you ought to give her a call."

Chapter 6

"It's the oats that mak' it grainy." She was sitting across from him, watching him, like his mother sometimes did, when she was eager to know how he liked a new recipe she had just dished up.

"It's pretty good," he said, taking another spoonful and swallowing a green leafy thing he hoped was something like spinach.

"It's kale," El said.

Ciaran sat on his cabinet bed across the room and ate alone. He hadn't said anything since he brought in the pot of snow and told El he had brushed away the visitor's footprints.

"Are you guys Amish?" Billy had read something about the Amish and Mennonites, religious sects, who lived without a lot of modern technology.

"Amish?" El hesitated and shook her head. "That is nae something ah know."

"Do you guys ever go to movies or watch TV?"

"Ah dinna know what those words mean."

"TV," he repeated. "Lost, Modern Family, The Simpsons." He desperately wanted her to say "yes," and call off the charade, but he knew his questions were pointless.

He hadn't seen anything that remotely resembled an outlet, an antenna, or cable. And he remembered not seeing any wires strung to the cottage.

"Do you live here year-round? I mean..." He didn't know what he meant.

He didn't know how to assess another person's life, a life whose inferences he had no way of reaching, of touching, of bringing into his own. Not only was he physically lost, he was in a dimension of time he could not reference.

"Ye shuid tak' off yer jacket," she said.

He thought he saw that same gentleness in her eyes that cleared the sadness from her face. He looked over to the fire. "Will that burn all night?"

"Nae."

"Can I sleep here?"

"Where else wid ye sleep, Billy?"

He couldn't wrap his arms around the magnitude of what was happening to him, but he was beginning to feel the shadow of trust with her. "I don't see a place here to sleep."

"Ciaran an' I'll make ye a bed."

"I have to tell you something." Billy set aside his soup spoon. "I'm not from here. I'm from another country, far, far away. If this is what you say about the time, about the year you're living in, fifteen hundred and something, I'm from a different century, too. Hundreds of years in the future. Five hundred, to be exact. In the future." He emphasized future. "Do you understand? Do you believe what I'm telling you?"

"Ah believe ye."

He reached into his parka and pulled out the cell phone. "See this? It's an iPhone. My mom bought it for me last

Christmas." He touch-scrolled through several pages and raised the iPhone again. "This is my mom."

"Bonny woman."

"And this," he said, flicking his thumb to the next page, "is my sister Kaylee. She just turned nine." Billy flicked his thumb again. "And this was my dog Cairo. He died last summer." He scrolled through several more pictures and handed El the iPhone. "This is my high school, Lincoln High."

Billy could tell by the expression on her face that she had never seen a building like this before.

"Sae many windows," she said. "Ciaran! Ciaran!" She held up the iPhone and again spoke in the language Billy didn't understand. Ciaran got off the bed, shifting his eyes with a wary reluctance. He came over and took the iPhone from her hand.

"Be careful," Billy's voice quickly rose in a cautionary tone. He watched El fire off a translation. Ciaran nodded, but he kept nodding, which worried Billy. That rubbery-mad smile came over Ciaran's face again. "El, tell Ciaran to give me back the iPhone." Ciaran spun and thrust the iPhone, like a punch, directly at Billy. "Thanks." Billy took the iPhone from Ciaran's hand, put it back inside his jacket pocket and managed a smile.

El continued talking to Ciaran in her same firm tone. He spun again and walked away from the table. "Ah told him tae prepare a bed fur ye," she said. "Ah'm sorry he got…" She wagged her head. "Bit he won't hurt ye. Ah can tell he likes ye."

Billy wasn't quite as convinced as El. He reached over to the lantern and moved it closer to her, curious to see more of her face and gentle, gray eyes.

"You told me before that you had a baby."

"Ah have a baby. A son, Bran, nine months auld, now."

"And you told me," he hushed his voice trying to be delicate, "Soldiers killed your father and took Bran."

"On ma heart ah told ye. Th' two soldiers came tae the door. They demanded tae ma faither tae give me up tae them. Ma faither said no. They threw him aside an' tied him up. They never stopped laughing."

"Where was your husband or the boy's father?"

"Ah told ye afore, he left when he found out ah wis wi' child. That's why the soldiers cam'. Thay said we were nivver married in the kirk. 'Church' as they say in England. So the baby could nae be baptized an' it wasn't mine. It belonged tae the Abbot."

Billy listened, as if he were hearing some dark episode from a brutally sinister country. He still didn't know how much he should believe, but he was certain, by the pain in her eyes and the grieving in her voice, that he was involved in something that he needed to know.

He leaned back and momentarily forgot about the pain in his ankle. He was rooted to her words, to the enchantment of her eyes and to the shadowy night that surrounded them. He thought to himself, *When do you start believing people and accept you are where you are?*

El had told Ciaran to bring straw in from the barn, but she hadn't stopped talking about what had happened when the soldiers came. How they threatened to take her baby and how her father begged them to take him instead.

"Then they looked at me. Thair eyes were eager an' greedy. Ah knew what they wantit. Ah told them they could have me if they let me keep mah baby an' let mah faither go." El rose from the table and stepped away.

Her gaze wandered for a moment, as if all the images of horror were flashing before her eyes. "They said 'aye,' bit they lied, Billy. They took me tae the floor. In front o' mah faither, thay had me. Both o' thaim, before mah faither's tears an mah baby's screams. Then, the one who finished me first took his long sword an' beheadit mah faither."

Billy's eyes filled with the horror of disbelief.

"Aye, Billy. The other pulled up his pants an' grabbed mah son. Ah lunged at him, grabbing mah baby's leg. The soldier kicked me awa', as if Ah wis a dog. They marched out as though they haed done something honorable, in th' name o' th' abbot, with Bran screamin' on the soldier's arm."

Billy stared down at the blade of light on the table. He forgot he was five hundred years and thousands of miles from his home. He only knew that somewhere in his heart was a cry, a voice he needed to hear, a voice that belonged to the wilderness of his being and spoke to him, not of past or future lives, but of where he now needed to be. He drew back his hands and finally found the nerve to meet her eyes.

"Where is your son now?"

Her voice dropped to a whisper. "Only God knows."

"I want to help you find him." The words jumped from his lips without a thought as to how he could help her. For the first time since he arrived at the cottage, he saw the glimmer of a smile in her eyes. "Ye can't even walk," she said. "Ciaran says ye fell, like snow, from the clouds."

El kneeled in front of Billy, rubbing warm oil on his ankle. His bare right foot, as she had instructed, lay against her thigh. The oil smelled woody and felt sharp against his skin. "This will heal ye," she said. "Mah mither, God rest her, wis a healer."

"A fortune teller and a healer, wow."

"Some women, Billy, born in the hielands, have powers from anither world." Billy felt her hands massaging his foot. He knew she was separate from him, centuries, language and lifetimes apart, yet the feeling in his heart was a warmth that filled his body. She finished wrapping his ankle in a thin, white cloth. "In the mornin' it will feel better," she assured him. "Ah promise."

"Can we go to a store, a place to buy things, tomorrow?" Again, his voice took on an anxious tone. "There's got to be a town near here." And again, Billy saw the glimmer of a smile in her eyes.

"Ye still dinnae believe me." She got to her feet. "I'll talk tae Ciaran i' the mornin'. Ah told ye to put yer stocking back on." El led Billy to a corner behind the table, where Ciaran had laid out enough straw to make a bed.

They knelt at opposite ends of the bed and laid two blankets over the white sheet she had placed across the matted straw.

"The fire will gae out soon," she said. "But dinnae worry, the door is boltit an' we have weapons."

Weapons? Billy's eyebrows fluttered up. The word made him feel a sense of fear and, at the same time, of unimaginable adventure. The heroes of the books he had read and of the games he played all faced danger and challenges. The cause of his father's death was in the perilous zone of war. The gladiator part of him soared to the surface of his heart.

El picked up the lantern. "Whit air ye thinkin'?" He shook his head.

"Think aboot me," she said. He thought he caught the glint of a smile in her eyes. "Sleep well."

Billy watched her open the small back door and close it behind her.

He took off his parka and fell to his knees on the straw bed. He felt his ankle, still throbbing but the swelling remained unchanged. Years of being an athlete had taught him when his injuries were serious and when there was no cause for concern. He covered himself with the red and black blanket. The pillow Ciaran had left him smelled of leaves and a hint of chocolate, but he knew that Ciaran hadn't stuffed chocolate bars into the pillow. He leaned back, with his hands clasped under his head, and tried to recreate his day: school, wrestling practice, Steve's warehouse, jumping on the tires, and then…. Then I'm here and I have no fucking idea how I got here. He looked through the legs of the table to the dying firelight. I told her I was going to help her find her kid. What was I thinking? I've got a Division finals wrestling match in less than two days. I can't even make a phone call. And she said they had weapons! Billy twisted his body, groaning and burrowing deeper into the straw mattress.

How can I explain this to Coach Anderson? Or my teammates?

How can I get out of a dream that has walls higher than my imagination? He reached for his parka beside the bed. He removed his father's dog tag from one of the pockets and drew it to his chest. "This is your son," he whispered. "Help me."

Chapter 7

The snowbanks and unshovelled sidewalks along the crime- riddled neighborhood were like a tableau, parts of a painting LuAnn could never escape, never take down from a distant wall in her mind, but that was okay. That was her past. The wall she knew was crumbling.

She parked the car in front of the old duplex. Sunlight was melting ice that clung to the gutters. She opened the stairwell door and climbed the broken steps to the heavy beat of gangsta-rap from a downstairs apartment.

LuAnn thought of leaving the pink box outside the door, without a note, like a silent offering from a grateful admirer.

As she bent, the door opened. At first, hardly more than a crack. Then wider, as the dark, round face behind the door took on a smile of recognition.

"I was napping, child," the Black woman said. "What brings you here? I heard a knock on the door."

The yellow scarf with the crystal broach was off her head.

All LuAnn saw was tight gray hair, shaved like a prisoner's cut. "I didn't knock. I'm sorry to disturb you."

The psychic thought she might have forgotten an appointment.

"No, not that. I just wanted you to have this." She handed Mrs. May the pink box. "It's just a little Christmas treat. It's from the bakery I work at. Blueberry strudel."

"Strudel," Mrs. May repeated softly, staring at the box in her hands.

"This'll go just fine with my coffee or tea." She raised her head. "Would you like to step in? We could share this together."

"Oh no, you enjoy it. Please go back to your nap."

"No, darling." She took a step back. "The pastry has its own mind. Its sweet voice welcomes you in."

LuAnn hesitated with an uncertain smile. She stepped into the familiar room, as if she were taking a second step into another life. Her impulse was to glance up at the gaunt prison photo of Mrs. May above the couch, making sure that all she thought and felt was still there, still real and worthy of her trust. But Mrs. May's shuffling about, pushing aside books on the coffee table and turning on the floor lamp, kept her attention near.

"I just want you to know, I had no intention of staying long. It was just a question about my son."

Mrs. May glanced back. "Sit down, darling. I can heat up some water for tea."

"No, no." LuAnn reached into her coat pocket. "I even have my own cigarettes. Would you mind if I smoked?"

Mrs. May smiled and took a seat on the couch. "We can smoke together."

"I feel less anxious about everything, but I'd still like to smoke a cigarette with you. My co-worker at the bakery told me tobacco can be spiritual."

LuAnn offered her a cigarette, lit it and then her own.

She took a drag and walked towards the window. "I felt something very strong when I was last here, almost five years ago. I looked at your picture above the couch, your prison picture, and something moved me.

Like an identification." For a moment, the clouded window held her gaze. When she turned back, her voice grew stronger. "I was a dropout in high school. I got pregnant and got married. Maybe you remember all this. Maybe not. Cash, my husband, the man you said I needed then, he dealt drugs and I went along with him. A certain excitement, busting up against the law. But it ended for me, the charm, the excitement, the foolishness ended."

A tiny, nervous laugh fell from her lips. She took another hit off her cigarette. "What really happened is that I fell in love with my son, with being a mother, and then we had a baby girl, Kaylee, and all of being a mother took over." She stopped and looked from the kitchen entry to Mrs. May who was sitting with a great silence on her face, and LuAnn wondered why she was telling this to a person she hardly knew, even though she claimed to be a psychic, and if she was just keeping Mrs. May from her nap.

"Go on," Mrs. May said, answering LuAnn's silent doubts. "I'm listening because I want to." She smiled. "I was the listener in prison."

"Well, I enjoyed all of this, getting into motherhood. The discipline and the schedules, making all the meals, the laundry, getting the kids off to day-care and school. All of that. It gave me a feeling of importance and a sense of purpose. And then Cash got killed fighting in Iraq, and everything, the lives, the dependency of my children, fell to me." She took a deep breath. "Am I making any sense?"

Mrs. May raised her head. "That's all you need, darling child. You only need the love that's there in your heart. And I see it in that blueberry strudel you brought me. In the little pink box." She put her hand on the arm of the couch and pushed herself up.

"And I'm going to have that strudel with my tea and the love you give is going to make it all the sweeter. Give me your hand."

Mrs. May led LuAnn to the door, still holding her hand. "You have a wonderful Christmas." A sparkle was in her eyes. "And you'll see the boy soon. He's on a sacred journey."

"But I didn't even tell you he was gone."

"I know."

LuAnn drove aimlessly for several blocks, her mind wandering in the same random pattern as the streets she was taking. She had just visited a woman who had told her that she was beautiful and that her son was on a sacred journey. Was it the word sacred or the pain in the prisoner picture above the couch that threatened to flood her eyes with tears? A few blocks later, she began to laugh, a sobbing laugh that sounded as though it was climbing a ladder and slipping back into tears every second step.

She pulled over to the curb, parked, and wiped her eyes with her last tissue.

The corner market windows were covered with the white, painted scrawl of weekly specials. LuAnn walked up and down the three narrow aisles, past the refrigerated cases and bins of withered produce.

The teenage clerk with moussed-up hair, almost like a black teepee on top of his head, seemed to sense her confusion. "Looking for anything special? We just rearranged the stock."

"Tissue. Facial tissue. Kleenex."

"Aisle one, next to the Pampers."

On the shelf above the facial tissue, LuAnn's eye caught sight of Catholic saints painted on tall, prayer candle glasses. She couldn't remember the name of the saint she chose, but it was one that Isabel had once shown her, embossed on a gold medallion.

"Two boxes of tissue and a candle." The clerk rang up the purchases. He wrapped the candle in brown paper and bubble wrap. "You wanna protect it. You don't want Our Lady of Guadalupe to break."

"That's right! Our Lady of Guadalupe. I was trying to think of her name. My co-worker at the bakery I work at, she's Mexican and she showed me the Lady." LuAnn glimpsed the name-tag on his shirt. "And you're Anthony." She smiled. "I've got all the names straight now."

"Perfecto. I'm not a religious kid, but my mother believes in the Lady. She always prays to her. We're Mexican, too. Look…" He pulled up a small gold medallion hanging from a chain around his neck. "Saint Anthony, my namesake. You know what he's the saint of?"

"No."

"The patron saint of lost things." He smiled. "Confirmation present from my Tia Luisa." Then, his smile disappeared with a youthful seriousness in his eyes. "Everyone puts the candle in their kitchen or their bedroom. They think God has time to look through every room in the house. For me," he said, putting the box of tissues in a plastic bag, "you put it in your front window. The Big Guy ain't gonna miss it."

LuAnn smiled. She hadn't expected a lesson in religious candle placement, not, at least, from a kid with spiky, black hair, moussed in a pyramid, and a smile as sweet as a slice of Max's strudel. "You know quite a bit about candles."

"Definitely light the candle, in the biggest window in your house. I grew up in a house of candles." He handed her back her change. "Candles and voices from the past."

"How interesting. A voice from the past might carry me forward." LuAnn smiled, thanked him and took her package. "Merry Christmas, Mr. Anthony, Finder Of Lost Things.

She stopped at the door, staring at something she hadn't noticed walking in. A Missing Person flyer was taped to the inside panel. She put her fingers to her lips and touched the face of her son.

"Mrs.! Mrs.!" He held up the package. "You took the candle and forgot the tissue!"

LuAnn started back to the counter.

"You kissed the boy's picture. You know him?"

"He's my..."

"Your son, of course! That's what the candle's for. And the prayers."

LuAnn picked up her forgotten package. "Thank you."

Before she had taken another step, Anthony's voice stopped her again. "Señora, my Aunt Tia Luisa, I told you, who gave me St, Anthony, she is a shaman. She can help you, yes, she can help you find your son."

"Thank you but really... That's very kind of you to..."

"Once I lost my dog; I was eleven. I cannot imagine what it would be like to lose a son."

LuAnn was quick to explain he wasn't lost. "Miss May, she's not a shaman, but she is a psychic just told me...

"My Aunt, don't worry, she will not take money... I can see in your eyes, the eyes that were crying when you came in here... I have a feeling in *mi carazon*..." Anthony glanced at the wall clock. "Look, we close in ten minutes. I'll close early. You have a car?"

"Yes, but..."

"Señora, drive away if I'm wrong. You already have your candle and the tissues for your tears."

The drive to his house was in walking distance from the store. Anthony remained in an upbeat mood, as if introducing this woman with the missing son to his Tia Luisa was a definite highlight of his week, a chance to do something for the woman immersed in a mystery and for his aunt to show off her remarkable powers.

Anthony's mother stood in the kitchen doorway with her arms folded. An apron with roses circled her ample waist. She spoke with a gentleness that engaged her smile. "She doesn't really do readings, not anymore."

"Anthony told me she's a shaman."

"My sister is seven years older than me." Her Spanish accent was like a sweet coating over her words. "When we came to this country, I was eleven, so Luisa was eighteen. She learned before she came here. I was too busy learning English watching TV."

"Is she married?"

"She went back to Mexico, Zacatecas, where we are from, and for fourteen years we did not hear from her."

LuAnn was trying to be polite, but, knowing this was something she really didn't want to do, she was getting anxious. "Is she a shaman or just what Anthony thinks a shaman is?"

"She will talk to you, and you will decide. She speaks some English, not like me, but enough to understand."

LuAnn looked over to a dark hallway. "What's he doing?"

Anthony's mother took a step into the living room. "Anthony! La Señora is waiting."

A moment later, a door in the hallway opened and the grocery clerk appeared in the hall entry.

"I'm sorry, forgive me. Tia Luisa wanted to know something about an order, las hierbas, I put in for her at the store." He gestured to LuAnn. "Come; she will see you now. She is happy to see you. I didn't tell her anything.. too much."

LuAnn turned a smile to Anthony's mother and followed the boy into the hallway. In only a few steps, they were at the partially opened door, which Anthony opened further and announced LuAnn. "Señora Blackwell, Tia Luisa." Then, abruptly he left, closing the door behind him.

The room had a single bed against one wall. The window, to the right of the chair, where Tia Luisa sat, was curtained, colorfully beaded in red, yellows, and greens and shaded with the darkness of night. In fact, the room itself was vibrant with rich, primary colors. The shaman, who LuAnn guessed to be in her late thirties, showed the same warm smile that her sister had expressed and that quickly engaged LuAnn.

She gestured with her hand for LuAnn to take a royal blue, cushioned seat across from her, less than four feet away.

"I speak English," she said, "Not like my sister, who says she speaks better than me, but I understand everything. Mi *sobrino* told me your son is missing. He did not go back to your home last night."

"Yes."

"But he will come home. He loves you."

"I want him to be safe. Not hurt, not in any trouble; do you understand?"

For a moment, Tia Luisa studied LuAnn's face. Her own face was not old, not ancient, but it had several marks on it, as if she had drawn lines on it, symbols, with a marker of some kind. Her black eyes were small but had a penetrating glow that reduced the attention to her wide, red lips. "How old were you when the child was born?"

"Seventeen. I was in school but I had to drop out."

"And you didn't go back...?"

LuAnn shook her head.

"But you need to find who you are."

"I know who I am, Tia Luisa. I'm a single mother of two children. My husband was killed in the war."

"Si. But those are titles: *madre, viuda*. Who you are never comes into your soul. Not in this birth, in this *encarnación*, we say."

"I don't think I understand." LuAnn looked over to the smoke rising from the incense at the feet of Our Lady of Guadalupe. "I understand your English, but I don't understand what it means. It's my son I want to find."

"Take away all the blankets, *las mantas*, that cover you and have covered you, and you will know who you are. Then, only then, will you find your son. He will see you and you will see him in the light of the soul, in *la luz del alma*."

"I think I should go. My daughter is…"

Tia Luisa raised her hand. "I wish I could show you when you are lonely or in darkness the astonishing light of your own being.' A poet wrote that. Hafiz of Persia. Have you heard of him?"

"Never."

"Close your eyes," she heard the shaman say. Her voice grew quieter and her Spanish accent grew stronger." Trust my voice. Ride *las olas*, the waves of my voice into a world you never knew existed. Yet, it is your world. and it is, deep in your soul, in that light we spoke of, who you are."

LuAnn's eyes closed. She could feel her hands relaxing in her lap, as if they were releasing a pressure, a nervous grip, she had carried over many years.

"But who will take care of Kaylee?" Her voice drifted into silence.

"She will be taken care of. The spirit be attending her.

You are here and you are there. You are in both worlds."

LuAnn felt as if everything of and from her body had disappeared. She said nothing and only felt the infinitesimal weight of light.

"See the sky…"

Those were the last words LuAnn heard.

Walking back to the farmhouse, she was looking up at a summer blue sky. Clouds darkened as she reached the de-cades- old, wooden door with the metal latch.

She stood in front of a dresser mirror. A candle in a copper holder burned next to a bowl of water. The name "Jody" was painted onto the ceramic bowl. Jody dipped a cloth into the water and raised it to wipe her face. She didn't look more than seventeen. A thin blue, cotton chemise barely hid her nubile figure. Her complexion was just dark enough to suggest Native American or Mexican blood.

A gust of wind rattled the shuttered window. Jody glanced to a reflection of the window in her mirror. She blew out the candle.

A rough-looking man in his fifties stared through the broken shutter. A shotgun hung from his shoulder.

Chapter 8

Billy didn't want to leave her gaze, but his head turned sharply to a loud, cough-like, rippling snort. A great brown horse with white markings on its face raised itself up from behind a crosshatch of wooden fencing.

"Tis Aedan." El laughed at the surprised look on Billy's face. "His name means 'fire' in old Gaelic. In wintertime he lives wi' us. All the animals do."

"All the animals?" Billy couldn't take his eyes off the stallion whose gaze seemed locked, as well, on the stranger. "There're more in there?"

"Two sheep. Maybe they're sleepin'. Come look."

Billy followed her to the crossed posts, built like a long, wall-to-wall gate, separating the far end of the bedroom. Almost hidden by bales of straw, he saw two sleeping sheep. He breathed in the dank barnyard smell of animals and hay. He thought of his own dog, Cairo, sleeping in his room, even on his bed most nights. "Do most of the animals stay in houses like this?"

"Tis called a màs an taighe." She smiled and patted her buttocks. "Backside o' the house. Can ye ride a horse?"

Billy was reluctant to tell her he couldn't ride, at least, not very well, but he didn't want to disappoint her. Yet he wasn't sure why he cared. "I've ridden a horse before, a few times, but I wouldn't say I was a rider." Billy turned away from Aedan's dark eyes. "Can you ride?"

"Ye don't see th' world, Billy, if ye can't ride. Ye have tae learn tae ride if you're going' to help me find mah son."

"I don't know how long I can stay here." The words spilled out before he caught himself in the promise he had made her. "I mean, maybe I didn't tell you I've got a very important event, a Division wrestling championship, like tomorrow night. It means everything to me, El." He could feel, as the last few words fell from his lips, the fading power of his own resolve.

"Ye told me somethin' like that, and ye told me ye would help me find mah son. A'm not standin' here with the king's army. Don't gae back on me now, Billy!"

She took a step away from the gate but quickly turned back with another storm raging in her voice. "Ye haven't haed yer heart ripped out by a lad who fled after he made love tae ye. Ye haven't been forced tae watch the faither ye love beheadit. Aye, beheadit, Billy! His head slashed off afore mah eyes. The blood runnin' ower the floor, the eyes starin' out like pieces o' glass. Mah faither, a breathin', lovin' man. Not dead parts on a stone floor. Ye have nev..." She stopped, tilting her head away from him.

"Haven't what, El?"

She walked over to a pair of tall cabinets, unlocked them, and turned slowly back.

"Haven't what, El?" Billy demanded.

"Ye have not grown into a man yet."

"I ain't no'child!" The words rocketed from his heart.

El's eyes still glistened with tears. She pulled open the cabinet doors. "This is where we keep our weapons. They were mah father's. But before mah mither died, he taught us how tae use thaim." She dropped her gaze to his foot, as if to make all things equal. "How is yer ankle?"

"What are you talking about my ankle for?" For a moment he was unnerved and looked away before he turned back to her. "You just told me I wasn't a man. My ankle's' fine… and I'm no child."

"Then you're ready tae fight? Tae leave yer life behin'?"

"I can't die five hundred years before I was born!"

"Any time in yer life ye can feel death, Billy."

She always had some word, some response, that preempted the tangent of his thought. He turned to the long shiny swords and bows the length of a man's spread arms that filled the cabinet.

"These ur the weapons we fight with."

"There's something I've got to tell you." Arching his back, he took a deep breath. "I want to make clear to you that I've never fought with a sword, not even a wooden sword. Just the plastic light wands from Star Wars, that you have never heard of, that I fought with against Justin when I was a kid." He paused. "You never even heard of plastic, either."

"Well, you're gonna have to learn, juist like we learnit from mah faither. Ye will learn from Ciaran an' me."

"You're sure of that?"

"Dinna doubt me, Billy. A' have never doubted ye, nor how come ye are here." She locked the cabinet door.

Aedan charged through the pale blue air, his nostrils streaming vapors of white steam. A cold wind whipped the rider's face as she rode bareback across a narrow plain squeezed between snow-crested hills. Billy had his arms wrapped around El. His heart raced with the gallop of the horse. He had no idea where she was taking him. He had given himself up to her cold, fiery world.

The Highland girl slowed the horse to a trot, maneuvering Aedan carefully between an outcropping of huge, thickly creviced boulders.

"Where are we, El?"

She brought the horse to a halt and dismounted. "Get aff," she said.

He was getting used to her abruptness. It wasn't in the manner of any schoolgirl he'd ever known, yet he wasn't offended. He dismounted, relieved he felt no pain, though he landed hard on his right foot.

"Whatever that stuff was you rubbed on my ankle, it really worked. I'd like to take some back for my wrestling team."

He watched El stroke Aedan's head. It seemed that she didn't think anything he said was funny.

"Do you come here often?" He was curious to know if this was some kind of hiding place in case the soldiers returned.

El grabbed his hand, as her footing gave way under the icy turf and loose stones. She stopped and pointed to a tree whose black branches scattered, like lightning had shocked them, against the sky.

"Dae ye see the rocks under the tree? That's where Ciaran and I buried mah faither.

We feared, if the soldiers came back an' the grave wis near our home, they would find it an' desecrate it."

Billy stared at three narrow rocks, tapered like missiles, and set in a triangle. "Why would they do that?"

"Mah faither didn't belong tae the Kirk. He wis a Lollard. Have ye ever heard o' thaim?" His blank stare was enough of an answer. "Jist as well. It's a group o' believers outside o' the Kirk. They feel th' Kirk has been corrupted, too much reverence on images an' relics, an' all the money they put intae Kirk artwork, from the meager sum the workers are paid."

"I can't understand a word Ciaran says, but you talk English so I can understand you. Do most of the people around here speak like Ciaran?"

"That's the way we speak. When mah faither wis fifteen, he joined the Scots at the Battle o' Flodden in support o' the French. Our King, James the Fourth, was killed." El told him that her father was captured and taken to England. He was put to work with other prisoners building forts and castles. He learned the English way and learned to be a carpenter. "Two years afterwards, he escapit with some other wee lads."

"I'm glad he did. Otherwise, you wouldn't be here."

"A'am glad, too," she said. The trace of a smile stayed on her lips. "So ah kin speak English tae ye."

As Billy shuffled down the snowy embankment, closer to the stones, El cried out, "Kiss the stone fer me!"

A gust of wind blew through the branches of the tree sweeping the snow off the rocks.

The high school boy stepped closer, inspecting the letters on the front stone of the triangle. He brushed away more of the snow. "What's it say on the stone?"

"My faither's name, Dubhuill."

"So that's your name?"

"Aye. It's the name the English gave him. Blackwell."

"Blackwell! You'er telling me your father was a Blackwell?"

"But he changed it back tae Gaidhlig whan he escaped."

Billy charged up the embankment. "I'm a Blackwell! I'm Billy Blackwell!"

El smiled. "It's the reason ye'er here, Billy lad."

"There's probably a million, billion Blackwells in the history of the world."

"Aye, bit only ye found me. Dae nae break th' spell."

He stared at her, his eyes blinking through the flurries of snow. She wasn't just pretty. *She's beautiful*, he thought. *But I have no idea where her beauty comes from.* "Let's go back," he said.

She handed Billy the reins. "Your turn."

He shoved his gloved hands deeper in his pockets. "I never said I could ride like you! That's like me putting you in a car and expecting you to drive," he protested. "Because you're in the car doesn't mean you can drive the car!"

"Ah have nae idea what you're going on about, Billy. Ye dinnae have to ride like me.

Ye juist have to get on the horse an' get us back." The sparkle in her gray, stormy eyes had a way of drawing Billy's hand from his pocket.

"I'll try. But don't laugh at me or say I didn't warn you. And if I start to fall off, grab my butt." "Your what?" He smacked his rear. My màs an taighe."

"Oh, ah promise ye." She laid the leather straps in his glove. "Aedan knows the way."

Billy watched El mount Aedan's backside. He pulled himself up and awkwardly swung his leg over, barely missing El, who smartly leaned down. "Hang on tight," he warned.

Aedan took off, racing with the same fury that had brought them to the gravesite. Billy leaned into the blast of numbing- cold air, ducking his head, digging his knees into the horse's sides. He could hardly feel El clinging to him, but he knew she was there racing with him across a plain of snow, under a sky of shredded, sunlit clouds.

"Go, Aedan, go," he whispered. "Go!" The fear in his nerves burned away with the animal's speed. He slapped the reins from his right to his left hand. Without thinking, he placed his right hand over the two hands clasped against his chest.

Then he felt the side of her face lean against his head and the warmth of her breath on his ear. "Ye can ride," she whispered. "Billy can ride."

Ciaran was standing in front of a small barn, behind the cottage, as Billy rode up. He grabbed the reins from Billy, all the while shouting to El, in a rush of words.

"Billy," she said, dismounting from Aedan. "Ciaran says he killed a rabbit an' already skinned it. I'll cook a rabbit stew fer us."

"Not exactly chicken, but really close." Billy gulped down another spoonful of rabbit and carrot stew. He smiled and looked around the shadowy room, from the cabinets and glowing fireplace to El's bedroom door. "It's really crazy but I feel at home with you and Ciaran. I miss my family, but in a weird way it's like dining with the Blackwells five hundred years ago."

"Mebbe this is yer home."

"I was being funny, El." He stared at the scar on her cheek, at her gray eyes, and soft, full lips. "I have a home I need to live my life in. I have a mother and a sister. And look…"

He drew his iPhone from his jacket pocket again and scrolled through his photo bank. "This is my home."

El leaned across the table.

"That's my house. You can't see my bedroom. It's in the back." He thumbed to the next photo. "And that's my dog, Cairo, but, like I told you, he died a year ago."

"Dae ye have more picters?"

"Yes. You can see them but…" He put the phone back in his pocket. "Not now."

"Whit's wrong?"

"What's wrong?" he mumbled to himself. "When I look at the pictures it makes me feel that I should be there.

I should be in that house. I feel like I'm ducking out of my own life, like I'm cheating on what that time would bring."

"Ye really feel that wey?"

"Yes. I should be working-out for a very important match. That's a part of my life, too. It's the real part of my life."

"But we are yer life now. Ye juist told me two breaths ago how much yer feelin' at home with Ciaran and me. We are the reason yer here." She reached across the table and took his hand "Ye must trust me."

"Why?" Billy couldn't escape the look in her eyes. "Why must I trust you?"

"Because whit ye do here will change yer life forever."

"Change my life?" He didn't want her to stop holding his hand, but he didn't want any more cryptic messages. "My father died, too." His voice deepened as if his throat were clutching each word. "He came home in body parts. His stomach and arms blown away. Nothing left of his face. And you want me to believe in your mystical, supernatural mystery? That was real!" He pulled his hand away and got to his feet. "Why, El?" He wiped tears from his eyes. "Why me?"

"Because ma' son is in yer hands."

"In my hands? You don't know who I am!" "Ye are a Blackwell!"

"You just found that out! Two days ago you didn't know I existed. Or the world in the pictures I come from!"

"Then leave, Billy. Leave." She stood up and walked around the table towards him.

Her temper raised the scar on her face. "Where will ye gae? If ye take Aedan, how far will ye ride back tae yer world, with no hoof prints tae guide ye?" She took back his hand. "Thae are ma' tears, too, Billy. Yer faither came back wi' a shattered face an' my faither's head rolled on th' floor. Is there any difference in death? We have both lost somethin' dear. Someone who gave us life. That's what binds us."

Her gray eyes wouldn't let him go.

"But somethin' binds us more. Th' lad ah' slept with will niver cross this door again. Ciaran will murder him, and Ciaran will niver have children. Niver. Bran, ma' son, carries the Blackwell name now. If he dies now, ye do not live. Not like Billy Blackwell. Time is here, in this room. Only here. Only now."

He knew he was lost. His world had become a centuries-old room lit by a single lantern, the shadows of two teenage searchers against the whitewashed walls, and the magnificent speed of a horse that would carry them into the depths of his unknown heritage, into the mountains and valleys of his soul, and the mystery of a child's disappearance.

Chapter 9

Jody was doing farm chores with her bother Tom, near the barn. He was three years older than her. His dark hair reached over his threadbare collar, and his unshaven jaw was cut square. At any given time, he seemed ready to lash back at whoever was near.

"He was looking out for some noises near the barn," Jody said. "That's what he told me, but I know he was sneaking peeks at me."

"He didn't go to touching you?"

"No, just sometimes brushin' up against me when he don't need to." Jody slopped a handful of feed to the pigs.

"Ma didn't want us to live here our whole lives."

"He's the only family we got," she said matter-of-factly, without a trace of feeling.

"Jody! You got them jars washed?" She heard the unfamiliar name "Jody" ringing in her ears and looked up at the voice screaming across the farmyard. Morrison was standing in the doorway, filling it up in his grey, washed-out shirt and overalls bibbed-up around his chest. He shot a look towards Tom. "Get the horses saddled!"

Tom set the hammer down on a storage bin. His pent-up frustration and bitterness glared back at the old man. But he said nothing and walked into the barn.

Morrison stepped back, with his eyes still on Jody, as she reached the doorway.

Tom hadn't given up on the thread of his morning thoughts. The clouds were low now, hovering across the fields with the threat of rain. He kept his voice down, glancing over to the kitchen window. "Maybe he ain't comin' back. Maybe he's leavin' this old farm to us."

"Maybe you're gonna marry the Spanish Queen." Jody stirred a soup pot on the stove.

"We're the ones that should be leaving."

"Takes money."

"The bank's got lots of money."

She looked back, sensing what he was heading towards. "Ma didn't…"

"Ma's dead ten years!" Tom's temper flared. "She didn't raise us to be thieves is what you want to say, but she didn't raise us to be slaves neither! If she knew how her own brother, her flesh and blood, was treating us, she'd put a knife through his heart."

"Don't be talking like that."

"Would talking bank robbery be easier to hear?"

She stared at him long enough to see the message he was sending. "That ain't our money, neither."

"It's his money locked in that bank. We're working for nothing. We got a right to spend it. Soon enough he's going to put his hands on you, and then I'm going to have to do the killing, anyway." He stared at her with a bullet-hard, haunted look. "You rather me do that and hang from a tree, or us rob a bank and start life somewhere no one will know who we are? It's a big country, Jody."

"You wouldn't shoot no one, would you?"

"You wouldn't even have to come in the bank. You stay with the horses outside."

"Where'd we go?"

"People come through here always talking about San Francisco, in California country. It's a state now. Gold brought lots of people and more businesses than we got businesses in White Rock." He could see her temper had shifted from fear to a mild interest. "This farm was just a place to keep us safe when we was young. It ain't that safe anymore. Not with his eyes on you."

Jody looked towards the unlit hallway. "He keeps his guns locked."

"I know where, and I ain't afraid to bust a lock."

A barking dog drew her quick look to the window. "That's him."

"You can't be scared your whole life, Jody."

Light broke through the clouds, not enough to shower the trees still cloaked in shadows. Jody waited on her horse, alone in the darkness. Her long black hair was pulled tightly back, tucked under a black cowboy hat that nearly reached her eyes. She wore a man's shirt, rancher coat and pants tucked into her boots. Her dark, nervous eyes scanned the distance for movement.

The shadow of a man appeared to be leading a horse towards the fences. The wind muffled any sound. Tom reined up beside her. "Don't be scared. Just don't say nothin'. They'll think you're a boy. Especially holding this." He handed her a steel-grey Colt pistol.

"You said I wouldn't be shooting."

"Not unless you get shot at… Let's go."

Tom spurred his horse. Jody tucked the gun into her belt and quickly followed.

In the ghostly morning light, Morrison's eyes shifted from the broken gun locker clasp to the hallway he headed down. He threw open Jody's bedroom door. His eyes moved from the empty bed to the tap of the wooden shutters against the glass.

The White Rock main street was busy. Shopkeepers unlocking doors, some unloading wagons, and a man wearing a straw hat walked out of the hotel saloon, mounted his horse, and trotted down the main street. He nodded to the "boy," on horseback, in front of the bank. "Mornin', son."

Jody nodded back, as the horseman passed. Her hand gripped the reins of Tom's horse stationed beside her. She turned back to the bank window at the same time bullets shattered the glass. Tom's horse reared back. Jody fought to keep her own horse steady, as Tom's horse lurched into the street.

The bank door burst open. Tom backed out, shooting, until all he heard was a hollow click. Blood streaked the front of his shirt. Jody drew her gun, firing into the bank. Tom scrambled desperately onto the back of her horse. Two bank officers rushed through the open bank door, firing at the fleeing horseman. The dressed-up boy charged the horse past the last fence lines and veered off the country road into an open forest. Tom's hands fell away from Jody's chest. She knew what it meant, but she couldn't risk stopping to administer aid or comfort. She grabbed onto his left forearm, pressing it against her stomach. "Don't slide off, Tom, keep to the horse."

Trees were starting to close in. Jody leaned the horse towards the sound of water, as it picked its way through the forest scramble. Finally, sunlight filtered through the leaves, and the horse drank from a shallow stream. With Jody's help, Tom had managed to get to the ground, finally resting his head in his sister's lap. He forced his words through every breath. "Go far, far away from here..." he gasped. "Where the old man can't touch you... Remember, you are strong... I love you."

The words held to his last breath. His eyes closed. Death transformed his face into a mask of unrelenting peace. Jody moved the gold coin necklace away from the blood on his chest. Her eyes dimmed with sadness.

A cold wind ripped over Morrison's land the following morning. Tree branches scattered across the yard. A chestnut mare tethered motionless to a post at the front of Morrison's house. In the kitchen, the gruff rancher stoked a fire in the wood stove. He didn't like any part of the law, especially the Investigator type that came in from a distant town.

"I never got along with him; don't know who could. My sister told me he had a bad fever when he was born. Probably burned his brain." Morrison looked up at the stout man, about fifty, standing a few feet from the kitchen table.

"The bank didn't hire me to investigate his mental state. A witness said his accomplice was a boy, about fifteen. You wouldn't know someone like that?"

The rancher didn't answer. The Bank Investigator, Philo Storm, rotund and neatly bearded, spoke in a deep, precise manner. His brown, vested suit showed off his upper-class taste.

"Town-folk say this fellow Tom had a sister they never seen much. How old would she be?"

"Maybe seventeen."

"Maybe? You raised them both..?"

"Since my sister died. Cholera took her more than five years ago. Their pa was mixed blood, Mexican, some Indian." Morrison went back to stoking the fire. "I told her not to marry him."

"Everyone have their own bedroom"?

The question seemed to rise out of the ether. Morrison lifted his head, knowing full-well what the Investigator was getting at. "What're you sayin'?"

Storm gestured as if his question was meaningless.

"She got her own bedroom if that's what your mindin'. Down the hallway, in back of you."

Morrison made it damn-straight clear, in the next minute, throwing open Jody's bedroom door. The wind was still rattling the shutters. The bed looked like it had been recently slept in. The picture of an older women sat in an oval frame on the dresser. Storm fingered the gold coin necklace draped across the frame.

"Present from you?"

"Her ma gave both her kids one. All she had. It ain't yours to take."

"It is until we find her." Storm slipped the gold coin necklace into his jacket pocket. "Where is she?"

"Maybe berry pickin'. She's got her own mind."

"You're saying she didn't mind you. And you're lying to me now." The Bank Investigator looked over to the shutter rapping on the window. "Must be hard living so close to a young woman so pretty. Especially, this far from town."

"You're just as big a fool as them agents who thought I killed my sister."

"Did you?"

"Raisin' two kids ain't my idea of somethin' you'd buy into doin'."

"Free help on the farm." Storm raised a brow. "When she comes back, tell her the gold chain is waiting for her. I'll be at the hotel in Rapid Falls. Maybe she knows the boy who was with her brother."

"What if she don't come back?"

"Then maybe I'll find her and return the gold chain myself. Good day, Mr. Morrison."

Sunlight climbed the snow-capped ridge. Jody stood on the bluff, looking down on a small wagon train creeping along the trail. She looked up at her horse. "We're movin' on, too.

Let's see what they're serving."

Chapter 10

A marble grey sky pressed down the loose ends of the day. It hadn't snowed all morning, but the only reprieve from the biting cold came from the rapid sword play, heating the bodies of two teenage warriors.

"Can ye dae this?" El whirled the silver broad sword and slashed the air up, down, and crosswise. "I telt ye before, death is always near i' the Highlands. Ye must be ready to fight."

Billy was mesmerized by the Scottish girl's speed and balance, as she attacked her imaginary foe with circular thrusts and swift vertical strikes.

"Who?" he shouted. "Who?"

Quickly he replicated El's moves, slashing the air with his deadly broad sword, inspired by her resolve and emboldened by his own innate agility.

"Sometimes ye don't have time," she said, catching her breath. "But, if ye do it quickly enough, like I juist did, then yer enemy doesn't know from where yer next shift is comin'. He steals a second to think, an' you mus' seize on that second!"

Ciaran's sleeveless wool coat hung from El's narrow shoulders, dwarfing her, like a stout lumberjack's vest, but didn't seem to impede her urgency or the deftness of her moves.

"Who must I fight?"

"Whoever has ma' son."

Ciaran stood close by, watching El and Billy as she continued instructing the boy her brother once called, "*an coigreach bhon speur*," the stranger from th' sky.

Billy shadowed her moves. Soon, however, his innate pride and natural aggressiveness, born of warring against countless opponents, took over. He fought with tenacious energy. As quick as he was, El was quicker, but she didn't have her brother's strength. Billy found it easier to repel the clash of her sword, even as her lightning thrusts caught him off- guard.

"Ye would be dead a thousan' times," she warned Billy. "Keep yer eyes on th' point o' ma sword, not on ma' eyes or ma' hands."

Back and forth they battled across the frozen turf. At times, he backed her against the barn walls. Moments later she forced him on his heels into a thicket of silver birch. They whirled, lunged, and dodged in a fierce combative dance, beneath the frosted arch of trees, as much a trial of courtship as it was a lesson in survival.

Again, they clashed. Billy pushed her sword up until both weapons pierced the air and their steel guards, the silver baskets she called them that protected their hands, met with a ringing clang. With their faces inches apart, she whispered, "You're learnin', Billy. You're learnin' tae kill, like the fighter yer faither was."

Billy was having a hard time reconciling the relentless, violent energy he was combatting with the nymph-like figure, in her flimsy white tunic. Instinctively, in one swift motion, he grabbed a thick branch, pulled himself up and leapt through the air. Caught off guard, El stumbled and fell in retreat. She lay on the ground, sprawled helplessly at the point of his sword.

"I wrestle to win," he said, breathing hard. "But now I know how it feels to fight for my life."

The loud, menacing roar of a mountain avalanche ripped through the air. Billy saw Ciaran standing at the corner of the barn with his mouth wide open and his sword pointing at him.

"Geibh thu bás mur leag do chlaidheamh bhuat air lar!" the twin shouted.

"What did he say?"

"You're a dead man if ye dinnae drop yer sword."

The violent warning in Ciaran's eyes drew Billy's arm innocently to the air. He dropped the sword.

"Now winch me," she said.

"Winch?"

"Kiss."

"He didn't say that."

She brushed her hand against his cheek. "Somethings are understood in the Highlands. Kiss me now."

Billy heaved a deep breath. "That might make him even more angry, El."

"His anger is brief, mine is for a lang time. Kiss me now."

"Not now," he protested.

"Billy, th' snow is cold on mah back. Kiss me to warm mah heart."

He shot a quick glance to Ciaran and turned back to her. "Just once." He kissed the scar on her face. He kissed her lips. They were the lips he had wanted to kiss since his first steps into the cottage.

Billy stared at the fire, but his eyes kept returning to El. She wasn't funny or quick with clever remarks, like the Senior Class president at his high school or busty like Roxanne, who let him kiss her boobs. He was only sixteen, just entering the chaotic world of sex and romance. Yet no one in his life had ever made his heartbeat with the same intense confusion, passion and desire. *No girl I know rides a horse like a jockey or sword fights like Luke Skywalker.* He shook his head and smiled. *Or has a scar running down the side of her face and haunted by the terror of a son who's been kidnapped.*

El turned from the fire, holding a clay pot she had just taken off a hook. "Whit were ye thinking?"

"When?"

"Dinnae be a school laddie. Ye know when. Ah turned an' ye had a look i' yer eyes."

"Is Ciaran coming back?"

She nodded and carried the pot to the table. "That's no what ye were thinkin'." El had changed into a white, long-sleeve dress that reached to the floor, and over that a plaid blue, red and green vest. She wore a red sash at the waist, but the dress still seemed ill-fitting, like something handed down from her mother. "Are the girls in yer school like me?"

"No one is like you."

She leaned across the table, kissed his forehead and then leaned back with a smile. "Ye didnae expect that, did ye?"

"No. I didn't expect that or the kiss in the snow. Was that to get me to stay?"

She put the pot down and stared at him. He wasn't sure if it was anger or hurt in her eyes.

"Ahm seventeen, Billy. Ah haven't bin many places or gone to school in a fancy building bit ah know whit love means. Ah know the deepness o' love that goes through the bottoms o` yer feet 'n' the heart. Ah gave mah heart once 'n' ah swore that when ah would give it again it would be to a laddie who would not runaway but would stay at mah side 'n' in mah heart forever."

"I'm going back to Cederburgh, El. That's what I'm trying to do."

"N' mebbie ye will. But ye will never leave mah heart. That's what love is aboot, Billy." "I only came here yesterday."

"No, Billy, ye came here when ah stood in th' meadow, out of the mist and th' dimming light."

He looked at her, not as if she were crazy but as though she, with her flowing golden hair, was speaking to him through the voice of a sea enchantress or forest nymph in one of the "mystical journey" video games he had played at his friend Justin's house.

And she repeated how Ciaran had told her that Billy had fallen from the sky.

Listening to the cadence of her voice and looking at her fiery gray eyes, Billy was beginning to believe something supernatural had actually occurred and that he was meant to be in the Highland cottage.

With the tin spoon, she filled his bowl with some kind of stew made of oats, greens and bits of leftover rabbit meat. "Hav' ye ever been in love, Billy?"

"I love my mom, my sister Kaylee. I loved my dog Cairo and I loved my father. I mean, he's dead, like I told you, but I still love him, even now. A lot of people in Cederburgh...." His cheeks reddened and his voice faded to a dry whisper.

"What?"

"We're both Blackwells." He forced a smile. "A lot of people thought he was a bad guy. He sold pot and stuff. That's what I heard from some guys. My dad had a reputation. I asked my mother and she said that he made some mistakes and she said, 'I made some mistakes with him.' Do you know what pot is?"

El hit the black pot with the soup spoon.

"No," Billy laughed. "It's a kind of weed; it grows in the ground and it gets you high, like a friend of mine said, 'Your mind gets cozy with the world.' So he got in a lot of trouble, but, see, he was never trouble to me. He was fast, he moved around, and when he moved, it was always about something or doing something. When he built me a basketball hoop and backboard in our yard, he said, 'Okay, let's do it,' and boom it got done. That fast. And then he taught me how to dribble a basketball, keeping the ball not exactly in front of me, at like three o'clock, so a kid couldn't slap it away."

El put down the spoon and moved closer.

"He wanted me to know that. He'd always say, that's the point, My Mighty Son. Keep your stuff away from trouble." Billy ducked his head in a bashful laugh. "That's what he called me. My Mighty Son. And whenever he wrote letters from Iraq, mostly to my mom, but sometimes he'd enclose a little note to me, with drawings on them, he was a really good artist, he always said, My Mighty Son."

"'An' he wrote about th' fightin' an' war?"

"No, not to me, no. He wrote about the mountains and the rivers they crossed and how little villages had markets in the street, and a lot of streets and roads were just ground, like the road to your house."

"Like villages here."

"That's what I've been asking." The anxiety in his voice mounted with his interest. "Where are these villages here, El?"

"We'll be gaeng to one soon enough."

"Yes, soon, I hope. Very soon." He smiled again and told her more of what his father had written about the desert sun and how it set differently than a Cederburgh sun. "He said it spilled across the horizon. I remember that because, when I read it, I never thought the sun could spill. I was nine, just before I was ten. That was the last letter I got from him. The last time I heard, My Mighty Son."

She watched him turn away from her, and she felt, in that moment, his whole body seemed like it was harboring or hiding a great sadness, almost as large as she felt for the loss of her son.

"He died in the war." Billy fished beneath his shirt and drew out Cash's dog tag. "I wear this all the time except when I fight."

"Aye, it's the light a' saw in the meadow, Billy. Ye canna see the meadow now because o' the snow, bit there's a pond in the meadow, just beyond the pines. A' would walk thare in the evening', whin the sun was settin. One day, a laddie was comin' towards me. Ah could not see his face because the sun wis shinin' so brightly on somethin' flashin' on his chest. An whin ye leaned over an' kissed me in th' snow, A' saw that metal thing fall open on yer chest an A' knew ye were the one who wis there that day in the meadow." She calmly set the spoon in the pot and stirred. "Gradually, the peace an' th' beauty o' the meadow took away ma' sadness an' hurt. The meadow is still in mah heart an' that's where ye are."

"You're telling me I was here five hundred years ago." His voice rose faintly, as if it were a question."

"Some part o' ye was. Some pairt o' ye came intae ma heart."

"So, I time-travelled. I went from one century to another?"

"Ye did… an did again."

"Maybe you're right. But it could be a dream, couldn't it? I could wake up a minute or ten minutes from now. I'd be in my bedroom and you wouldn't be there." He got up and looked around, as if to make sure everything was as he had seen it minutes before. "None of this, the table, the bench, the hearth, would be there. When will Ciaran be back?"

"Before the dark."

"El, I am still there, in that Cederburgh house. My love is there, too. My mother is there. Kaylee is there. Friends and memories are there." He looked over to the small window, starting to darken. "Pictures of my father are there. My little sister was born the same year my father joined the Army. He called her My Beautiful Daughter just like he called me My Mighty Son."

"Th' soup is getting cold, Billy."

"I'll eat it. Don't worry, I'm hungry. But I was just think-ing of how we'd get on his motorcycle." He noted her blank stare. "A motorcycle is like, well, it's got two wheels, one front, one back and there's a seat you can sit on and a motor, so you don't have to use your legs. Anyway, I can draw you a picture of it later. It was a black Harley and we'd ride up the hills to the quarry. "Hang on tight," he'd holler with my arms wrapped around him, just like my arms were wrapped around you when we rode Aedan."

"Did ye love th' feelin'?"

"I loved it, loved it, loved it! I'd rest my head against his back. I'd close my eyes and feel the summer breeze. Yes, with you and with my father." He took a deep breath. "But with you the breeze was a winter wind that froze my lips, and still I loved it." He smiled, as much in his brown eyes as on his lips.

"Do you know what a quarry is?"

"Nae," she shook her head.

"It's like a giant hole or pit where they used to dig up stones for buildings, like the stones on this floor." He stubbed the stones with the toe of his boot. "But then the rain and the snow-run-off fill the hole like a giant swimming pool. And even though it was spring, 'spring-cold' my father would say, he'd jump in the quarry water and then he'd raise his arms and shout, 'Jump in, My Mighty Son!' And I'd tear off my clothes and leap fifteen feet into his arms, creating a splash as big as a geyser. And he'd hug me.

My teeth were chattering, like this, (tapping his teeth together) and water would run down my eyes." Billy's smile was broad and filled the fading darkness with light. But he could see on her face that something he had said moved or disturbed her.

"Finish yer meal," she said. "A' don't understand half o' what ye said, but a' know the other half is the laddie in the meadow."

He hadn't thought he'd need another blanket that night as he lay cushioned in his straw mattress. He felt warm, even without his parka, but after a few moments, he pulled a second blanket over him. He closed his eyes and let her kiss come back. It ruled out every fear of where he was or how he would get back to his world. Her lips pushed aside any thought of who she was or why the boy in the meadow appeared. It was a kiss unlike any he had felt before.

He was entering El's world. A world of love betrayed, beheaded death, a lost child. He was being challenged to embrace a past that clung to him with messages he didn't understand, as if he were being swept into a mystery of dark hallways filled with a wavering light he dimly saw. Was this my past? he wondered. Am I the hero of my own beginning? He turned toward the wall, clutching the blankets against his chest. Are we always the hero of our own beginnings?

This is my second night sleeping here. The Division Championship is tomorrow night. How can I get there? How does anyone leave the anchor of time? How will anyone understand what has happened to me when even I don't know what has happened or how it happened. Nothing is lost forever, my father said. Unless I wake up from a dream, I've lost the chance to win my weight class. But it will come back to me, the chance will come back to me, to win it back. And I will. I'll get a scholarship, too.

The wind howled. Billy glanced up, thinking the thatched roof would topple or fly off to the moon. *If I grabbed the roof maybe it would carry me back, like riding a boogie board, surfing across the winds of time.* He hummed Harvest Moon and fell asleep.

"Ciaran would nae have struck ye unless a' told him to." El sprinkled herbs into both cups and filled them with hot water.

"Maybe so, but I've wrestled a lot of guys and I know the look in the eye of someone who wants to do serious damage."

She sat down at the table across from him. "When a' sword is drawn agaisnt ye, ye don't wait for th' man you're facing tae explain his reasons. The scar on ma' face isn't from a kiss." El stared down at her cup of tea. She brought her hands to the gray morning light that circled the cup. "When a' tried to grab Bran back from the soldier, he slashed me wi' his dirk. A' don't know what world ye live in, but Ciaran an' I live in a violent world. Th' clans are constantly fightin' each other." She grabbed the edge of the table.

Every word sounded like her fist pounding against the boards. "They burned down villages like they did ours. They rape women, steal livestock, set fields a-fire. The English armies invade us, while we simply try tae keep alive and find some kind o' happiness amongst our own. 'Oh, 'tis political,' ma' faither would say an' spit on the ground. It's no' about people. It never is."

El turned her eyes to the fire. Her voice fell to a trembling whisper. "Th' kings have their castles. All we have, Billy, is the air we breathe, an' much o' the time it's filled with lies an' terrible news." She got up from the table and walked back to the fire. "I ask, how come I was born? Tae suffer? Tae have a son a cannot lay against ma' breast?"

She has no idea how violent the world is going to get, he thought. *She doesn't know about atomic bombs or nuclear fuckups or chemical rain.*

"Look at me, Billy. Am a' bonnie in yer eyes?" Billy looked up, caught off-guard by her question. "Am a' bonnie in yer eyes? ah ask."

"Yes."

"Dae ye care that soldiers raped me?"

"No." He got to his feet in an effort to explain himself. "I mean, I care that you were hurt, that you were taken against your will. Of course, I care about that."

"But a' mean, dae ye think less o' me that a was stained by the monsters?"

He shook his head. "Never."

"A' feel so stupid." Tears started down her cheeks. "Ma dignity has bin taken away. The faither o' Bran hurt ma pride, but what happened in this room, on the floor you're walkin' on, tore apart ma' soul. A' have to be tough, a tell myself. A' have to be strong fur ma son an for Cirean who, half the day, is helpless." She walked away to the dark corner of the room, threw her arms out and sniffled up her tears. "A' can't always be strong, Billy.

It hurts to be strong. I've got to be a man whan I'm wantin' to be a wife, a mither. But a' think o' ma mither an' I'm tough because she was strong." Her gray, tear-filled eyes looked up at him. "Say mah name, Billy. Say mah name so A' know I'm here. When you've got nothin' left, ye don't know yer anywhere. Even the ground you're standin' on is some-where else."

Swaying her back and forth in his arms, he repeated: "El... El... El... You are here, and you are beautiful."

She put her hands on his erection, her *bod*, she called it, and guided him into her. El raised her knees. Billy felt her hands on his back, pulling him down, closer, deeper inside her. Her breath grazed his neck, her tongue licking his skin. He knew he was supposed to hold back, he wanted to, but when El arched her pelvis and moved her hips again, teasing his cock with a rhythm his own hand had never rehearsed, he surged inside her.

"No, not that soon!" he exclaimed in a harsh, self- reproaching whisper. He raised his head, squeezing his eyes shut with both relief and adolescent regret.

"Kiss me again," she answered, hushing his lament. "Kiss me now."

Regret was gone when his lips touched hers. "I'm hard, I'm still hard," he whispered.

El drew his hand to her chest. He kissed her nipples, *buds o' mah soul* she called them. Then he opened his mouth to the sweet, warm curve of her breasts. He grabbed her wrists and pinned her arms against the wrinkled sheet. Again and again he thrust himself into her mysterious world.

"Stop," she said.

Neither he nor she moved. Inside of her, inside of an abandoned teenage waif from centuries ago, he felt, at last, despite the thousands of miles that separated him from his birthplace, he was at home.

"Slowly," she whispered. "Gae slowly now." Again, she arched her pelvis and began a slow, loose rhythm that seized his blood. He watched her eyes close and her lips clench tightly. Her head fell back into the pillow. "Yes, yes," the voice cried from inside her. The muscles of her vagina beat against his swollen bod.

He had entered a universe he sensed at once was his, yet one in which all the colors were new to his heart. He felt a distant pleasure come over him as if he were adrift in a summer sky, and all he could feel or think of was freedom.

How can her small body fill me like a thunderstorm? Then he felt El's foot rub against his calf.

"Did ye like it?"

"Yes."

"Wis it like other girls you've made love tae?"

"I've never made love before."

She rolled her body against him and wrapped her arm across his chest. "Ye must niver forget me."

A lantern burned on a table next to the bed. Looking across the room, Billy could see Aedan's dark, glossy eyes. They weren't directed at him, but he thought Aedan was letting him know he was there. Billy slept the night in El's bed, the bed her mother and father had slept in, where she was born. "I can imagine making love to you anywhere and everywhere in the world," he told El. "But I don't ever want to sleep with you in my parents' bed."

She laughed. "Billy, ye showed me pictures o` yer house. Ye have enough rooms and enough beds. Ye don't have tae worry about that. More's the problem o' getting me there." She blew out the bedside candle.

"More's the problem of getting me there, too," he mumbled.

He closed his eyes. Somewhere in time the Division Finals were over. He heard the cheering crowd. He saw Coach Anderson smiling and his teammates beaming with pride in the ebullience of victory. Justin had a white towel draped over his shoulders and was high-fiving teammates. "I missed it," he whispered.

"Missed what?" she echoed. "Goe tae sleep, Billy."

He was certain he had missed the school victory. But he knew he had made love to the most beautiful girl in the universe. And he had learned that it wasn't his triceps, his deltoids or any other muscle, but the heart was the muscle to be protected and cherished.

Cold air rushed in. Ciaran slammed the door and set a wooden box next to the fire. Billy watched him take bricks of peat from the box and set them on the flames. All morning Ciaran had said nothing to Billy. It wasn't that Billy understood much of what Ciaran said or that Ciaran spoke to him very often, but now his face had a troubled expression.

"He's jealous," El said. "An, disapprovin'."

"What's he so jealous of?"

"He knows ye didnae sleep in yer bed."

"He's your brother," Billy fired back. "Not some guy who's waiting to be your boyfriend."

"We are twins, Billy. He's protective an' loyal tae me. A' told ye that."

"I'm very protective of my sister, Kaylee, but she's going to get married someday and I'm not going to try to kill her husband."

El laughed. She put plates on the table and told Ciaran something that sent him outside again. Despite the brief spate of laughter, Billy could tell something was bothering her.

"Ciaran rode Aedan into the village this morning lookin' for any kind o' work." She recounted how he talked with a man he had worked for before. The man's shop had been burned to the ground and he had no money to pay Ciaran. "People ur sellin` whatever they kin, whoever has money to buy." The man had told Ciaran that now people were willing to sell their daughters into marriage for a meager fee. She turned away and went back to the fire. "The Macleod clan burned an' destroyed everything, just like they did ma life."

"If the man has no money to pay, why's Ciaran going back to the village? Does he want to buy a wife?"

El burst into laughter, but, like a dashed wave, the laughter died. Her cheeks turned red and tears wet her eyes.

"I'm talkin' aboot somethin' more serious an' terrible." She took a deep breath. "He told me that a lad wis sold, a baby boy. 'That's how desperate folk are' the man said." She sat on the stool and started to cry again. "I cannae tell ye everything. Ciaran doesn't always git things right. His attention doesn't bide in one place." She reached out with her hand to the table to steady herself.

"You think it's your baby?"

Billy stepped back and looked around the room. In three nights and not even three whole days these whitewashed walls, this burning hearth, and this turbulent young woman and her mysterious twin had become his locked-in world.

"If what Ciaran says is true, then we've got to find the baby, we've got to find if it's Bran. If it is, we'll get him back. He's a Blackwell." Billy kneeled and put a comforting hand on her. "If he is lost or dies, I am never born. Not to the Blackwells of Cederburgh."

He didn't know if she believed what he was saying or even understood what he was saying. It only mattered to him, naïve as he was, displaced in a war-torn, chaotic century, that he was ready to fight for her. "I've never lost a match."

El rubbed her forehead against his hand, sniffled up her tears and raised her head. "I'll make some tea an' put out some cheese an' bread."

Billy followed her back to the hearth. He watched her poke with an iron rod at the burning peat.

"Ma faither built this chimney," she said. "Most o' the cottages like this dinnae have a chimney, just a hole in the roof. But ma fatiher built this house, th' bed we slept in, the tables an' cabinets, an' chairs. An', like a' told ye, he taught me the English language."

Billy let her ramble on, hoping it would keep her mind away, for a moment, from what Ciaran had told her. "Did he work for many people?"

"Aye." She told Billy that he built furniture and rooms for landlords and shopkeepers in the village and barns and sheds for farmers. "He wis a wonderful man." She brought the pot of tea to the table. "He didn't deserve tae die. Not like the filthy pigs who murdered him."

Billy pushed his cup in front of the pot she was holding, hoping she wouldn't break down and start crying again.

She smiled. "I'm no gonna cry again, Billy, if that's whit ye're afraid I'll do. A' want to, but a' won't." She filled his cup and sat down across from him. "Is yer life anythin' like this?"

"No." He paused and looked over to the fire. "Nothing like this. Absolutely nothing. We have amazing things you don't have. I wish I had a picture of our kitchen at home or of cars. Look." He reached in his back pocket and pulled out his wallet. He handed her a piece of folded pink paper. "This is a driver's permit. I can drive a car. It has wheels and an engine and can take you anywhere. You don't need to walk or ride a horse to get where you want to go." He smiled and watched her unfold the paper. "I would drive you over all the streets in Cederburgh and a big city like Chicago."

"A can read some o' th' words bit they don't mean anything." Billy reached over to his parka and pulled out his iPhone.

He scrolled through several school pictures. "Look at this one. See all those cars, those things, in front of that building. Those are cars. That's what I'm talking about.

You put gas in them, and they move." He looked into her eyes and stopped. Gas doesn't make any more sense to her than Sugar Pops. He set the iPhone down.

"I'm sorry," she said.

"I shouldn't expect you to know anything about gas and cars. I only know something of your world because it's the past, but how could I expect you to know anything of the future? Almost five hundred years from where we're sitting now. That's the crazy miracle. That we're together, El. I'm eating food in your house and sleeping in your bed. Whether it's for the time we've spent together or the weeks and years to come, the miracle is we found each other and maybe nobody understands our love, but we feel it and know it." He leaned back and raised his brows. "Let's face it. Like I said before, it's time travel. You eat some kind of herb or you drink a potion, or wormholes, or super high-tech, light speed stuff."

She leaned forward with her hands flat on the table. "Did ye swallow a pill or dram or potion?"

"No." He shook his head slowly. "I don't know how I got here. I fell down a tire hole in my boss's warehouse."

Billy noticed the change in her tone and expression. For the first time since he entered the cottage, she seemed more like a girl in his high school class anxious to hear about the latest Facebook post.

"What's a wormhole?"

"A magic hole, like a secret door you go through. And when you step through it, you're in another world, another dimension." He got up from the table. "I'm not a scientist, El, but, if I had to explain it or describe it, I'd say that you move into another place or time. You could go into an ancient, prehistoric civilization or future-travel onto planets and cities we don't even know exist!"

"Someday I'd like to hear more aboot that. I'd like to gae someplace far away."

"You could come to Cederburgh with me and Bran. I think you'd get along really well with my mom."

She knew he was joking with her, but she also knew that her life had imprisoned her. Unless she found Bran, there was no way she would ever go anywhere. Her sadness would keep her in the cottage where the boy was born, and she would spend the rest of her life caring for Ciaran.

"Really, I don't think we know anything about dimensions or wormholes or history, how time works or what happens between people." He sat down and placed his hand on hers. "Just like us. Unless this is a dream."

"Don't keep sayin' that!"

"But would you tell me if this is a dream? Can you be the dream and the dreamer?"

El turned away to the iPhone on the table. She brushed her finger across the screen. "Who is she?" They both stared at the face of a teenage girl. Brown hair framed her oval face with bright eyes and a pretty smile. "Ye showed me yer sister. That's no yer sister."

"She's a friend from school."

"Have ye kissed her?" She raised her gray eyes like two bullets aimed at him. "Have ye kissed her, Billy? Did ye ever make love tae her?"

He shook his head. "I told you I've never made love to any girl before you."

"Good." A smile crept onto her lips. "A' could tell the way you made love it wis yer first time." Her fingers passed across the light on his hair. "Shall we do it again?"

He looked into her eyes. One minute she was crying her eyes out over the loss of her son. Then she was cursing her father's killers. Now she wanted to make love. "What are you using me for?"

"Do ye know what emptiness is?" she shot back. She didn't flinch or look away. "You know what cars are an' wormholes," she said, "but do ye know what emptiness is?"

Before the next word had reached her lips, the heavy door blew open. Ciaran stomped in. "Tha an leanabh sa gh-leann, seachad air croit MhicGilleFhada!"

Billy turned to El. He couldn't tell if it was fear or joy that crossed her face. "What's he saying?"

"Th' baby is in the glen, past the Laing croft!"

"The baby that was sold?"

"Aye."

"How far is that?"

"A long journey, Billy." The words fell softly from her lips. "A long journey. Will ye gae with me?"

"Yes! Yes, of course!" He didn't hesitate. He was following the girl with a scar five hundred years ago. "Yes," he repeated. "I'll go."

"It could be muckle dangerous."

"But we have weapons…?"

"Aye, we have weapons."

Ciaran waved his arms, rolled his head and pounded a fist against the wall. Billy jumped up from the table. "Stop! Enough!"

"Ciaran wants tae take his sword an' find the baby."

"Does he know where the baby is?" Billy's voice rose anxiously. "He said it was past a croft. That's a farm, you said."

"Na."

"No, he doesn't really know where the baby is? Or no, a croft isn't like a farm?"

"Na, he doesn't really know where the baby is. Stop these stupid questions!"

Billy saw the frustration cross her face. The long journey to find her baby was imminent. He didn't want to be left out. "How long ago was Bran taken from you?"

"Seven months."

"You told me he was two months when the soldiers took him. So he's nine months now." Billy crossed his arms and thought a moment. He remembered being still seven when Kaylee was born, and she didn't look any different than any other pink, wrinkly baby he'd seen in a baby carriage or on TV. Okay, he thought. "How would Ciaran recognize him?"

"Whit?"

"Dè tha e ag ràdh?" Ciaran interrupted them from across the room.

El shot a look to Ciaran. His eyes were flaming with anger. She rattled off some words in Gaelic and turned back to Billy. "A' told him ye were no sure he would know whit Bran looked---"

Before she had finished the thought, Ciaran yanked his head to the side, grabbed his patched coat and stormed out of the house.

El crossed the room and shut the door. "Now ye have pure upset him."

"I'm sorry. I wasn't trying to get him upset." Billy was trying to be conciliatory, but his voice shot up in frustration along with his hands. "But we've got to be realistic! How will you know a baby you haven't seen since he was two months old?"

"If he's ma son, he will know me. An A' will smell him, A will taste him, A will know him." She walked over to the hearth. "If ye met me a hundred years from now, Billy, would ye know me?"

"My heart would know you." He was certain of that, but he had no idea why the words welled-up or where they came from.

"Well," she turned to face him. "Ma son is in ma heart." She whacked a tin serving spoon against the black kettle over the hearth and stomped from the room.

Billy watched the bedroom door slam behind her. He pushed his hands deep into his jeans pockets and stared at the burning hearth. *Maybe she makes love to me so she'll have a baby in case we can't find Bran. Or I'll stay here because of the baby, as if anyone can stay in a dream or start a new life in another dimension.* His gaze drifted away from the embers. *Or could I?*

He pulled open the heavy, barn-like back door of the cottage. It was high enough to let Aedan through with his head bent and just wide enough for the procession of two or three sheep. Billy watched El shuttle the animals out. Her expressionless face made her scar appear more threatening, as if the pain in her heart were stamped in a burning pink line on her cheek. Her Gaelic voice was subdued and dispassionate. The sheep needed no instruction. They were eager to graze on the sprouts of grass that poked through the melted snow.

"They won't run away?"

El shook her head. She looked up at dark clouds moving across the sky. "We will have tae wait till tomorrow before we can ride Aedan to the village."

Billy had already reflected on the possibility, having seen these same dark clouds burrow their way across the Midwest skies, dumping heavy, traffic-stopping rains or snow. The language, clothes, and rituals of this world were foreign to him, but the sky, at least, was vastly familiar.

He watched the clouds butt-up against each other in a long, ominous train. He had finally come to believe El's insistence that he was in Sixteenth Century Scotland, but something about this moment was different. The natural world was ringing through him. He knew deep inside his being that he had been transported. He could feel through his body, in his heart, in the nerves of his fingers, that a different world engulfed him. He saw the trees, the snow and rocks, but he knew they told a different story. It was a thin, almost invisible filament, yet a remarkably present line that separated this furious world from his Cederburgh life. He had traveled through time. "Damn!" He kicked the snow. "I'm in Scotland!"

"Dae ye see somethin', Billy?" El shouted.

He looked over to her. *She wants to talk; she doesn't want to stay mad at me.*

"If we stay out here much longer, we'll get caught i' a storm. Ye bring the one over by the trees." She pointed to a fat, brown sheep with a white mask from his eyes down his nose. "A'll get this one."

Billy walked slowly toward the sheep. He didn't want to scare it and have the animal scuttle deeper into the thick pine forest. He picked up a branch the length of his arm. "Come on," he said to the sheep. "Come to papa." He got closer, repeating, under his breath, some fragment of a song he remembered from preschool. "Lambzy-pamzy, lambzy-pamzy."

The words drifted into silence as he circled the animal, tapping the frozen ground with the stick. "I need you to go back to the house." Billy jumped and the sheep raised its head. "You probably don't know me, you don't recognize me, Mr. Fluffy Head, but I'm staying at the house with you. I'm a guest from another century and I made love to El. I was in her bed. If you looked through the gate, you could see me, like Aedan did. El's still pissed at me for something only she knows, I don't understand, but I can tell she's getting her chops back." Again, he circled the sheep. "We're lovers across five centuries. Isn't that amazing?"

The sheep munched. A green blade of grass stuck out of its mouth, but it didn't budge. Rain was coming down harder.

Billy lunged forward, ramming his chest into the sheep's backside. "Damn it, move!" he commanded, whacking the sheep's haunch with his stick. He dug his fingers into the wool on each side of the sheep's flanks, letting the sheep drag him from behind. "You're on the way!" The sheep headed towards the back door. "Keep going!" Billy shouted, hanging on the sheep's backside. A crack of lightning split the sky. Thunder roared through the last of his words.

Chapter 11

A trail of three covered wagons rattled slowly down the mountain. Men on horseback rode alongside. Inside the lead wagon, Jody sat with several older women. The strain of the journey, the sacrifices made, were marked on their faces.

Except for Jody, no one in the wagon was younger than thirty. Two of the women were nursing babies. A few of the women knit and sewed. Their eyes intermittently, like stolen glances, looked over to the stranger, Jody. She had no fear of looking at the women, but most of the time she kept her head down, shelling peas into a large porcelain bowl resting between her crossed legs.

Like so many of the days they had traveled through, the evening sky was dusty rose and grey. The wagon train had found a wide gravel arc that curved to the side of the trail. Some of the passengers were walking about, stretching their legs, looking over the mountain side to the valley below.

Kids, seven and eight, were chasing between the wagons, and some of the travelers stood at the fire pit eating stew from shallow tin plates.

Jody joined with two other women in serving the travelers.

As each passed with their plate, the server would dip her ladle into the steaming, iron cauldron that hung over the fire and fill the traveler's plate. One handsome, young man held his plate out for Jody. When she was about to fill his plate, he playfully pulled it back. After the second effort, the Trail Boss behind him nudged him to move ahead. The two older women watched the young man return Jody's smile with a wink before he moved on. The Trail Boss stuck his plate in front of Jody, not at all amused. His look was more a stern warning than a polite exchange for his meal.

The following morning was mountain cool. The passing clouds still hadn't moved far enough to let the full breath of sunlight shine through. Jody had just scooped a bowl of water from one of the huge wooden casks in the rear wagon. She set the bowl down on the rock and wet her face. A shadow crossed the bowl.

"We can't keep you any longer, Jody."

She looked up into the face of the Trail Boss. "What are you sayin'?"

"We'll be down the mountain soon enough. The town there will take you in."

"Take me in? I'm not a ward of some charity house! No one need take me in. We had an agreement."

"It depended on you working the trail and keeping up a moral conduct."

"That's just what I've been doing!"

"Not what some of the ladies say."

"Them old ladies haven't been kissed since their marriage night. What do they know about morals? I traded you a good horse for the promise I'd get to California!"

"You got a month of travel from us."

"That ain't the worth of a horse!"

"It is when you're crossin' mountains." The Trail Boss walked to the cliff edge. "We'll go through the town below. We're gonna leave you off there. You're young n' pretty. Too pretty for the women in the wagons. Town'll do you better.

Besides, I've got some of the young guys wantin' to fight over you, and that ain't helpin' us get to California."

"You ain't about to drop me off like a sack of old clothes. I'll do my walkin' into town."

Jody watched the wagons slowly creep away. Only the young man who winked, getting his food, paid any attention to her. He was bold enough to put his hand to his lips in a token of love, as the wagons descended the trail. She looked back to the town a thousand feet below.

Jody had walked a thousand feet just crossing the fields on Morrison's farm. Besides, this was mountain-down making it easier. All she carried with her was a cloth bag, holding two shirts and a comb she had stashed in her saddle bag the night before she and Tom had left the farm. Still, her feet were sore when she crossed the dirt, town road and walked into the hotel bar. A handful of scruffy cowboys stood at the bar drinking shots and bottles of beer. Jody looked around at the few men playing cards at the mostly empty tables. She turned her eyes back to the bar. A man in his fifties, wearing a stained white apron, spoke up quickly.

"Can I help you or who you looking for?"

"Like your father?" One of the men at the bar piped up, drawing scattered laughter from the men at the tables.

"I was just on the wagon train that passed through. I wasn't going to California, like them. I thought this would be a good place to settle." Jody had worked out parts of her story on the way down the mountain. "I'm looking for some work, as well."

"No work here. Maybe the dry goods store down the road."

"You could use a pretty face servin' us beers." A young man at one of the tables shouted across the room. "We're tired of seein' your old face. Give her a couple of days."

A few more men at the tables joined in. "Yea! Don't hurt to give the girl a try-out! We're payin' you for the beers. We get a voice in who's servin' it!"

"What's your name?" the man behind the bar fired back. "Jody."

"Jody's the name of my first wife!" someone shouted out.

"No point in me talkin' to you through this drivel of laggard men," the bartender shouted. "You can sit at one of the tables and see how many of these scoundrels buy you beers or go down to the river and watch the ducks for a while. Maybe buy a couple of apples at the market."

Her brother's death hadn't left her. The men looking at her, making all kinds of offers, didn't draw her smile. "I'll come back at sundown."

Jody walked out of the bar. She past a market. A box of apples sat on a stand in front of the store window, followed by a store selling boots and another with the word 'LAUNDRY' lettered on the window. Across the road she noticed another bar. Lettered on a wooden sign painted gold above the door were the words in red: "The Golden Slipper."

A few more steps led her to the sparse grassland along a narrow, sloping hillside. Medium size rocks lined the streaming river. Why it reminded her of another life, a life faraway in her past, she didn't know. But it brought back memories of another village, of people busily attending their needs on a warm, sunlight day. A feeling of love overwhelmed her.

She didn't know the village or recognize any of the faces, as small and as fleeting as they were, but if she could reach into the river and bring the village into her heart, she would have done just that. It was love she wanted back. The love of a mother who passed away years ago. The love of a brother who only weeks before was riding at her side. She watched the flow of the river and said goodbye to love.

"You're not twenty. I know you're lyin'!" The boss, Riley Wilson, with the white apron covering his big tummy, shouted at her.

"It don't make no difference. I can bake and cook and clean the tables that all the people comin' in dirty up."

Wilson didn't want to give up to her so easily. He liked the fact that his customers took a liking to her, but he didn't want to mess with trash or runaways.

"Plus I can add," she said. "And subtract so people won't be cheatin' money on you." She had learned enough about the people on the wagon train and where they came from to weave a fictional but plausible backstory of her own life. Wilson took a hard breath, staring at the empty tables. "There's room in the kitchen to sleep." He looked back to underscore his point. "Best be up at dawn. Work ain't easy here. Hotel folk want some kind of breakfast."

A pale half-moon was running away as a bolder sun came over the hills. Jody closed the kitchen screen door and looked over to the brown-spotted beagle standing beside the baking table.

"Jack, it's not your birthday so don't think you're getting a cake, but I'm making cookies and you can have one *sin* the chocolate. That's "without." My mom was Mexican."

She was wearing a white apron over her jeans and blue shirt embroidered with flowers, one of the two shirts and a brush she had stashed in her saddlebag the night before she and Tom had left for White Falls. Jody mixed up some flour, working hard, moving from one task to another. Jack, tongue hanging out, begged at her side, wagging his tail, following every step she took. With pillows and blankets, she had made a bed for herself in the kitchen. Jack was sprawled, a heartbeat away.

Nights were spent hustling back and forth in the barroom, serving up bottles of beer and whiskey to the cowboys at card tables and those alone. More than a few locals and strangers kept their eyes on her. She was getting used to once or twice a night some guy setting an extra coin on her trey.

She stood in the back kitchen doorway. The sounds of music and voices from the barroom were all but gone. She was adrift in moonlight, arms folded, looking up at the stars.

Her eyes filled with loneliness and longing. Jack looked over, sad- eyed, wagging his tail. "We're a long way from a lucky star, Jack."

The following day, most of the afternoon it rained, a soft June rain in the twilight. It was too early for a barroom full of customers, even if it weren't raining, but a tall, handsome man came through the door. He was better dressed than the ranchers and miners who frequented the bar. He took a seat at a table in the middle of the room.

With his dark hair slicked back and a tweed vest beneath his jacket, Jody thought he might be the town banker.

"You eatin'?" she called from the bar.

"No, Mam."

"Drinking?"

"No… Just talking."

"I'll get the boss." Jody started for a private door behind the bar, but his voice stopped her.

"It's you I come to talk to."

Jody turned back. "Me?" A thread of fear went through her, as she stepped to the corner of the bar. *Has this got something to do with the bank robbery?* was the first thought that raced through her mind.

"You're Jody, is that right?"

"Yes."

"Lot of boys in this town think you're a mighty pretty lady."

Jody blushed, feeling a little less nervous. "Thank you."

"You'd make a lot more money if you got up the nerve to sing."

"I don't sing. Besides, Mr. Murdoch don't want entertaining here."

"The saloon down the way does."

"No one there's asked me to sing."

"I just did. I'm Glen Martin, owner of The Golden Slipper." His quick smile grabbed at her lonely heart.

Chapter 12

"They are called trews." El handed Billy a pair of brown trousers.

He slid one leg after the other into the tight-fitting pants. "Should I button them?" He stared down at a row of buttons at the calf of each trouser leg.

"Ciaran might laugh at ye if ye dinnae. Ye look fine in ma faither's clothes." She picked up Billy's wet parka and jeans. "Ah will hang yer clothes on a chair next to the fire."

"What about the parka? Don't you think people are going to notice it's not from here?"

"Aye, we kin tell them it's from France an' ye took it from a fighter."

Billy watched her leave. He sat down on the bed and looked over to Aedan munching on hay. "Aedan, tell your sheep friends: if it's not on your phone, it ain't real, and if you ain't on Facebook, you're not in this world." He finished buttoning the bottoms of his trews and looked over to the horse. "I'm starting to talk to animals. First, the lamb, now you. Of course, I talked to my dog all the time, and he wagged his tail, but he never really answered me either."

"Guess whit?" El pushed the door open with a perplexed look on her face. "Ciaran told me the man never said anythin' about a baby bein' sold."

"He's lying." Billy shot straight up from the bed. "He doesn't want me to go with you. He wants to go himself."

"He's never lied to me. He's always protectin me."

"He didn't protect you when the soldiers took your baby and murdered your father!"

"He was not here, Billy." She looked at him crossly. "That's mean for ye tae say."

"I'm sorry. I shouldn't have said that, but don't you see, he's jealous? You said yourself before that he was jealous." He waited for the rumbling sound of thunder to ebb, but his voice remained agitated and he wouldn't let go. "Jesus, maybe I don't know anything about swords and sheep, but I know what jealousy is about. It's no different in my town, in my school!"

El raised her voice over another spike of thunder. "I'm tired o' hearin' about yer school an' all the girls in yer school!"

"I never said anything about girls! You don't get it, do you?"

"Get whit?"

He followed her across the room. "I've never been in love with anyone before. I'm just a guy at Lincoln High in some stupid century you don't even know exists. But I feel this thing for you!"

She kneeled and opened what looked to Billy like a chest. "We call this a kist," she said, averting his look. "What thing are ye talkin' about, Billy?"

"It's in my heart. I can't get my arms around it. It's bigger than my heart. It's you. You are in my heart!" In the next step, he turned towards the door and made sure it was shut before he looked back. "I didn't plan this. I don't even know if you're real or if I'm real anymore. But I know something in my heart is bigger than anything I've ever felt before."

El rose slowly with an armful of colored material. "Bran is in ma heart. Ma mither and faither are in ma heart. Ma brither is close to ma heart." She laid the wrappings on the bed and started to sort them.

"And me?"

"If ye're not in ma heart, where are ye?" He watched her carry the sorted material to a table against the wall. "He's nine months now. He's no a wee baby anymore. None o' these are gonna fit him, but A can use the cloth."

Are we looking for a baby that was sold or that doesn't exist? he wondered. *Is all this sorting baby clothes just a part of her delusion?* A raindrop hit his forehead. He looked up at the thatched ceiling. "The roof is leaking."

"We always get a few drops in a rainstorm."

His blue eyes shifted back to her. "Do you believe Ciaran or is he lying? Just answer the question."

El unfolded a small brown tunic. "Ma mither telt me when A wis a wee girl that Ciaran had whit she called a 'condition.' She did no say there wis somethin' wrong with him. She said he wis touched by a spirit. As I grew older, she explained more tae me. A asked her, if I am Ciaran's twin, why didnae the spirit touch me, as well? She told me that the spirit touched everybody in the house. Because we were all a pairt o' Ciaran's condition. How we treated him, how we reacted and how we tried to help him were part o' the condition. That is how the spirit touched all o' us." El unfolded the last of the baby's clothes. "But Ciaran is like any laddie."

"So maybe a baby wasn't sold. Is that what you're saying. Maybe there is no baby?"

"Aye. But I know thare is." She lit a splinter of wood from the lantern flame beside the cabinets and carried it to the bedside lantern. "It is nae a game he's playin'. It's a hurt he's nursin'." She blew out the flame and turned to Billy. "Now kiss me."

He held her in his arms. Their bodies fell together to the feather quilt.

"The rain will stop an' ye will go with me tae find ma Bran." She put her finger to his lips. "A'm older than ye. Five hundred years older. Dinnae say another word."

He felt her hand slip beneath his trews at the waist.

Ciaran sat on his bed, his arms wrapped around his pillow, rocking back and forth. It didn't seem the Scottish boy cared who was looking at him or was even aware of anyone's gaze.

Billy had seen enough TV documentaries and had glimpsed into Special Ed classes on his way through the school hallway to know that what Ciaran had, what El called a "condition," was actually some kind of autism.

"Ye can put bowls on the table," she said, turning from the hearth. "They're in the cabinet." She pointed to a dark wood cabinet along the wall where Ciaran slept.

Billy got up from the table. "Where do you wash all the bowls and cups?"

"Ciaran washes thaim. He heats water an' pours the hot water over thaim."

Billy took three wooden bowls and tin cups from the cabinet. He smiled to himself, thinking of his mother telling him to put dishes on the table. By the time he had placed the last cup next to its bowl, the smile had faded. *She's worried. I know she's worried. She has no idea where I am and I can't tell her, I can't text her, I can't call her.* He looked up at drops of rainwater falling through the thatched roof. *I don't know how to get out of this Century and nobody I know can get back to it.*

"Yer mither will forgive ye, if that's what yer thinking." El looked over to Billy. "She'll be proud o' ye someday."

"You don't know that."

"A'm a mither, Billy. Mibbie A'm young, but so wis ma mither when she had Ciaran an' me."

"And my mother, too." Billy sputtered a nervous giggle. "Maybe you were my mother five hundred years ago."

"Then maybe we shouldnae be makin' love." El smacked the black pot again with the tin spoon.

"I take it back." Billy raised his hands. He didn't want to see her mad again. "I ne—"

Lightning burst across the window. Thunder ripped through the sky, ramming its crescendo against the little cottage. The pots and plates rattled with what seemed the same nervous fear that crossed the faces of those inside. Ciaran jumped up and raced to the door.

"Ciaran!" Before the name had left El's lips, the door slammed.

"He'll catch pneumonia in the rain!" Billy looked over to El. "Why don't you do something? You said we were all a part of his condition. If he gets sick, we'll never get out. We'll be stuck here, and Bran will be lost forever! And I will never be born!"

"Is all ye can think aboot is yerself?"

"If I'm not thinking about myself, myself can never be here! The journey will end! That's his plan!" Billy flung his parka over his shoulders and raced out the door.

He stood in the pouring rain, calling out the twin's name. Waves of mist rolled through the torn veil of evening light. He took a few steps into the downpour, barely able to make out the silhouette of trees. "I need to talk to you, Ciaran!" But he knew, even as he shouted the words, there was nothing he could say to Ciaran that the boy would understand.

He ran down the path that led to the grave of El and Ciaran's father. A jagged blue spear of light rocketed through the sky illuminating everything around him.

Ciaran was clinging to a tree, his head pressed against the bark, like a pained animal hanging on for its life or trying to escape back into the heartbeat of the tree.

"Ciaran!" Billy rushed to his side and threw his arms around him. "Ciaran, I am your friend. Friend! Like on the road. Friend!" He could feel Ciaran pushing his head into the side of his parka. The boy was sobbing, wailing, and muttering in his own incomprehensible language.

"Look!" Billy wormed his hand inside his jacket and pulled out the iPhone. "Look!" He raised the phone in front of Ciaran's face.

"I will show you things that you have never seen! I will make you happy again." Billy shouted out every thought that came to him. "I'm putting this back in my pocket. It can't get wet. Not like us. We're soaking wet and we'll get sick. We'll die if we stay here!" He grabbed Ciaran's arm. "Listen to me, Ciaran. El will never forgive us! We've got to get out of this storm." The shock of thunder rode across Billy's words. "Together, Ciaran, together! We're friends!"

Ciaran threw his head back under the bare branches, letting the beating rain exalt his pain and wash away his tears. "Frien…" he gurgled.

"Yes, like we were on the road. Friends." Billy dropped his arm and muscled the boy off the tree. "Come, come with me."

El stood in the doorway, holding a lantern. Her gray eyes filled with disbelief, as she held out her hand. "Get in here afore ye die on me."

Ciaran scuttled quickly to his bed and plopped down, shivering in his wet clothes and stamping his feet against the stone floor. El glanced back to Billy. Rain dripped off his forehead and cheeks, reddened with exhaustion. His drenched, buzz-cut hair was flat on his scalp. "Now ye're a part of us," she said. "Thank God, Billy, ye're here." She banged the hanging pot.

Chapter 13

She stood at the corner of the piano. The man accompanying her at the piano looked to be in his mid-fifties. He wore a pressed, black suit jacket and matching pants. His straight, white hair fell across his forehead, and a glass of bourbon sat on the piano top within his hand's reach. Jody was nervous, but she wasn't afraid. This was her chance to show off who she was, and, at the same time, to liberate herself from the demeaning kitchen work and leering customers at the hotel bar. She knew she would miss Jack. She already did, but the brown and white beagle would easily befriend someone else running the kitchen.

She wore a pale yellow, flowered, summer dress the club owner, Mr. Martin, had bought for her. The dress flattered her figure and seemed to brighten the spirit of her voice which, not withstanding a slight case of nerves, was sweet and engaging. She charmed the men who had moved their chairs and gathered closer.

Glen Martin stood at the bar, watching, with a steady, encouraging gaze. The evening was a small but definite triumph. Still, Jody slept on a straw mattress in the storeroom filled with cases of beer and whiskey. She didn't want to think ahead. She couldn't imagine singing in bar halls the rest of her life, but she was eighteen now and she had no education but what Tom had taught her.

She couldn't go back ever again to the farm. It was not something she wanted to do, anyway. Mr. Martin was paying her a meagre wage and she was allowed to keep the tips her admirers put in the glass jar on the piano top. Almost half of those, forty percent, however, went to the piano player. Neither did she forget that she was a fugitive from the law. She had changed her last name from the day she stepped into the hotel bar. The town knew her as Jody Daniels. That's what the painted sign said outside the Golden Slipper front door: "No Charge! Nightly – Listen to the Songbird – Jody Daniels – from the High Sierras!"

"Are you the young lady they call the songbird?"

Jody turned to look up. She was on her knees picking flowers. "Maybe, if your talkin' about The Golden Slipper."

The old man smiled. He was creeping into seventy. That's what Jody thought. He was hunched and his knotted hands held the reins of the one-horse wagon. Half the wrinkles on his face were covered with grey whiskers.

"That's why I'm here. Back of me is six cases of beer."

Jody looked to the rear of the horse-drawn wagon. "You want some help carrying those in? I'll go in and get you some help."

"Is the boss around? Tell him he owes me some money."

"When I see Mr. Martin, I'll tell him."

Jody hurried back into the saloon, still clutching the flowers. But when she got inside, she stopped. Martin was standing at the bar talking to a young woman, a year or two older than Jody. The woman had a smile on her face and her right hand was reaching out to touch Martin's arm. "Mr.

Martin, beer wagon's here!" Jody's voice cracked across the empty room. "The man wants to talk to you." She put the flowers in the vase on the piano and never looked back, until he passed her walking to the door.

That night Jody and Martin made love in his upstairs bedroom. It was not the first time she had slept with him.

She had staked too much of her heart on a man whose heart had nowhere to go.

"Who is she?"

"A friend, looking for work. Don't worry. She doesn't sing."

"It wasn't her voice I was thinking of."

He moved her closer and put his hand against her leg. "You're my songbird, honey."

"Then maybe we should sleep together every night."

Jody sat on the piano, a glass of champagne in hand, singing a risqué Music Hall song. She wore a sparkly dress, with her silk-stockinged legs crossed in a showy pose, her hair done up with ribbons, her eyes and lips brightly colored. Her small-town fame had spread. Each night she filled the room with cowboys and locals. Even some women showed up, taking a look at who was keeping their husbands from dinner with them. The men hooted and clapped along with the rhythm of her voice.

Martin, pleased with the crowd's reaction, watched from the back of the room. Later, at night, he took Jody into his bed, as if this were her reward for a successful performance.

In the back of her mind, perhaps in her soul, Jody knew she was playing a dangerous game, trading her body, her deep- felt sense of self, for the comfort of an affirmation that someone in the world found her worth something. She watched the rainclouds pass overhead and heard a voice from the back door of the saloon.

"Señorita Jody... Señorita Jody..."

Yolanda, the young bar server, was coming towards her. "It soon maybe raining," she said. "No one is coming." Her Mexican accent rolled softly from one word to the next. "I have a song for you. It is for you because many days I see you standing out here looking at the sky and wondering."

Jody smiled. "Thank you, Yolanda. Gracias. I don't know many Spanish words, but I will try."

"Many are the nights I think of you..." Yolanda sang. "Many are the days you fill my heart... In many of the worlds I've searched for you... In many of my dreams you are the starring part..." Yolanda smiled. "Do you like it?"

"It's beautiful... so beautiful. And so is your voice."

"And in Español," she began to sing again, "Tantas son las noches pensando en ti... Tantos son los días que llenas mi corazón... Tantos son los mundos que he buscado a ti...

Tantos son los sueaños en que estamos juntosâ¦"

"We will sing it many times. The rain is coming. You can practice in front of me and maybe at the two tables with people." She laughed.

That night, Yolanda was very right. The storm blew in.

Most of the tables were empty. Jody, in a red, sequined blouse and jeans, sang to few patrons, to Yolanda and to a man sitting at a table closest to the door. He was short, stocky, and seemed less interested in the music than in the reactions of the few people in attendance. Even though the rain made a racket on the roof, her voice carried the lyrics across the room in English and Spanish. Some of the patrons even wiped tears from their eyes.

Martin wasn't there to see Jody perform her new song. She was told he had gone out of town.

The rain didn't stop for several days. Yolanda wanted to know if Jody was interested in learning another song.

"No, mi amiga. I am sad." "Triste."

"Si."

She was unmoored, without a family or home, singing in a saloon to people, many of whom were more interested in her body than her voice, and would go home when the doors closed to their own families or lovers or dreams. The days passed, taking the rainclouds with them. On her way back from a walk, Jody saw Martin standing in front of the saloon with a short, stocky man she thought she recognized as the man who had sat at the back of the room the night she first sang a Spanish song.

"Jody," Martin yelled, "come over here. I want to introduce you to someone."

"Mr. Beckwith, this is the voice that so enchanted you." Jody offered a nervous smile. "Mr. Beckwith wants you to entertain at his establishment in Redhorn."

"What?"

"He heard your voice and got a good look at how pretty you are and contacted me for hiring you in Redhorn."

"Where's Redhorn?"

"Maybe sixty miles from here," Martin answered. The tone of his reply made it clear that this wasn't up for discussion.

"A long days ride, at the base of Mount Carmel," Mr. Beckwith added. "You'll feel very much at home there."

Jody sounded more frightened than confused. "Why would I want to go there?"

"Because that's the deal I made with Mr. Beckwith." Martin answered in a cold, unequivocal voice.

Whatever sense of self-worth Jody thought she had was destroyed in a transaction over which she had no control. But she wasn't going gently, screaming at Martin in the bedroom they shared. "I'm not going! I don't care whose deal I mess up, it ain't with me!"

"And I'm telling you you're going," Martin answered in a louder voice.

Jody picked up a bottle of perfume from the dresser and threw it at Martin. Martin turned quickly, as the bottle shattered the bedroom window. "Now look what you did!"

"I ain't going!"

Glen took two steps towards her and grabbed her arms. "You're going 'cause I say you're going!"

"Let go of me!" She tried to twist away. "You're hurting me!"

"Tell me you're going!"

"You don't own me! You don't love me! If you loved me, you wouldn't be sending me off!"

"Love's got a market value like any other business." He threw her onto the bed. "I gave you a chance and a career. Be thankful for that. You was sleepin' on a kitchen floor with a dog when I met you."

Jody leaned back on the pillow, sobbing uncontrollably, the first time she had let anyone see her cry.

The night sky glimmered with stars. Beckwith's DeerShot Saloon was lit-up, with people still coming in on the frosty night. Jody, tarted up in a tight, sexy, black satin dress and heavy make-up that turned her farm-girl youth into a made-up burlesque doll's face, strutted onto a small stage and began singing her trademark, risqué Music Hall songs to the delight of the customers. She knew her talent was sufficient, and her poise had matured. But she never sang in English or in Spanish the song she loved the most, "Many are the Nights."

At night, after the saloon lights were out and the last customers had left, Jody climbed the steps to Beckwith's upstairs living quarters.

She sat on his bed, in a black satin chemise while Beckwith filled two glasses with whiskey.

"The men like you, Jody." He handed her a glass. "Why don't we make ourselves a little business deal?"

"What kind of a business deal?"

"It's not fair that I keep you all to myself."

She stared at the short, paunchy man who had become her lover.

"There's a room down the hall that's empty and you've got plenty of time," he continued, "when you're not singing." He took a sip of whiskey. "What are you thinking?"

"I traded my horse for a ride through the mountains and my body for a song." She touched the gold coin necklace on her neck. "I may as well sell my soul for the upkeep."

Jody sat, bundled up, on the bench of a one-horse buggy. Down the street, two men, both her ex-lovers, were in a furious argument in front of the Golden Slipper Saloon. She was close enough to hear them shouting.

"She's pregnant! She was pregnant when she came to me!" Beckwith screamed.

"You don't know who the father is any better than I do!" Glen Martin was no match for Beckwith's fury, but his powerful physical presence offset any threatening gesture.

"I know damaged goods when it's staring me in the face! You take her back!"

Sadness and humiliation filled Jody's eyes. The words she had just heard reduced her to a piece of cloth traded between two penniless hobos. She climbed down from the buckboard. Her eyes welled-up, as she walked through the desolate street, away from the saloon.

"Take her back!" Beckwith shouted again.

But Martin had his eyes focused on the lone figure walking further down the road. "Jody! Jody!" His shouts were lost on the dust in the wind. She kept on walking. "She'll come back," Martin muttered. "She's got nowhere else to go."

Jody sat against a tree. She pulled the shawl that covered her shoulders closer. She had walked deeper into the forest than she knew either of the men would venture. Nor would they send men on horseback to find her and renew the battle over caring for a pregnant woman of no value to either of them.

She wasn't worth the effort. No song was in her soul. Darkness claimed her dreams. She had no idea if Martin, Beckwith, or any of the other men she had entertained, were the father of her child. But the life growing inside of her was hers, the very first thing she ever had that was hers, that her mother would have loved to hold in her arms, and that Jody swore in her heart, that night of darkness, to sustain and protect.

Mrs. Quellum, the fifty-plus-year-old, dyed-blond woman who ran the brothel, was sympathetic to Jody. She had seven girls working for her in an old, two-story New England style house, complete with gables and a wide front porch. Built just after the Civil War by a wealthy farmer, it sat on the outskirts of the rural town and was referred to by its residents as a "social club." Nearly all the business came from soldiers stationed at an Army Fort nearby.

Most of the young woman were supportive of Jody. They were desperately careful to make sure they didn't get pregnant. For her stay and keep, Jody did laundry and cooked meals for the girls. It was cold enough to be snowing the morning Jody waddled down the upstairs hallway, shouting to anyone who could hear. "The water's runnin' on my legs. I think the baby's comin'!"

Minutes later, she lay on a bed with her knees propped up and one young woman on each side of her hollering, "Push! Push the baby! Push!"

Jody's red face was knotted in determination. An older Black woman, Claire, just past her twenty-fifth birthday, stood at the end of the cot ready to receive the baby. "Push harder, honey. Harder!" Claire kept hollering "You're doing it! You're doing it! The baby's coming out whole!" She leaned forward between Jody's bent legs and took the baby in her hands. "It's a boy, honey," followed by a four female chorus of "It's a boy!"

"A beautiful boy," Claire added, in a hurried voice. "We gotta get someone to cut the cord."

Jody was dripping wet. Her face was a mixture of happiness, exhaustion, relief, and the loneliness of knowing there was no father to hold her hand or embrace her son.

Rain tumbled through the sky. It was a warm Spring rain that brought the same warm feeling to Jody's soul. She stood on the front porch, holding Danny in her arms, wrapped in blankets the girls had either knit or bought for him. They carried mixed feelings about Danny.

On the one hand, they enjoyed the excitement of new life, of indomitable youth around them, but it also brought into view the sexuality they were expending, the trafficking in favors that brought them no permanent happiness or spiritual grace. Mrs. Quellum, too, was growing impatient. "It's four months now," she pointed out. "Plus the three, four months before you had the baby. You've got to start earning your keep again, Jody. Lots of those Army boys liked you. Besides, some of the girls are getting jealous. I don't want them thinkin' they can all have babies and live here."

"My strength is getting near," Jody said. Mrs. Quellum patted Danny's blanket. "How's the little fella?"

"Perfect, 'cept his left foot's just a little bigger than his right."

"God hope that's the only thing. Hard for me to see."

"I can. I know every inch of my baby. Ain't that many inches to him."

Mrs. Quellum watched the soft rain fall for a minute. "I'll see to it that someone watches the boy." Her voice was firm. There was no room for discussion. "Now, the Sheriff's getting on me for your condition, and me and him never had problems before." She turned and went back into the house.

Jody cradled the baby against the rain. "You've been kissed by my mother angel before you came to earth, Danny boy." She kissed a strawberry birthmark on the boy's head just above his temple. "Nothing bad's never going to happen to you."

It was a rowdy night at the bordello. Smoke, laughter, and a hunchback cowboy playing the banjo filled the parlor. The Army boys had been paid that day, and they were buying the drinks that night, along with tipping the girls and dropping money in a jar for Danny's upkeep. Jody was sitting on an officer's lap, her arm around him, nuzzling him with kisses. She was wearing a red, satin corset which gave the soldier a good idea of the package he was going to unzip when he followed her upstairs. He was telling Jody how much he loved girls with a little color in them, when a loud disruption at the front door pulled their attention to the hallway.

Soldier ready, his body straightened. Jody swung her legs to the floor.

Three men were standing in the hallway. "Where is she?" Jody recognized the Sheriff, and the man standing next to him she thought was his Deputy. The tall man with a gray beard and gray hair was a stranger, but in a black robe and a loud, castigating voice, raging above the commotion, she knew he was a Priest or Father from the church.

"She's raising the child in Satan's house!" he bellowed. "She keeps him locked upstairs, unable to see the glory of God's creation! Seize him! Seize the child now!"

The Deputy started up the stairs as Mrs. Quellum got in the middle of the ruckus. "This is my establishment. You can't do this without a warrant! The child has done nothing wrong."

"No!" Jody screamed, racing into the hallway. "This is my son! My child!"

The Sheriff grabbed her, holding her back. "Don't make this more difficult on yourself. The Priest petitioned the court, and the judge issued the warrant."

"How could you?" she screamed at the Priest, trying, at the same time to desperately break away from the Sheriff's grip. "This is my child, my baby! He came from me! He came from my soul" Tears streamed down her cheeks and a choking cry rose from her lips. "You can't do this!"

"You don't even know who the father is!" the Priest declared. "He is a bastard child whose soul must be saved! God steals from Satan what He can."

"The thief is in your heart, not in God's," Mrs. Quellum shot back.

"And the silver's in your pocket!" the Priest snapped. "All you care about! Not this poor child living in sin!"

"He has my soul," Jody cried. "My soul!"

The Deputy came rushing down the stairs, carrying the baby, like a package wrapped in a blue blanket. He raced out the open front door.

"Help me, Mrs. Qeullum! Don't let them take my Danny."

Mrs. Quellum stared at the Sherriff, with a helpless, re-grettable look. She had a business to protect.

Jody pushed past her through the open door to the porch. "You're interfering with the law!" the Sheriff shouted.

She rushed down the porch steps, screaming, "No, no, you can't take my baby!" Like a mad woman in a red corset, she raced into the night, chasing a horse-driven carriage.

The Sheriff and Mrs. Quellum stood on the porch, watching Jody stumble to her knees in the dusty road, sob-bing hysterically. A man, half-dressed, pushed his way to the front of the crowded porch. He saw the fallen woman on the road.

"What happened?"

"Sadly, Mr. Storm, the woman just lost her child to the church." Mrs. Quellum looked over to the Bank Investigator, tucking his shirt at the waist.

"How old is the child?"

"Four months."

"And the mother has worked here long?"

"Since well before the baby was born."

Mr. Storm looked back to the woman in the red corset fallen on the road, lit by the moon.

Chapter 14

Billy leaned in, placing a firm but gentle grip on Ciaran's hand. The Scottish boy sat hunched at the table, staring at the thin, black object in front of him, while his time-traveling friend guided Ciaran's finger, first tapping on one of the pink airplanes, then dragging the digital image across the iPhone screen to a landing strip. Mesmerized by the moving images, the bright colors and music, Ciaran ignored the water still dripping off his hair and rain-soaked clothes. His attention had settled on the small iPhone screen. Within minutes, without Billy's assistance, he began safely guiding the pink planes and amber choppers to their landing strips.

Billy turned to El, astonished at how quickly Ciaran had caught on, how skilled he was at playing a game he'd never seen before, with a device he'd never even imagined could exist. "He's amazing. He's a video game genius. He plays Flight Control better than me!"

"Ye would likely have a friend for life if ye stayed long enough. That's nae th' only game on yer phane, is it?" El's tone turned sharper before Billy could tell if she was being sarcastic or hopeful. "He's gaun to die if he doesn't get out o' those wet clothes, an' I'll likely have tae bury ye beside him."

Her threat was lost in the rattle of pots. Billy looked up, past the oak beam, to the sound of rumbling thunder "It won't stop. It'll rain through the night."

She pointed towards Ciaran's cabinet-bed and her voice sounded more like a command. "Feumaidh tu aodach tioram a' chur ort. Bheir me feadhainn dhuit." She turned to Billy. "He's got to get dry clothes an' so do ye. Come wi' me."

"Wait!" Billy's gaze shifted between El's stirring spoon and Ciaran's hand still poised over the iPhone. "I can't leave the phone with him."

"Dinna worry. Ye have made him very happy."

"Everybody's happy with a five-hundred-dollar phone," Billy grumbled. Reluctantly, he followed El into her bedroom.

She took a pair of browns trews and a white tunic from the kist. "A'll be back," she said.

Billy sat on the bed in his underwear, nervously tapping his foot, ready to jump up and get his iPhone back. He could hear Ciaran's raging words and the shuffle of his chair against the rough stone floor.

He closed his eyes and felt a creeping hollowness reach towards his heart. Finding El's son is more important than winning any match. If Bran dies, maybe I'm born somewhere, in another time, like the wind scattering my seed in some unknown galaxy, but I won't be able to draw the same crazy line back to El, back to her heart. Aedan whinnied softly, as if he agreed.

Billy heard the voice of the horse, opened his eyes and got to his feet. "Look at me." His voice was directed towards Aedan, but, in the next moment, his gaze drifted away along with his voice, and he opened his heart to the room. "I love my mom and my sister, but this isn't family love. This is someone in the world. It's a part of me I never felt before, like finding an island inside of me I never knew was there."

Aedan raised his head, stepped back, and whinnied louder, as the bedroom door flew open.

"Ye're a good friend, lettin' Ciaran use yer phone," El said, closing the door.

"He's not using it now?" The serenity of Billy's thoughts disappeared in the jittery uptick of his voice. "You took it away, right? That's an expensive phone, El. My mother–"

"A heard about your mither afore, bit ah don't think yer phone costs as much as ma brither's life." She swooped in, cutting Billy off. "Or his pure happiness."

"I know my phone is just a phone. It's who gave it to me… that's what means something!" He threw up his arm wildly. "Don't you have something, anything your mother gave you that you…" He groped for a word, finally seizing on, "cherish."

"Anything ma mother touched means something tae me. Anything ye see in this house. Aye, it's only two rooms. Not like the rooms ye showed me in yer house. But it's ma world. Ma mither wis in this world, under this roof, 'til she died. Her hands were on everything ma hands touch."

Billy backed off and took a breath. "I'm sorry El. I'm not sure what f'n for, but I'm sorry."

"Know this, Billy. You're here because A'm here. Ye will help me bring ma child back tae me. An ma mither, who gave birth tae me, is a part o` yer journey, too."

"Then let's get on with the journey. If that's why I'm here, and I've already forfeited a title match, let me, at least, do something right."

The racket of fists turned their startled looks to the bedroom door flying open. Ciaran was standing in the doorway, throwing his arms up, blathering in Gaelic. "Air do shocair, a Chiarain. Dèan air do shocair!"

El looked over to Billy. "Something's wrong wi' the phone."

"Holy shit! I knew it!" Billy leapt across the bed to the doorway. The three rushed into the main room. Billy grabbed the iPhone off the table.

"He says the game went away."

Billy swiped the screen with his finger. "It's here. He just pushed a wrong icon and flipped to a different page." He cast a relieved smile in Ciaran's direction. "But tell him he can't play anymore tonight. We have to save the battery."

"Whit's a baah… tury?" El stumbled over the word. She kept one hand on Ciaran's arm, anxious to explain the problem to him.

"It's the thing that makes the cell phone work." Billy caught Ciaran's glare. He was staring, with ownership- intensity, at the iPhone in Billy's hand. "The more you use it, the weaker it gets. Just like Aedan. The further you ride him, the more he needs to rest, eat, and drink water." A surge of confidence and finality, in something he knew something about and she didn't, took over in his voice. "The iPhone is Aedan. The battery is food and water."

Billy wasn't sure El heard him over the blast of thunder. All he could make out from her explanation to Ciaran was the word "Aedan." He watched Ciaran rotate his head.

"Will he quit and go to bed?"

"He hasnae eaten. Juist like yer baahtury, he needs food, an so do ye." Her disapproving tone turned to a rare childish smile. "Ye realize ye're standin' in yer underclothes and A'm seein' yer baahtury is a wee bit low."

"I think it's stopped raining." From the warmth of the bed, Billy stared at the thatch above him. He rested his hand on El's thigh, a gesture as comforting as it was a source of pleasure.

"Go back tae sleep," she whispered. "Ye're gonna need yer rest."

"How long does it take to get to the village?"

"It depends on if we ride without stopping."

She told him that there was always the chance they'd run into drunken or hostile soldiers. Then, before the two of them were spotted, they'd be forced to hide or take a longer route.

"Are we going to take our swords?"

"I will decide in the mornin'. Go back tae sleep."

She's had experience with soldiers, he thought. They raped her and murdered her father. She knows the terrain and where she's going.

My father is the only soldier I've ever known. I never saw him drunk or hurt anyone. Billy clasped his hands behind his head and let the thoughts roll through his mind. *He was brave enough to die. Nobody understood him, my mother says. Maybe I will. Maybe that's why I'm here.* He closed his eyes and listened to the rain. *Maybe if I fight for Bran's life, I'll understand who my father was.*

"I can't do that. I can't leave the phone with him." Billy got up from the table and pointed to Ciaran's untouched bowl of porridge. "Look, he hasn't taken one spoonful of his breakfast. He's been playing Flight Control since I gave him the phone."

El reminded him of how upset Ciaran got the night before. "He's gonna get pure upset again if ye take it away now."

"That cell phone is the only thing I've got that ties me to my world," Billy countered.

"Who have ye talked to from yer world synce ye came into this house?" She hit the black pot with a spoon. "This is yer world, Billy."

Billy looked over to Ciaran sitting cross-legged on his closeted, straw bed with the phone in his hand. "That's just it! This is my world and I can't get a signal! I can't call my Mom. I can't call my coach. My coach who was banking on me. I can't call anyone! Who am I, El, if I can't connect to the people I know?"

"Am I not good enough for ye to talk to?" She dropped the spoon to the floor and folded her arms. "Answer me, Billy... Answer me!"

Billy turned away from her to the sheet of gray light that hung across the window. *I'm arguing with someone five hundred years older than me... or is it five hundred years younger?* He clenched his fists, took a deep breath, and drew on the only thought that made sense to him: *Am I supposed to stay here and live my life with El?*

"Well, A'm not in yer fancy high school with all the windows. But ye've got a commitment tae me, don't ye? Who's bin sleepin' next tae me at night? Who's puttin' his sixteen-year-auld hand on ma fud?"

Billy glanced over to Ciaran, hoping he was still buried in Flight Control and not watching the two of them arguing, not watching his sister's temper flare and giving him a reason to jump up and intercede.

For the first time in his life, the first time since he saw his father's casket lowered into the earth, he felt something wasn't right. He had fought strength, boys with muscled arms and legs, with speed and strategy. He had never fought a woman's heart.

His voice dropped to a whisper with his only defense. "That little phone is something I need as much as you need swords and food for your survival. It's different worlds, El. We're from different worlds."

She responded with a look of disappointment Billy didn't expect. He watched her march over to Ciaran. In one sudden sweep of her hand, El scooped the iPhone from her brother's grasp. Ciaran looked up as if she had slapped him across the face.

"Ciaran," she said, and rattled off a torrent of Gaelic.

Then she turned to Billy. "Here's yer bloody phone," she snapped.

Ciaran got to his feet. He didn't look directly at Billy, but the Cederburgh boy could see there was as much confusion as anger in his eyes. Ciaran grabbed a heavy cloak and stormed out of the house.

"Ciaran is gonna bring Aedan tae the front o' the house an' post him there." The grim look on El's face had softened.

"I told him that if he takes the sheep out an' lets them graze, ye'll let him play with the phone when we git back."

She opened the bedroom cabinet that held the broad swords and long bows. "This is a biodag. Some folk call it a dirk." She held a long knife in front of her. "It fits in this sheath an' belt. Wrap it around yer waist."

Billy had never seen a knife as sleek with a point as deadly. The silver handle wasn't jeweled but it still sparkled in his eyes. He deftly stashed the dirk into its sheath and tightened his belt.

El did the same with her belt and slipped a silver dirk into its sheath. She looked down at Billy's boots. "Ye canae wear them. No one has ever seen boots like those." She opened the other cabinet and removed a pair of brown leather wrappings. "These are called cuaran. Wrap them over yer calves, from the bottom o' yer trouser. Then over the foot."

He stared at the long leather straps dangling from her hand. "You want me to wear these instead of my boots? Why can't we tell people the boots are from France, just like the parka?"

"Aye, Billy," she said, handing over the cuaran. "A'm wantin' ye to look like a lad from the Highlands. The parka could be a French fashion. No one will believe the craft o' those boots." She watched him struggle with the wrappings. "Ye're no afraid, are ye?"

"I'm more afraid of these damn things falling off my feet." He grunted and stood straight up. "I'm anxious to see what the village looks like."

Billy followed her to the bedroom door. She turned back and raised her hand to his cheek. "Kiss me."

Billy stopped. "This isn't our last kiss?"

"Only if ye get us killed." A smile peaked on her lips. "Now kiss me. Don't be afraid. Aedan has traveled this road afore."

They kissed. She grabbed his hand and rushed across the room to the front door.

"You still haven't told me. Is it far?"

"How far is the journey of any life to find yur heart?" She opened the door.

Chapter 15

The covered wagon travelled along the country road. The two drivers, stationed on the bench, kept the four horses at a steady pace. The drivers were bundled in sheepskin jackets against the cold prairie wind that whipped the wagon bonnet.

Inside, on benches that ran the length of the wagon, a dozen girls sat, ranging in age from late teens to almost thirty. They looked tired, despondent, showing no attempt at conversation or any sign of laughter or even a smile. Silently, they ate rice and beans from their tin plates. Jody sat between a Mexican girl bundled in a shawl sweater and Claire, a woman whose face was already hardened by the rigors of her trade and whose hands had brought Danny into the world.

Jody pushed aside her plate of food. A hacking cough and fever kept her from eating. "You'll be a ghost if you don't eat," Claire whispered. "The men ain't gonna want what they can't grab and feel." She scooped up a fork of rice. "Change of scenery's gonna do us all some good." The setting sun bathed the hills in a fraudulent light, projecting warmth when only cold winds blew through the passes. The moon came next, leading the wagon into a stony darkness. Jody sipped from a bottle of rum. But nothing Jody drank or ate seemed able to stop her coughing.

Claire leaned to her, whispering. "They say you got some kind of disease." Jody turned her glassy eyes away, coughing into a piece of cloth. "The girls want you out of here."

It rained through the night. Claire pulled back the canvas flap and peered out. "Glass lamps and big city buildings. Holy damn. We're in San Francisco, ladies."

Some of the girls smiled. Jody didn't look up. She slumped off the bench. The two drivers, covered in black slickers, guided the horses through the pouring rain. Until the wagon stopped. The drivers ducked against the rain and trudged to the rear of the wagon. They pulled the canvas flaps back and lifted out the body wrapped in oilcloth. They carried the bundle over to the shelter of a porch casement.

"She'll die out here," the driver said.

The other man pulled back the top corner, exposing Jody's scab-pocked face. Her eyes were closed. "She's dying anyway. We can't bring Mr. Capps a dead girl. He'll start wondering how sick them others are."

From the rear of the wagon, Claire watched the men hurry through the rain back to the horses. She crossed herself and closed the flap.

A heavy fog rolled in from the Bay. The sun struggled to find a place in the leaden sky. A few rays of light caught the door of a fashionable, two-story Victorian townhouse. A slight, Asian man, perhaps in his early forties, stepped out, dressed in black pants and a black shirt that fell below his waist. A terrier dog beside him scampered down the steps into the street. The man watched the dog sniff, pee, and scurry to the side of the casement beneath the steps. The dog barked. He raced back and forth between the casement and the steps, barking incessantly.

"Gibbons, stop!" Quickly Li came down the steps. He ducked under the casement to observe Gibbons' latest discovery.

The full morning sun streaked through the curtained bedroom windows. Jody lay unconscious, beneath a heavy white quilt. Dr. Reed, a thin, mustached man, holding a stethoscope in one hand, turned back to the Asian houseman Li and the elderly, bespectacled man standing next to him. "I don't think she'll live out the day, Professor Stone."

"What will she have died of?"

"Basically… neglect."

That night Professor Stone sat in the parlor, in his favorite leather chair, his hand gently stroking Gibbons. The Professor stared vacantly at the fire blazing on the grate. Still, it was evident he was deeply absorbed in another world of thought. His shock of silky white hair crowned a kindly, wise face. By the time Li came in to tell him he would be busy stabling the horses in the rear of the townhouse, Professor Stone had moved to his desk in the study. Writing letters, he occasionally glanced over to a framed, sepia-tinted picture of a young woman, perhaps in her twenties, with a vibrant smile. He ate dinner alone. He had thought of inviting a friend over. Though he was born and raised back East and had advanced his professional life at the foremost East coast universities, five years ago, upon retiring, he had moved to San Francisco. His reputation was such that almost immediately he established friendships in both the scholarly and social worlds. As he spooned honey into his tea, the houseman appeared in the study doorway again.

"Professor Stone…"

"Yes, Li?"

"The young lady has stirred."

"Anything said?"

"No."

His instinct was to immediately get up and visit the guest bedroom, but just as quickly he had second thoughts. I'll know more in the morning. I'll call the doctor again. He didn't want to be disappointed. He knew, almost grudgingly, that he had to admit this to himself. The lady in the photograph on his desk had died too young. He prayed for the woman on the bed.

The following morning Professor Stone visited his unexpected guest. Li was at his side, with a tray holding a glass of water and a cup of honey. The Professor leaned over the bed, whispering to Jody. "You're going to live."

"I don wana…" Jody mumbled back in broken words.

"You have no choice, my dear. In this house, I'm in charge." Professor Stone dipped a spoon into the glass of water Li was holding. Gently, he passed the water across Jody's lips and then a touch of honey.

That night, he worked on a letter to his lawyer. He set his pen down, picked up a scrap of turkey from his dinner plate and placed it in direct line with Gibbons' panting mouth.

"Has she taken any food?" Stone looked up as Li entered the room and proceeded to draw the heavy, grey drapes across the windows.

"She sipped some broth, Professor."

Late the following morning, Professor Stone again ventured into the guest bedroom. Li had assured him that the girl, whatever her name, was alive and willing to talk to him.

Jody sat up against the pillows. A plate with bread, jam and butter was on a tray resting on her lap.

"When you're strong enough to walk, you'll dine with me," the Professor said. He was amazed that, having seen her on the steps of death, her face had taken on some color, the sores had declined, and she could make understandable sentences.

"Who are you?" she asked in a still, lifeless voice.

"Professor Jeremiah Stone. Recently of Boston. Do you know where that is?"

"No."

He assessed her ignorance. "The better question is: who are you?"

"Jody McDee,"

"Recently of?"

"The Castle Rocks."

"Hotel close by?"

Softly, she answered. "A brothel."

Professor Stone raised his white brows. "Whore house?"

"The same." Jody's answer seemed neither to surprise nor dismay Stone.

"Finish up your breakfast. You need to fight now to get stronger, to get back your life." He paused. "You can read; is that correct?"

"Yes."

The Professor started to leave, but, as weak as her voice was, she was still able to stop him. "Professor Stone, why are you doing this?"

"Why not? We're both fairly recent arrivals. I just happened to have gotten here first, in better health." His answer came with a twinkle in his eyes, as he continued out of the room.

Jody looked down at her bread and jam. No man that she could remember had ever talked to her with such kindness in his voice. It was after she had finished her soup that same evening that Li came into her room with an armful of books. He lit the candle on the table next to her and set the books in a stack on the floor.

"Professor Stone said to start with these." Li spoke in a quiet voice. His Chinese accent rounded each word, without being confusing. "He said to pay special attention to Gibbons' theories."

"Gibbons?"

"Not the apes or the dog. Gibbons is a writer of history. The professor's favorite subject."

"Thank you, Li."

"And the cream I gave you for your face… do you need more?"

"I still haven't seen myself, but yes, I think so."

She watched him leave the room. Her eyes gravitated to the pile of books. She picked up one with a blue cover, brought it to her lap, and began leafing through the pages.

Exactly a week later, Li announced to Jody that she would be having dinner with Professor Stone in the dining room. Jody had spent the past week absorbed in reading books, playing with Gibbons, briefly discussing things she had read with the Professor and taking short walks with Li, dressed in a selection of loose-fitting outfits from Li's Asian wardrobe. She had taken her first bath, in the servants' quarters' bathroom, for the dinner occasion. She was seated at one end of the long, mahogany dining table, with Professor Stone directly across from her.

"The large spoon, on the left, is for the soup," the Professor instructed. "You draw it away from the rim of the bowl, never towards you."

Jody noisily ingested a spoonful of her favorite chicken soup.

"And never slurp, my dear."

Jody blushed. "I was just letting the cook know how good the soup is."

Professor Stone smiled. "Evidently, a bordello custom."

The following afternoon, Li drove the carriage with passengers Jody and Professor Stone to a fashionable dress shop. The Professor, guided by his sense of taste for a young woman entering fashionable society, as well as Jody's own aesthetics, and Li's subtle input, managed to purchase six outfits, as well as a few leisure dresses, under garments and three pairs of shoes. Of course, some of the feminine items were chosen while the men chatted in another part of the store.

"She's taking a trip," the Professor explained to the Saleslady. "She's going back to visit the royal family in Spain."

"Oh, perhaps you'd like to visit our luggage department?"

"That will come another day," Jody chimed in.

The crash of thunder sent Gibbons racing, room to room, through the house, finally landing in the study, at the Professor's slippered feet. Jodie had just handed him a paper, which Stone was carefully studying. "Your second argument needs more elucidation. Your opinion is important, but you must, as well, support it with facts and the thoughts of others."

"But not as many spelling mistakes." Jody smiled triumphantly. "I really appreciate this, Professor Stone. Like I said, I never went to school."

"Intelligence doesn't come from school. It's a gift." He handed her back the paper. "And, I might add, it's a gift I believe you have."

The Professor got up from his chair and carried a parcel of books to the tall bookcase centered between the windows. Jody stared for a moment at the photo of the beautiful young woman on the desk. She looked up. "What do you want of me, Professor?"

"What do you think I want?" The question caught him off guard. "A wife? That woman in the photograph is already in my heart. A consort? I'm too old, my dear." He chuckled and set the books on a middle shelf. "I came West because that's the very last thing in my life I wanted to do, the last place I wanted to see. This is the end of the continent, a different spectacle than our European roots. I'm too old to start over. But never too old to learn."

"There ain't—"

"Isn't."

"Nothin'—"

"Anything."

"Will you let me finish!" Her cheeks flushed. She had never raised her voice, let alone challenged him before.

"There isn't anything you can learn from me! Except maybe some manners not to interrupt!"

He raised his fluffy, white brows. "My students were never this rude."

"How many of them was whores?"

"Just answer my question."

"It's not a trademark, Jody. You talk as if, like an 'A' on your forehead, your mistakes are emblazoned on your soul."

"Some things don't rub off so easy. You never buried a brother with a bullet in his heart or lost a child four months from your womb."

"I buried a wife and lost the same. The woman in the picture was my wife, lost to influenza at your age. My only son was killed at Richmond one week before the Civil War ended."

The knowledge stopped her. She felt the heaviness of a boulder rush across her heart. "I'm sorry."

"No one leaves the world unscathed, Jody. But there are riches in it, as well. Not all of them in a bank... I want you to be a lady."

He watched her leave the room. She was crying, and he was thinking again of that other woman who had slipped from his life so many years ago.

With Li at the reins, the carriage sped through the night. Jody sat across from the Professor in the cab. She looked quite elegant in her new finery, and, having had a few glasses of sherry, she was a bit loquacious.

"Was I too argumentative for your friends?"

"Argumentative. Five syllables. Excellent articulation."

"Professor, you know what I mean. Did I embarrass you when I misquoted President Lincoln?"

"What I found embarrassing was the ruthless arrogance of my friends." Professor Stone, in his tailored grey suit, looked resigned. "They really can't hold winning in abeyance."

"Claire would probably die herself if she knew I were riding in this carriage."

"Who might that be?"

"A friend from the past."

"The past, we agreed, is behind you."

A disturbance in the road forced Li to pull the carriage to a halt. Jody glanced over to a man's profile in the window of the carriage beside them. The man lit a cigar and glanced over to the anonymous, beautiful woman, in classic finery, staring at him. His carriage pulled ahead, and the face of the Bank Investigator Philo Storm disappeared.

"I'm only repeating what Professor Wingate's butler told me." Li set down a box of produce on the kitchen counter. "He overheard Professor Wingate say that you were making an old goat out of yourself and ruining your reputation."

"He's a jealous curmudgeon who doesn't think women should have ideas or sit at the same table with men, much less learned men, which, frankly, is giving himself and his colleagues a good deal more credit than they deserve." The Professor picked up his glass of water.

"He doesn't believe that she's your niece."

"Did you say anything to the contrary?"

"You've been here five years. I've been here since the beginning of time. For the past four of those years, I've served you. I find your insinuation unkind."

"Forgive me." The professor turned and started to leave the kitchen. He stopped abruptly, dropping the glass of water and clutching the edge of a table for support. His pale face tightened. Li alertly took a step towards him. "Is something wrong, Professor?"

"Nothing's wrong. I'm sorry about the glass. Just clumsy." He regained his step and left the room.

Chapter 16

El galloped the horse down an icy road, wracked with fallen branches and mud holes. The bright sun bellowed across a cloudless sky, pushing swords of light through the barren trees and skimming the snow-crusted hillsides with an eye- blinding, silver veneer. They were in the tangled grip of light and darkness, ceding no warmth to the rider or her passenger, yet leading them deeper into the mystery of her son's disappearance. With a turn in the road, Billy could see a huge island off the coast to his left. A thick mist rolled across its rocky slopes, blowing towards the mainland with a blast of northern wind.

El reined-up Aedan to a trot. "That's Eilean a' Cheo," she said. "Some call it the Isle o' Skye. The Clans Macleod an' Donald fight over it aw the time."

"Everyone fights over land," Billy barked. "It's in our DNA, El!" He glanced back between the island and the road. "God didn't make the world big enough!"

"Or She didn't divide it fair enough! Now we're alongside Loch Carron," she said, dismissing Billy's rant. "We'll come tae the village soon enough."

The road veered to the left, following the river inland.

The fitful sun that had been their only companion, if not their source of comfort, disappeared in clouds of thick gray mist streaming off the sea. Loch must mean river, Billy thought, glancing over to the fast-moving current. The mist was at his back. He could feel its wetness on his neck. He pulled up the collar on his parka. "Are you sure this is the way?"

El cocked her head so Billy could hear. "This is the only wey." All Billy saw was a heavy, foreboding sheet of fog. He could hear the beat of the horse's hooves across a wooden bridge he barely saw. El slowed Aedan to a trot. "This is the village."

What's she talking about? There's nothing here. The sound of the wind seemed the only living thing across the desolate landscape.

"Get off the horse," she said, reigning up Aedan.

Billy didn't hesitate to put his feet on the ground. "Aren't you getting off?"

"Na, A'm going to ride off an' let ye find yer way back. 'Tis an old Gaelic trick." She dismounted the horse. With a smile he could only see in her eyes, she added, "A'd niver leave ye. It's ye who will leave me." She turned away and led Aedan down the empty road.

Billy stumbled through the snow, reaching down every few steps to keep the cuarans, the leather wrappings, from unraveling on his legs.

"Take ma hand," she called back. "But whan we see someone, quickly let go!"

He caught up to her and grabbed her hand. "No one's going to see us. It would be great if someone with a kerosene heater and sandwiches gave us a shout out."

"Ye're talkin' like the wind`s swept through yer brain," she said.

Charred, snow-laced timbers across a broken wall were all that remained of a cottage they passed. Further on, Billy could make out taller buildings. Wind drove the mist through huge, gouged-out holes in the shattered walls. Engulfed in desolation, there were no campfires, no shadows, no scavenger's hunched over refuse seeking a treasure left behind. Billy remained alert, ready at any moment for an armed soldier to jump out, just as he had seen on TV news of the enemy leaping from behind walls and abandoned buildings, strafing the streets with bullets and bombs.

"Where did everyone go?" he asked.

"Folk will come back tae git whit thy can, find whit they lost. That's how life is here. We're at the mercy o' the feuds between the clans, or the Reformers fightin' the kirk. The poor are trapped in the middle." Despite maneuvering around snowdrifts and rock piles, she didn't stop talking. "We don't make the rules or laws. We juist sacrifice our blood fur someone else's ideas." El looked up at Aedan. "Isn't that right? It's not a world o' cars an' schools, like yours, Billy."

"You don't know what my world is like. You have no idea! You couldn't point to the U.S.A. in a five-country quiz!" Billy forgot about his frozen fingers and the baby. "What about Iraq and Afghanistan? Or the Atomic bomb! That's what history is, El. Not just your world. War didn't end with your century!"

She looked straight ahead, again ignoring his rant. A few wooden signs swayed in the wind, chained to posts above the burned-out hovels. Gusts of snow nearly blinded them. El buried her face in the arm of Billy's parka. The catastrophic world of wars fled to silence on the numbing wind. Aedan snorted again and pawed the ground. El stopped. A man stood alone on a hillside next to an outcropping of stones, mostly covered in snow.

"Fynn!" As if he were frozen, the man didn't move. "Am A talking to Fynn?" El shouted again in Gaelic.

Billy followed her closer to the lone figure. He was leaning a hand on some kind of steel rake that he seemed to be using as a staff to steady himself on the icy grade. He was taller than Billy and at least fifty pounds heavier, Billy thought. The collar was up on his ragged cloak, and his steel gray moustache and beard hid the width of his neck. He answered in Gaelic, though his accent was such that Billy thought he was catching some of the words.

El turned to Billy. "'Tis Fynn. A remember bein' at his home, helpin' ma faither. He says that the room ma faither bult` wis burned tae ash with most o' his house. He killed one o' the soldiers but another cut intae his leg afore he ran off."

Fynn looked over to Billy and raised his voice.

"He wants tae know where ye're from. A told him London, but he's one o' us, A said."

With an uplifted hand in the man's direction and a few head wags, Billy tried to convey that somehow, they were brothers in a secret society. He turned to El. "Ask him about the boy."

"That's what A'm doin' if ye give me the time!"

Snow flurries were beginning to deepen the mist. Billy's feet were freezing in the leather wrappings. His instinct, like in the matches he fought, was to always take charge, but the language barrier stymied him. El repeated the story Ciaran had told her about an old couple selling a baby boy. Fynn shook his head. He lifted his rake and slammed it into the hillside. "How come do A know this?" he blustered in a hoarse brogue so the strange boy would understand. "What happened tae our world when we sell children in order tae feed our stomachs? They crossed themselves in praise o' Christ, our Laird, but they wallow in sin."

"A'm not asking ye aboot the world, Fynn. A'm askin' ye aboot ma son!" she shouted back. "Ma faither built ye a fine room. What ye know, ye owe me!"

"Ma house is gone," he howled. Like an angry prophet storming into the mist, shouting about the end of the world, the distraught man pulled his wounded body up the hill.

"What more did he tell you?"

"He doesn't know the man's name or where he bides exactly, but it's somewhere in Laird Kinnaird's estate. He's certain o' that, an' the fella' has a black horse."

"Do you know where it is?"

"Na."

"How many people have black horses?"

"They're not that common here. Dinnae ask me anymore questions."

"If you don't know where this old man lives and all you know is that he has a black horse and maybe there's a hundred black horses where we're going, how do we find him?" Billy threw up his hands. "How many days or maybe even years will it take to find the guy who has your son?"

"Dinnae shout at me!" She turned and stamped through the snow to the far side of the road.

"You don't understand," he yelled. "If we don't find Bran, all of this is pointless, and I've lost my Division match!"

"Dinnae blame me! Dinnae ever blame me!" Even from across the road, Billy could see the flames in her eyes. "Is thare nothin' else in yer life," she shouted. "No room for someone else's sufferin' o' for yer own growth?"

"What do you think I'm doing here? Why do you think I'm standing in these stupid leggings freezing my nuts off?"

He had no idea if she had heard him. The flames of anger had turned to tears in her eyes, but he had no idea, either, if they were caused by the relentless wind or the torment in her heart. El's back was to him as he crossed the road. He didn't bother to brush the snow pelting his face. He wrapped his arms around her and felt her chest heave with the pain of her silent whimpering. "El..." Billy turned her towards him, letting her body sink into his arms. "We'll do what you want to do. That's the plan."

She rubbed her forehead against the face of his jacket. "We canae go any farther," she said. "We'll only get lost in the storm."

Aedan had made the trip back and forth between the cottage and village many times, mostly with Ciaran. In the blinding fog and snow, Billy and El had to trust the horse's instincts, the horse's memory, the horse's connection to the world in which he was born. And somehow, with Billy's arms around El and their eyes closed against the storm, with each of Aedan's steps, they felt that same kind of trust being born within them. It was deeper than love, or might that trust be the soul of love? Perhaps Billy, holding her like a lost treasure, was still too young to understand this, but he was wise enough to know that his world had somehow, quietly grown larger.

He knew he was holding a life that was older than his history, older than the reach of his thoughts and that, when the storm lifted, they would begin this journey again.

"Tomorrow," she said.

"Tomorrow!" he echoed in the impending darkness. "We will find Laird Kinnaird's estate tomorrow!"

Bran's fate was suspended on the hearsay of a bitter old man who had lost everything.

The horse trounced into the mas an taighe, shaking his coat, unaware or simply dismissive of his heroic trek through the deadly fog and treacherous roads. Billy watched Aedan munch the hay. He was getting more comfortable with the great horse. He still wasn't certain that Aedan trusted him, but, like some computer-generated stallion, Billy believed in the horse's magical power.

He stepped outside and ran a plank across the rear doors, shutting in the sheep and horse for the night. The cold, the darkness, the gleaming snow on the barn roof caught him in a breathtaking, outer dimension of time. He stood for a moment staring at a scattering of stars finding space among the train of weighty clouds. He wondered if his friend Justin would believe his story of landing in Scotland centuries ago. Of making love to a girl who tore his heart from him and of her terrifying, tragic family story.

He leaned against the doors and imagined himself climbing on a rope ladder hanging down from the clouds, lifting himself up with the same strength and dexterity he had practiced on the ropes that hung from the rafters in his family's backyard garage. The thought of channeling a tunnel through those same clouds, a wormhole, back to Cederburgh delighted him. It was his secret, a secret of the imagination that would keep him sane in a world that had ripped the framework from his adolescent structure of reality. Would he remember any of this, he wondered, when somehow he found his way back to Cederburgh? He dug his hands deeper into his jacket pockets. The fingers of his right hand fumbled with the smooth, cold metal of his father's dog tag and brought him back to who he was and the secret in his heart. "That's it!" His eyes lit up. "I was transported by this!" he whispered louder, clutching the dog tag in his fist. "The dog tag is my talisman and the wormhole to this world!"

He raced around to the front of the cottage. He stood at the door watching El move around the table. He looked over with a sense of relief to see Ciaran still asleep in his box bed. Everything was in its place.

Billy could tell she was still in a quarrelsome mood, as she set slices of white cheese and bread on the plates.

"Dinnae juist stand there, ye can help me. Take the gairdingis from the cabinet an' bring thaim tae the table."

Billy marched over to the cabinet and pivoted back to El, with a stumped look. "What are gardenies?"

"Gairdingis. Ye pronounce it, gairdingis. Say it."

"Gairdingis." Billy made an effort to sound Gaelic, as a favor to her, but he didn't like her sharp tone. "What are they I asked you."

"The brass plates next tae yer arm. Bring thaim here. We put thaim under the bowls o' hot food so as not to ruin the table." She wiped her hands on her apron. "Is thare anythin' A don't have to teach ye?"

"Yes! How I got here and how I can get back!" He broke into a wide, exuberant grin. "El, I've discovered the key to the wormhole while you were slicing cheese!"

"Whit hole?"

"The wormhole I told you about. The time-travel portal. It's my father's dog tag! That's what brought me here and that's what's going to get me back to Cederburgh!" He looked to Ciaran, making certain his excitement hadn't wakened him. "I'm not a prisoner."

El's face lost its sharpness, but what replaced it was a look more dire. "Who said ye were a prisoner?

Is that whit ye've been feeling? Is that whit poundin' me in the kip felt like?"

"No, that isn't how I feel. That isn't how I've ever felt.

Love isn't a prison. No, it's dimensionless." He instantly realized how his words had sounded, and he couldn't risk losing the first love he'd ever had. "Because I know how to get back doesn't mean I'm leaving you."

She glared at him, unsure of the subtlety of what he was saying. "But ye're sayin' ye can go back at any time, whether we find Bran or no."

"No, I'm not saying that at all. I don't know any secret words to get me back and I've touched the dog-tag many times. You've seen me touch it, and that hasn't sent me back."

"Sae what are ye sayin'?"

"The owner of the tag will tell me how."

"Yer faither…"

"Aye."

"Ye're believin' yer dead faither will speak tae ye?"

"I'm believing your dead mother spoke to you from the flames." Billy pointed to the hearth, "and your dead father was a Blackwell!"

"Bring me the gairdingis."

He brought over three brass plates and watched El set a bowl on top of each one. She told him to bring the pot hanging on the hook over the fire. "Be careful ye dan no burn yourself," she added, in a less abrasive tone. "Use that cloth tae protect yer hand."

Billy grabbed the puffy cloth hanging on a peg and returned with the black pot. He watched El ladle out the steaming porridge into each bowl.

"I didn't make the decision to come back from the burnt-out village. Is that why you're so f'n mad at me? It was your plan. I said I'd follow your plan, whatever it was."

She brushed back a golden strand of her hair. "Whit's 'f'n' mean?"

"F'n?" The question caught him by surprise. "It doesn't mean anything. It's an expression, El, that's all. A hoodoo expression."

"Whit's hoodoo?"

"It's whatever you want it to mean. That's the beauty of hoodoo." He picked up the pot and carried it back to the hearth. He didn't want to get involved in something that would spark her anger even more. The excitement of his wormhole revelation had already been trashed into doubt and a senseless argument.

"We could have found a place tae rest."

"Where? In a burnt-out, snow-packed building?" He came back quickly to the table. "We couldn't see in the fog. Night was on us. If Aedan hadn't known the way, we'd still be floating in an icy river."

"Ye do no trust me, do ye?"

"What's trust got to do with this? We were supposed to be looking for an old man and a black horse and that's not a lot to go on in a whole country, especially at night!"

"Do not dare raise yer voice tae me. A'm yer lover like ye told me. Show some respect."

"You're a lover with a crappy attitude. And own it, you're the one who made the decision to come back here!"

She set her hands on the edge of the table and leaned across it. "Ye're a coward."

Anger shot, like a bullet, through Billy's clenched fists and heart. "I'm not a coward. I've never backed down from a fight, on the mat or in the street!"

"Then tomorrow mornin' we gae back."

"I never said no."

"Will ye ever say 'no,' Billy?"

"Never to you."

Everything in Cederburgh was lost. His title fights. His team victories. But he knew he had to go forward. He knew it was the path his father would have taken. And he knew in his heart what he wanted to say, he said: "I love you."

"Open yer jacket."

"What for?"

"Open yer jacket an' kiss me."

Billy kissed her lips. She pushed the plates and bowls aside and lifted herself to a seat on the table's edge with her legs draped over the side. She hiked up her white dress, pushing back its multiple folds until all Billy could see was the lantern light on her thighs. "Now make love tae me."

"We can't wake Ciaran."

"Ciaran sleeps through Highland storms. 'An we can't leave 'til it's over. Make love tae me now."

Chapter 17

"Do you mind if I say something?"

"You will, anyway."

Jody looked up from her plate, at the dining room table. "You look pale."

"Merely a reflection of my thoughts. I've been invited to the annual Christmas Ball. My "niece" has been included in the invitation."

"And that's what pales you with fear? The fact that they think I'm your niece or that I'll somehow embarrass you again?"

"The bluebloods of San Francisco are like pariahs. As for the men, they're mercenary fools."

"I'm not afraid."

"Of course, you're not. You're running from the law and you've slept with men who were killers, robbers, and thieves. But," he paused and stared at the candlelight that blazed between them, "you've never danced with me."

"I've taught more than one man to dance, Professor Stone. Some on my lap and some on the floor."

In a posh, resplendent ballroom, glittering with San Francisco's high society, an orchestra plays to the crowded dance floor. Professor Stone, in tails, and Jody, in a beautiful gown, are dancing. He's not a master of every step, but neither is he a bumpkin trying to find the tempo.

"You dance beautifully."

"You're being too kind, my dear. But that man has been eyeing you the entire evening." Jody followed Professor Stone's gaze to a tall, handsome man standing next to an empty table. He had sparkling dark eyes. and black hair combed straight back, long enough to be tied at the back.

"Do you know who he is?"

"Aidan Campbell. His family owns half of northern California. Remember, you're no longer Jody McDee. You're Miss J.D. Stone of Boston.

"I don't really think I'll be talking to anyone but you tonight."

"I didn't expect the evening would be that long." Professor Stone smiled. "I'm just teasing."

At another table, near the dance floor, two women, in their late thirties, shift their gazes back and forth between Jody on the dance floor and Aidan Campbell at an empty table. Abigail Ralston wears her long brown hair tiered in soft curls. Her friend, Emma Tinsdale, pale and thin, with blond shoulder- length hair, appears more subdued than Abigail, despite enjoying the mild social intrigue.

"Mr. Campbell has had his eyes on her all evening, Emma.

Who is she?"

"J.D. Stone. Professor Jeremiah Stone's niece. So I was told. But I'm not saying I got all the information right."

"I didn't know the old buzzard had family. Is she from here?" Emma forked a bite of chocolate Christmas cake.

"I was told she arrived from Boston a year ago."

"J.D. Stone. What an odd name for a woman. More for a bank robber," she laughed.

"Everything about her is a mystery, Abigail."

Abigail turned back to Emma. "Her complexion isn't exactly English, is it?"

"I believe England once had a Spanish king. Or was it French?"

"Don't bother with history. We should invite her to lunch with us, before Aidan Campbell sweeps her off to his ranch."

Campbell, unaware they were talking about him, looked over to the society ladies' table, as the music swung into a jaunty foxtrot. He pointed to Emma and back to himself.

"Go, Emma. He wants to dance with you. Maybe he'll marry you and not the lady from Boston, who, for all we know, may not even be from Boston."

Everyone in the Stone household slept late the following morning, even Li who had stayed the night waiting in the carriage for the Christmas Ball to end. But he was well-awake when the door chimes rang, announcing the Messenger Boy with a sealed envelope addressed, in elegant calligraphy, to Miss J.D. Stone. Professor Stone, bundled in a shawl, sat in the study, by the warmth of the fire, gazing at the invitation he had just been handed.

Jody stepped away from the fireplace. "I've never been invited, or accepted, or encouraged by anyone before." The words hadn't left her lips for half a second when she realized the horror of her remark. The pain on Stone's face amplified the egregious mistake. "I'm sorry. You've done all those things. You've been the world to me. You saved my life. I can't say anything right since my name change. I meant, among younger people, my age. That sounds wrong, too. I mean, God knows, since my mother died."

"These women don't see life as you do, Jody."

"That's the point, isn't is? I want to see life the way they do. What was all this education for if I can't use it? Why did I learn manners if I can't show people I have them?"

"I know these pretenders, all too well." His voice was dry and weak.

She was too caught up in her own thoughts and defenses to hear him. "And the beautiful clothes you've bought me. What good are they stuck in an armoire? Professor Stone, I'm about to enter a new life! I'm going to wear the pale blue dress and the pearls you gave me for Christmas. Don't worry.

I shall never forget who I am and how I got here. That's a promise," she said, as she left.

He stared at the empty doorway. A wan smile faded from the old man's lips. He shuddered, coughed, and pulled the shawl to his chest.

Jody, wearing her new pink and white dress, beamed with excitement as she walked into the dining room of a fashionable, downtown hotel. Abigail and Emma had already been seated, as the maître de brought J.D. to their table. They were as anxious to see her as she, notwithstanding her bene-factor's caution, was delighted to be with them. The setting was resplendent with mirrors, starched white tablecloths, people in expensive finery, and crystal on ever table.

She knew then, as she took her seat, she was ten million miles in her mind and in her heart from any barroom stool or rowdy brothel.

"And how are you this lovely summer day," Abigail asked.

"Very well. The summers back East are a little warmer, but I'm getting used to San Francisco weather."

"Do tell us," Emma asked enthusiastically. "Were you married and have you children?"

"No, not so lucky or not," Jody smiled. "Depending on what you think of marriage."

"But I take it you were active in social affairs?"

"Social affairs…" Jody hesitated with the phrase.

"Emma means, did you engage with society." Abigail quickly made it very clear.

"Yes, of course. Different kinds of meetings and…" she hesitated. "Dances. Every holiday brings out a different dance."

"So it seemed at our Christmas Ball. Did you, by any chance, have the opportunity to dance with Aidan Campbell? He seemed to be looking your way."

"No. I didn't, not at all."

"Well, Emma did."

"Of course, you know, Aidan Campbell is the most eli-gible bachelor in these parts. He has a reputation, my dear. Not as a scholar, mind you."

"He inherited the largest horse ranch in Northern California," Abigail added. "My husband does his banking so, believe me, we know. But look how we're going on, Emma. We don't even know if Miss Stone is interested in marriage."

"Please call me J.D."

"Initials?" Emma raised her brows.

"My parents were anxious for a son. They wanted so much to name me after my Uncle Jeremiah. As fate would have it, I didn't get his full name, but I came to live with him, which has been a blessing."

"We heard that your parents died at sea."

"Yes. But it isn't something I prefer talking about. It brings back very painful memories, as you can imagine."

"Were they sailing from Spain?"

"Spain?"

"Emma, we mustn't pry. We'll learn everything, I'm sure, as we become friends." Abigail called the attention of a passing waiter. "Sir, please bring our guest a glass of sherry." She turned back to Jody. "Which is one of the reasons we wanted to get together with you. Several of us women from the very best families, the upper echelon of San Francisco society…"

Emma jumped in. "We've established a foundation to help the poor. So many children living in such terrible conditions." The waiter set down a glass of sherry in front of Jody. She thanked him as the two women exchanged a self-congratulatory smile.

"And, as you can understand, foundations are time- consuming, as well. Isn't that right, Emma?

Emma nodded, with her toothy smile. "We've been made to observe the most wretched conditions. Sick, dirty children, squabbling and playing in filth. All one can do when one gets home is nap or play the piano. Do you play?"

"I sing... a little."

"We've been asked to invite you to join our foundation."

"And we don't want you to think this is a way of soliciting a large donation from the Campbell estate," Abigail quickly added.

"As much as we would appreciate Mr. Campbell's contribution, our invitation is based solely on our highest respect for Professor Stone and the gracefulness we observed in your Christmas debut."

"I am deeply honored. Thank you, ladies."

Abigail lifted her wine glass. "To our lasting friendship." The women exchanged smiles, toasting to friendship and the foundation.

She threw off her cape as she rushed through the downstairs hallway. "Professor Stone! Professor Stone!" A step later, she turned into the study. "Professor Stone..."

She saw his favorite leather armchair facing the window. "Miss Abigail and Miss Emma invited me to..." By the time she reached him, her smile and words had faded from her lips. Her eyes shifted from his lifeless face to his pipe on the floor.

"No.. no!" The wail could be heard through every room in the formidable townhouse. "Li! Li!" She fell to the floor, her arms wrapped around his legs, laying her head against his knees, sobbing uncontrollably into the same chamber of her heart that she kept for Danny.

It was a week later, after the funeral arrangements had been made and various organizations had been notified, that J.D. Stone received a call from Mr. Harrington's law office. It was arranged that she see the lawyer on the following Tuesday.

Mr. Harrington was a balding, intense man in his forties. He wore gold-framed glasses, a neatly trimmed beard, and a grey, vested suit. He trained his eyes on several documents before looking up to Jody, seated across the desk from him.

"Apparently Professor Stone, as he indicated in these written statements, had no living heirs apart from you. He's deeded his scholarly papers to the Harvard University library, as well as those of his books which, when no longer of any use to you, you may wish to present to that formidable institution. That's how he wrote it. He also left a sum of money to his houseman, Li, and the right for him to live at his residence, in your employ, as long as you reside there, dependent upon his own arrangements." The lawyer looked up from the documents. "Did Professor Stone ever speak of his financial affairs to you?"

"Not really. Never."

"Well, fortunately for you, the professor was not only a brilliant scholar, but, in the years he lived in New England, he invested heavily and wisely in the import-export trade.

The bulk of his estate he's left to you, which should afford you, Miss Stone, a modest, dare I say, substantial annual income, to be administered by Crown and Duncan Financial Services, here in San Francisco. I'll have my secretary give you all the necessary contact information plus there are several papers that will need your signature."

"And the house?"

"The deed has already been transferred to your name. He had that done several weeks before he passed." Mr. Harrington paused before adding, "Evidently he liked you quite a bit." A faint smile crossed the lawyer's putty-thin lips. "I can see why."

Chapter 18

B illy looked over to the window, shaded with evening darkness. Ciaran sat on his bed and wolfed down the cheese and porridge. He had no interest in the cell phone. El explained that he was in one of his moods. "He gets lost in a thought. It could be any thought," she said. "A spider crawlin' on the wall. Whit happenit tae a cloud that passed over a hill. But usually, when he comes out of it, he wants tae gae outdoors or he wants tae ride Aedan."

Billy swallowed a spoonful of soup. "It's too late for that."

"Bit ye can go outdoors with him, if that's what he wants.

Ye pulled him out o' a tree in a storm." She leaned forward and sweetly cupped his face between her hands. "Ye kin walk with him with what's left of yer energy from seeing the village an' makin' love."

It was a longer walk to the burial site than Billy would have volunteered to take. The mist had lifted, and moonlight shone on the tall, standing stones that marked the grave of Ciaran's beheaded father. The night was achingly cold. Even at that, a few ravens crossed wings through the leafless trees. Ciaran nodded his head in the shadow of the stones. His lips were sealed. He was the boy who had worked with his father, who had carried his father's tools. Billy imagined that, under his breath, the boy might be chanting something sacred, like a Gaelic prayer or the fragment of a song. The vision of a splattered ghost jumped through Billy's mind. The words, "I am still your father," dripped, like movie poster blood, across the filmy skull.

He knew that it wasn't his father's remnants, the mosaic of flesh and bone that was buried in one of the stones. It was the jigsaw puzzle of memories that was the man he loved. It was the spirit of someone a billion, trillion miles away, blown into unrecognizable atoms, that pounded in his heart. It was the talisman he wore on his chest. Go, Billy, go, he heard his father calling when he wheeled his blue bike down the driveway. Hang on, My Mighty Son, hang on tight, he heard his father yelling back to him, as they raced on his Harley through the narrow roads in the hills above Cederburgh.

He opened his eyes to Ciaran's shadow, broken across the ceremonial stones. It was a pain, Billy instinctively knew, that reached through the centuries, burdened by love and death. Billy had rounded a corner in the depths of his soul. He was older than he ever imagined he could be. They walked back in silence. The Cederburgh boy couldn't tell if Ciaran was sniffling tears over his father's death or from the winter wind that mercilessly beat at their faces.

"How often do you do this, Ciaran?" He didn't expect an answer. He wasn't even sure the Highland boy could hear him above the wind. And he wasn't naturally outgoing but, in the absence of anyone he knew, he felt the need to open-up to whomever was there.

It didn't annoy him that Ciaran couldn't understand a word he was saying, though he missed some faint kind of acknowledgment. "You go work in the fields around here when it warms up. That's what El told me. She said it keeps you two alive." The wind whipped up a flurry of snow across their faces. Billy thought of pulling out the hood on his jacket. "I really wish I could get through to you. We could be friends. On the road I met you, we were friends. Remember that? In the tree we were friends."

He heard a yelp, like the cough of an animal, jump from Ciaran's throat. Tears got lost in the boy's unshaven cheeks. "I'm sorry, Ciaran. I kind of know what you're feeling." Billy extended his arm and reached around Ciaran's shoulder. "It's not easy to lose a father you love."

Ciaran made no effort to pull away from Billy's arm.

They stepped into an empty cottage, still lit by a slowly dying fire. Billy crossed to the bedroom and yanked open the door. All he could see of his love, lying in bed, snuggled in the feather quilt, was her face, lit by the lantern's glow. Minutes later, having said goodnight to Aedan and the two sheep, Billy lay in bed wondering: Did I ever think this would happen to me, not even a hint in all the Chinese fortune cookies I opened.

He slid his hand under the quilt and laid it gently on El. "Are you up? Can you feel my hand?" he whispered.

"We leave early i' the morning," she said, without raising her head. "Ye must get some sleep."

He turned back and rested his hands under his head. He listened to the wind. His thoughts mingled with the moaning sound through the trees and clumps of snow falling from the roof. *Maybe that's it, I'm in an alternative universe. A world that copies ours, where people go to get their life back or learn about their life. Why else would my father's dog-tag have taken me here?*

Then he remembered hanging his parka on the back of the chair by the table. The iPhone was in one of the pockets. Maybe *this late at night I could get a signal.* He smiled at his own joke: *Verizon can't get a signal when I'm swimming at the quarry. How can it find an alternative universe?*

"El, El," he whispered. "I left my parka on the chair. My iPhone's in the pocket!" He slipped to the edge of the bed without making a sound.

"Phane..." She mumbled in a thick accent that stuck to her slumbering lips. "Where are ye going?"

"You're up?"

"Twistin' an' turning, talkin' tae yourself, like ye got the whole world rattlin' around in yer head. Only a dead body could sleep through the storm."

"My cell phone is in my parka. Ciaran knows I keep it there. If he wakes up and tries to get it, it's game over." Billy pulled away and got out of bed.

"Whit's game over?"

"It's an expression, El, like f'n." He adjusted the belt buckle that held his sheath and dirk. "It means we're in trouble. Besides, it's just more wasted battery time."

As Billy reached the door, Aedan suddenly reared back, his front legs striking the air. With a terrifying cry, his legs crashed down against the gate.

El sprung up. "Someone's here!"

Billy pulled his dirk from its sheath and threw the bedroom door open. His eyes darted from the dark space behind the table to the cabinets in the corner. He could see Ciaran standing next to his bed, scrambling to put on clothes.

Still in her nightgown, El came out of the bedroom. She was breathing hard and held a lantern into the darkness. "Who's there?" she shouted in Gaelic. "Who's there?" She grabbed Billy's hand and pulled him along to the front door. "Ciaran!" she called out.

El lifted the bar and pushed open the door to a cold blast of air. She raised the lantern and shouted in Gaelic. "Is someone out there?"

"Is anyone out there?" Billy yelled, knowing there was barely a chance his words would be understood. "Are you a friend?"

"Ay, A'm a friend!" the man answered in halting, heavily accented English. El turned her lantern from side to side but saw only the moonlit darkness and clattering branches in the wind.

"If ye're a friend, come tae the future with yer hands free at yer sides," she said.

They heard the snap of a branch. El swung her lantern. Billy clutched his dirk. A shadow emerged on the snow. A figure stepped out from the grove of trees. It was bundled in pieces of tattered cloth, like a casualty of war. A scarf covered most of its head. The certainty of its gender became clear to Billy as moonlight caught the bushy black beard, mostly hidden by a scarf.

"I am a friend," he said in Gaelic. "Caraid dha?"

"Oisian Allaway Blackwell."

Billy saw El's face suddenly charge with surprise. She took a step onto the frozen ground. "Why dae ye come here?"

"Seo mo dhachaigh. Bha mi an-seo mòran bhliadhnaichean air ais."

"What's he saying, El?"

"He knows mah faither's name 'n' he knows this is his house."

"Ye're Elspeth an' ye have a brother, Ciaran."

"Come tae the future," she called again.

At the second step, the intruder fell face forward into the snow.

"Ciaran!" El glanced back into the house. "Ciaran!"

Billy turned as Ciaran entered the doorway. His broadsword was raised, and his left arm boarded a shield.

"Put the sword away," she yelled in Gaelic. She told him to help Billy carry the man into the house. "Can we start our journey on the steps o' a dyin' man?" she whispered. "Is this an omen, Billy?"

Billy had seen homeless people wander the downtown streets of Cederburg, but the man on Ciaran's bed, mumbling incomprehensible words, looked more damaged and hopeless than any drifter his eyes had ever come upon. El kneeled beside the stranger, loosened his scarf, and placed a cup to his lips. "This will help ye feel better." She told Ciaran to put more peat on the fire. She bent to feed the man again. "Whit's yer name?"

Tea dribbled off the side of his mouth. "Adel... Adelard."

"Ye're French?" she asked in disbelief.

His eyes slowly opened. "*Oui.*"

"How did ye know ma faither?"

"Lo..." He grimaced, pushing his answer through a halting, feverish breath. "Lollards." He wagged his hands close to his chest, as if his ragged clothes were suffocating him.

"He wants you to take off—"

"Dinnae tell me to take off what A can see," she snapped. The desperation of the circumstances, the bleak possibility that anything could be done to save someone who knew her father, unnerved El. She started to unravel the dark swatches of material that bound him like a patchwork mummy. Red streaks and splotches of blood oozed up with the removal of each layer.

Billy winced. "He's bleeding to death."

"Be still, Billy. A can have a go at savin' him. Don't let him close his eyes again." El stood up and told Ciaran to bring in more water.

Billy stared at the half-naked man on the bed, the first living or dead victim of violence, not on TV, he'd ever seen. Blood gleamed on the deep slashes below the stranger's ribs. His black hairy chest was threaded with pieces of flesh. Billy knelt and put the pewter cup to his lips again. "Drink a little, just a little, Adelard."

Adelard's eyelids rolled back. "Ye're English?"

"American. I'm from Illinois." Billy caught himself. *He has no idea what I'm talking about. I'm meeting more people from five hundred years ago.*

"A speak English." Adelard uttered the words as if he'd read Billy's thoughts. "A understand."

"What happened to you?"

"A'm a Lollard. Dae ye know whit that is?" Billy told him the little he knew from El's account of her father's beliefs. "That's how A know him." He winced again, coughed, and grabbed Billy's hand. "Where is he now? Where is her faither now?" he gasped.

Billy hesitated, unsure of his right to reveal a secret, but frantic to keep the man from falling into unconsciousness.

The terrible report of what happened to the family gushed from his mouth. He told Adelard how El was raped, her father beheaded, and how her infant son was stolen. The stranger sneered and clenched his yellow teeth, desperately trying to stymie the bolts of pain shooting through his body. "Nowhere is thare freedom. We all bide under a fool's boot." He gasped; his eyes closed.

"El! El!" Billy shot a look to the hearth but quickly turned back, leaning as close to the dying man as death and fear would let him. "Keep the faith. Think you're going to live. My father taught me to think positive. You must fight, Adelard, for your life!"

El stood over Billy. "He doesn't know an' he cannot hear ye."

"He understands English. We talked." Billy eyed the bowl and cloth in El's hand and stepped aside. She wiped the sweat from Adelard's brows and brushed back the few locks of black hair that curled from beneath the tattered bands that circled his head. She dabbed the cloth in and out of a bowl of dark brown liquid. "Adelard, Adelard, we want ye tae live." She rose from her knees and turned to Billy. "What did he tell ye?"

"What he said before. That he's a Lollard and that's how he knew your father."

El turned her gaze to the window. Light was breaking above the trees. "We must pray that he lives."

"Yes, pray he lives. Ciaran can watch him. Today is the day we start…"

"Start whit, Billy?" She looked at him with an icy glare. "It's my life or his life, El."

"Whit?"

"If Bran doesn't live, if somehow something terrible happened to him, I will never be born a Blackwell and my father, the man I loved, whose dog-tag I wear, will never have been mine!"

"Enough aboot ye 'n' th' Blackwells! A'm wantin' ma son back more than anythin', but A cannot let a man die. Not in ma faither's house." Billy followed her towards the window light. "Whit good am A, if A let a man die an' abandon the healin' ma mither taught me? Answer me, Billy!"

She walked back to the bed, kneeled again, and bathed Adelard's wound in the same brown solution, darkened even more by the man's blood. "Gae outside an' help Ciaran with the sheep." El's voice, weighted with anxiety and sadness, put an end to Billy's thoughts.

Chapter 19

The front door opened with a rush. "Li, Li... I'm home. The horse and buggy taxi went just fine." Jody removed her gloves, setting them on a marble stand in the foyer. Her eyes fell to a sealed, white envelope inscribed with her name.

"Li..." She started for the study at the same time Li appeared.

"Yes, Miss Stone."

"When did this come?" She held up the envelope.

"Mr. Campbell's gentleman dropped it off while you were out."

That afternoon Jody paid a visit to the Emma Tinsdale estate. She followed the butler to a garden where Emma and Abigail were already seated. A maid served tea.

"You must respond." Emma handed the gilt-edged invitation back to Jody. "I'm sure you know exactly what to say, but I'd let Mr. Campbell know that your grief, over the passing of Professor Stone, if it can be diminished at all, has been assuaged to some extent by your many activities.

Noting, of course," Emma continued, taking a French macaron from the silver platter, "the Benevolent Foundation for Destitute Children as one of your prime activities."

"In fact, we do have business at hand." Abigail noted. "Our Charity Ball is at the end of summer, which gives us less than four months to organize the event. Part of which is actually visiting the orphanages and church relief programs we sponsor, so that we can properly assess where best to put the funds we raise."

Emma nodded wisely. "We feel that would be something you might excel in."

"Of course. I'd be happy to do it."

"Only because we're more at risk."

"Risk..?" Jody's look made it clear to both ladies she was not quite understanding.

"You see," Abigail said, setting down her cup of tea, "Many of the children you'll visit are infected with diseases which we, in contact with them, could easily pass on to our own children. You don't have children, somewhere, do you? A private boarding school?"

Danny raced through her heart, but her pause soon ended. "No... I don't have children."

Hours later, as sunlight faded from the study windows, Jody sat in the Professor's chair at his desk, writing a note. "Dear, Mr. Campbell, Your flowers are as lovely as the thoughts behind them..." She looked over to the beautiful bouquet set in a vase on the table. She raised her voice, "Li..."

Moments later, Li appeared in the doorway.

"Read this please." She handed him the note. "Check for spelling mistakes and is it too childish, too swoony?"

"Swoony?"

"You know, too emotional, too needy."

Li looked down at the brief note. "*Thoughts* is with an *ough*. Otherwise, I believe it's quite acceptable. He'll probably want to…"

"Want to what?"

"See you more often." He smiled and handed her back the note. "I'll be excused now."

She watched Li leave and looked back at the note. "See you more often," she repeated softly.

Abigail was tending to a lavish floral arrangement. Morning tea, toast and jam had already been served to the three women seated in the Ralston's parlor. "This will brighten your day, J.D. We've commissioned Alexander Bukhov to design invitations. He's one of our most prominent artists."

"And we're having them printed at Hall's, Stationers," Emma added. "They handle the most prestigious accounts."

Abigail set down her pruning shears. "You don't seem pleased."

"I just thought that if we kept our expenses at a minimum, we'd have more money for the children. They're in desperate need."

"J.D., no one's going to attend if our presentation looks shabby. You mustn't forget, this enterprise reflects on us, as well."

That same night Jody stood in front of Li. He was dressed in a short black robe, tied at the waist, over loose black cotton pants. He moved his arms and legs with deft, sweeping, gestures. "Breathe deeply," he said. "You must learn to breathe. From your breath comes strength and the vital energy you will need."

Jody, dressed in black cotton pants and a loose-fitting black shirt, followed Li's movements, haltingly at first, but slowly, gradually, with more speed and agility. Candles lit the room. Their shadows crossed framed pictures of a younger Li, striking martial poses, as well as drawings of his teachers and famous warriors.

"Professor Stone understood the nature of human be-ings," Li explained, between his lightening-like moves. "The evil of power and the pettiness of fools."

Jody walked the waterfront district, plagued by derelicts, street ruffians and homeless children whose gaunt faces and desperate eyes stared back at her. But no one, she could tell in her heart, was Danny.

Each night she learned from her Master Li, as the move-ments become more complex and athletic. Li raised his hands, stretching his arms above his head. He whirled, spun, and vanished! The candles flickered in the empty darkness.

"I will learn to do that," she said to the candlelight.

As he had promised in his invitation, Aidan Campbell took Jody to an elite city restaurant. He moved the lighted table candle to the side and unfolded his white napkin. "It's not often that business takes me into town, but sometimes it's worth the ride."

"Thank you. I accept that as a compliment. I'm told you have a wonderful ranch north of here."

"My father built it up. I've managed to keep it going since his death."

"Very well, I'm told," she smiled. "An excellent reputation precedes you."

"Well, I'm pleased to tell you that you also come highly recommended, though no one seems to know quite who you are. The details are rather sketchy."

"Do I look sketchy?"

"No, in fact, you look quite beautiful. Do you ride?"

"I've been on a horse or two."

"It would be my pleasure to teach you. I often find city girls just a trifle stiff in the saddle."

"Really..."

"Shall we order?"

"Why not? It's a restaurant."

Aidan gave her a double take. "You didn't learn that in a boarding school." He signaled for the waiter.

The following weekend Jody accepted an invitation to the Campbell ranch. She sat alone in the carriage wondering what new phase in her life she was entering and would Aidan care if the young society woman he had extended an invitation to was once a fifty-cent-whore in a bordello and was wanted for a shoot-out bank robbery. Jody glanced at the ocean, as Li drove the carriage horses along the Pacific trail. Less than an hour later, on a sleek black mare, Jody galloped across a sun-lit valley. Aidan rode alongside, glancing over to the profile of a woman keeping her eyes focused ahead. He had never expected this kind of equine proficiency from the Back East society girl. As the grasslands turned to the forest trees, they reigned their horses, resting them at a nearby stream.

"You don't ride like a city girl." Aidan remarked, trying not to be overly complimentary.

"Are you in the habit of inviting young ladies for the weekend?"

"Well, I might ask you if it's your custom to accept invitations from eligible men for out-of-town excursions?"

Jody smiled. "Li protects my reputation."

She nudged her horse away from the stream. Aidan watched her ride through the shafts of forest light.

Evening dinner was served in the Campbell estate dining room. The thick adobe walls were decorated with colorful Native American tapestries. Standing out, among the tapestries, was a slightly larger fabric, a square of dark green stripes of varying widths, centered with a Scottish family crest, a golden lion. Polished silver and candlelight warmed the long white tablecloth.

Aidan sat at the head of the table, with Jody two settings to his right. "You read quite a bit, don't you?" he asked, lifting his glass of wine.

"I inherited a library. You either read what's in it or you wind up listening to people who've read what's in it."

"You're not one of those women who thinks women should think?" he asked, leaning more to a comment than a question.

"Heavens no, that would be awful. We don't want two people in a household doing the work of one person. That would be as silly as if both people slept together, when they could just as easily sleep alone."

Again, her wit outdistanced his celebrity. "You make a damn fine point," he answered, grudgingly.

"I'd like to make another, Aidan. I'm on the committee to raise funds for aid and relief to impoverished children. Eventually, we'd like to build a new, larger Settlement House. But, of course, this all takes a great deal of money."

"Is that why you accepted my invitation?" His temper was as quick as her wit. He put down his fork. "Is this all about a Settlement House contribution?"

"No. But this is something I do, I'm interested in, I care about. I accepted your invitation because I find you charming, but I'm not blind to the fact that you're wealthy. If you saw the faces of the children, if you…"

"I've heard quite enough." Aidan rose from his chair. "I expected this was going to be a social engagement, not a solicitation for funds."

Jody, as quickly, got to her feet. "You wanted to know more about me. I've told you what I care about, what I feel. You've never been where I've been. If my feelings offend you, then I'm offended by your lack of trust." Jody turned away from the table and started out of the dining room.

Aidan followed a step behind. "Where are you going?"

"Home!"

"You can't ride back to San Francisco at night!"

She stopped at the door and turned. "If you have no interest in my concerns, I can't believe you'd have any interest in my welfare. Li will have the carriage ready in minutes. I'm safer with him."

"What's that supposed to mean? J.D!" He stood in the entry, red-faced, with his white napkin flaring down from his collar.

Into the night, they rode. Li held the reins, but Jody sat on the box-seat beside him, still very upset.

"Li…" "Yes, mam."

"Suppose I wanted to sell something…"

Li didn't bother looking. "Something could be anything."

"Jewelry."

"There are many merchants in San Francisco."

"I thought that a Captain of a ship might find a larger market overseas. And no one here would be the wiser."

The carriage passed miles of fenceposts, and empty, weather-beaten barns lit by moonlight. As they crossed a wooden bridge, Li's quizzical look suggested what Jody was getting at. "Professor Stone gave you those jewels."

"He was very generous, but I don't need everything. This is what he would want me to do… for the children."

Chapter 20

He wandered into the snow-covered strip of land between the back of the cottage and the barn. He saw Ciaran tapping the backs of the sheep with a long branch. The Scottish boy raised his hand close to his shoulder and offered a small, dispassionate wave, from a boy who never had friends nor ever knew how to create a friendship. Billy watched the wind barely stir the pines beyond the barn. Huge bulkhead clouds spread briefly, sending shafts of light through the crowded Highlands sky. He kicked at the wet snow crossed with Ciaran's footprints.

Maybe Adelard dying is making us wait for the perfect time to find her son. Maybe if we'd left this morning, we'd never find the boy. Billy looked around him at the flash of sunlight that had covered the snowbanks and white sleeves of the trees. *Like me biking through the snow to Steve's place. If it hadn't snowed, I'd had gotten to Steve's earlier. If I hadn't jumped on the tires. I would never have found Scotland.*

Billy reached for the iPhone in his jacket pocket. I've got to take pictures of everyone. El, Ciaran, the cottage and Aedan. He stopped. *Of course, I can't take a picture of the past! How dumb am I? I can paint the past, but you can't take a picture of it.*

Adelard's breath sounded like the rasp of a broken pump.

Billy watched the man's eyes barely flutter and close. "Is he dying?"

"A dinnae know that he wants to live. He's between both worlds." El walked back to the table.

"He told me his heart wis heavy with sadness. He haed seen many folk slaughtered, juist like ma faither was. He saw folk tortured, burned to death, churches set on fire with the folk locked in."

Billy couldn't tell if there were tears that streaked the scar on her face or just a faint shadow caused by the window light. She sat down at the table and lit the lantern. "He wis born in France an lived in Spain, England, an' now here. 'It's all the same,' he kept sayin'. One time he looked at me an' said, 'Whit is freedom?' A didn't know what tae say. But then he tapped his heart." Her gaze fell to the clay bowl and bloodstained cloth across from her. "A think it was the only time he moved his hand." She stared for a moment at the bowl. "We'll find a spot in the back, next tae the trees."

Billy jerked his head back, startled by a deep, frightening moan that rose from the deathbed. He looked over to the window. Light was closing into darkness. Something was pulling at him. He didn't want to be the guy who gave up on the dying man. Remembering his own words to Adelard – "you must fight for your life." The thought wouldn't let go of him. His father threw his body over a live grenade. You must fight, too, for another man's life, he heard his father say. Billy turned back to her. "Let's try one more time."

"Try whit?"

"Try anything." He pointed to the bowl "You know, to save him."

"A've been tryin', Billy" She got to her feet and leaned over the table. "Before A sent ye out, ye thought this wis a' futile task. He's a stranger tae ye."

"He was never a stranger. Death has never been a stranger to me. Not since my father died."

"Adelard," El whispered at his lips. "Can ye hear me?" Again, she put the pewter cup to Adelard's mouth. The tea spilled across his lips. Another groan rose, louder, more frightening, as if he were summoning strength from every moribund atom of his body. He raised the hand that had touched his heart, now fell lifeless, to his head, to the ragged scarf that covered his thick black hair.

"Le vôtre!" he cried out. His hand dropped to the bedding.

His mouth fell open with the last exhale of breath.

El made the sign of the cross on Adelard's chest. She kissed his lips. She got to her feet and put her head against Billy and wrapped her arms around him.

"You were right," he said. "You were right to stay."

"He is the second man tae die in this house, Billy. Ma faither an' now ma faither's friend." She raised her head. "He said *le votre*. What daes that mean?"

"I think it means your or yours."

"Is it Spanish?"

"No. But in Spanish *a su salud* means to your health.

There's a girl from France in my Spanish class. She told us in French they say a *votre santé*. It means the same thing."

"*Yer?*" She gave Billy a puzzled look. "Mine, he meant mine. He wis confused with fever."

"No, he speaks French, El. That's his language. He meant your."

El looked back at the corpse. "He put his hand tae his forehead." She stepped to his side and touched the scarf, soiled and sticky with blood and sweat.

"What are you doing?"

"Somethin' is inside. A can feel it." She pulled the fabric apart and opened the scarves folds.

Billy stared at four gold coins couched in Adelard's tangled hair. "Those coins are for you, El."

"Me?"

"That's what he was saying. They're yours. It's part of the message."

"Why?"

"I don't know, but that's why he came here."

"He came here tae die."

"Yes, to die but maybe to save your son, in your father's name!"

Clouds crossed the moon. Again, and again, Billy and Ciaran struck their shovels against the frozen turf. They placed the gravesite far enough from the trees to keep the shovels from hitting the ancient roots. Billy wasn't sure if Ciaran thought they were in a contest, but frantically the Highland boy pitched his shovel, throwing more dirt onto the surrounding ground. It amazed Billy how Ciaran, without so much as a grunt, could slam the shovel down with his foot covered in a leather cuaran. Billy wasn't sure what he was going to tell his mother about his journey, but, for sure, he was going to tell her about the death of Adelard and how he and Ciaran dug his grave as the moon rose and the snow fell on the eve of a Highland night. The burial act seemed to Billy more a validation of his manhood, than any number of wrestling matches he had won or girls he might someday sleep with.

Looking over to Ciaran, compulsively throwing shovelfuls of earth on the small hill behind him, Billy thought back to the image of Ciaran mourning his father at the gravestones. Who dug my own father's grave, he wondered? Did he care at all about the man he was burying or was his mind set on his troubles at home or the movie he watched the night before? Billy was knee deep in the hole when he caught El's eye, making her way across the snow. She spoke to Ciaran first, but Billy was certain, by the weary look in her eyes, she had been crying.

"I've washed him 'n' wrapped him in clean linen," she said. The scar on her face looked darker, even in the moonlight. "We will eat before we bury Adelard."

"Tis a fine time tae snow," she said, looking out the window. El turned to Billy sitting at the table. "We shouldnae wait much longer. Finish up."

"Hang on," Billy protested. "I just sat down." He could feel the tiredness in his muscles and the back of his neck. He grabbed another piece of cheese and looked over to Ciaran, sitting on his cabinet bed, sopping up some porridge with a hunk of bread. "Ciaran and I are going to need all our strength to get him to the grave. He's got to weigh almost as much as you and me together."

"He'll be lighter now that he's dead. His blessit soul has gone tae God."

Billy put his spoon down. "How much does a soul weigh?"

El lifted a brow, knowing she was being challenged. "More than your thoughts, but not as much as yer love for me."

Billy took a bite of his bread and cheese thinking to himself, a high school girl doesn't have a chance against her.

She walked over to him, ran her fingers through his brown, buzz-cut hair, and kissed his head. "We must go."

It was still snowing when Billy and Ciaran carried the body of Adelard across the frozen field. Dressed in a white robe, El walked in front of them. Her head was covered in a long, white scarf, and in each hand, she carried a burning lantern. Both sheep followed her. Moonlight glowed on the carapace of white sheets covering the Frenchman. The boys slipped and stumbled. The body swayed. Ciaran laughed and even Billy, as solemn as he held the occasion, laughed at their bumbling, zigzag trajectory across the knee- deep snow.

El set the lanterns at the head of the grave. "Lower Adelard wi' his head facin' the moon," she said.

Using the bottom sheet as a kind of stretcher, the boys carefully lowered Adelard into the depths of the pit.

"What are the sheep for, El?"

"The lambs o' Christ. They represent th' peace an' purity that surrounds his soul."

Billy stood motionless. A young woman robed in white was standing across from him. A tall, ruddy boy with hip-pie- length hair, in a gray blanket coat, was tapping his hand on the back of one of the sheep.

The snow had stopped falling, as if it were drawing its white curtain back in respect for the solemnity of the occasion. Billy looked up and realized that, for the first night since his arrival in the Highlands, the sky was starless and clear, with only the beacon of a white half-moon to light the grave.

"Shouldn't we say something?"

"Let the earth cover him, first an' foremost," she said.

Billy scooped up a shovelful of dirt. Gently, he sprinkled it across the linens. Ciaran saw what Billy was doing and instantly grabbed his shovel and began the same crazy dirt race he had started when they dug the grave. El grabbed his arm, commanding him in Gaelic, "Not yet!" She stepped forward to the head of the grave and lifted her arms. Her golden red hair fell across the white shoulders of her robe. Billy imagined her, just as he had seen in mythic drawings, a sorceress calling forth the rough, hidden world of its forest gods.

"He died on Scottish soil, far from his home, but the soil is God's soil." El's voice floated through the silent December night. "Like grain has the measure o' His will an His love, so has its sister soil in France." She crossed her heart. "May Adelard's soul an all the souls o' the departit rest i' peace. Beannachdan Dia dhuit." She looked across the grave to Billy. "Blessings of God be with ye. Repeat the words, Billy."

"Beannachdan Dia dhuit." Billy mumbled, stumbling through the benediction.

"Amen," she said.

"Amen," he repeated.

She motioned Ciaran to begin covering the grave.

Billy tossed and turned in the darkness, unable to sleep. Who really was the stranger Adelard? Why did he die the night before we were leaving to search for her son? If he was French, why were Spanish coins buried in his head-scarf? And why, he wondered, did the girl lying next to him feel more like his centuries-old friend than the seven-teen-year-old teenager with a scar on her face that he had met only a few days before?

"Billy, be still." El turned and put her hand on his arm.

"I can't sleep. Everything seems so crazy." He flipped on his side. His face was a breath away from hers. "Are you taking the gold coins with us? That's probably more money than the man with the black horse has ever seen."

"Gae tae sleep," she said.

"If it starts snowing again, will we still go?"

"Ay."

"I will go with you anywhere, you know that."

"E'en tae the steps o' death?"

"If that's where you take me." He kissed her. "Are the steps up or down?"

"Be quiet, Billy. Ye're no so funny. Adelard wis a sign." She stroked her hand across his cheek. "Death is near. The steps are going upward. Now f'n sleep."

Chapter 21

A bigail, Emma, and Jody, dressed for a day-outing and carrying parasols, walked rapidly along the parkway, towards the grand Palace Hotel. "What was it like? You must tell us," Abigail said, most interested in J.D.'s weekend at the Campbell ranch.

"Ladies, we have a lot more work to do than jabber about a day spent at a dusty ranch."

"But it was a weekend," Emma quickly noted.

"Most of that was in the carriage, Emma, traveling with Li."

"But," Abigail quickly pointed out, "if we don't insure our social status, the children will get nothing, J.D. It's important what happens to us and between us."

The Christmas Ball had been held at a convention hall, beautifully decorated for the occasion, but, in Jody's eyes, it did not compare with the stunning Palace Hotel ball room.

"Picture the orchestra at the far end, in front of the organdy drapes." The Hotel Manager's hand fluttered towards the windows. "The dance floor is laid over the carpeting, and the beverage court will be set up along this wall, convenient to our service doors, as well as the buffet table, closer to the kitchen." He turned to Abigail and Emma. "Follow me"

Abigail and Emma exchanged a look and nodded, ignoring J.D., as Mr. Dunnigan led them through the ballroom to a meeting with the chef. "He's temperamental," the Hotel Manager advised. "but, if he insists on his native language, I'll happily translate."

Emma looked back to Jody trailing behind. "Come along, J.D., food is one of the fun things we get to choose."

The day had been somewhat exhausting, certainly emotionally, but, at home in the study, Jody felt more secure and hopeful. She moved from one piece of furniture to the next, dusting and thinking back to the barroom songs. "Many are the nights I think of you.. Many are the days you fill my heart.." Softly she sang, "In many of the worlds I've searched for you… In many of my dreams you are the starring part…" Danny never left her.

"Miss Jody." Li took a step into the study. He was holding a white envelope. "It isn't necessary we eliminate all our expenses."

She smiled. "I can clean as well as anyone, Li."

"I've been told in some homes you're regarded as a martyr."

"Who told you such rubbish?"

"The servants talk, you know. They tell me that those who employ them think you're foolish for bringing books to children who want toys."

"I have brought toys, as well."

"Behind your back, your own friends are saying the children will only grow up to steal your money."

"Then they're not my friends. I should steal their money and buy the children toys." She added with a defiant look, "Shouldn't I, Li?"

The Houseman looked down and remembered the envelope. "I almost forgot; this is for you, from Mr. Campbell." He handed her the envelope.

For a brief moment she stared at her name. Then, impulsively, she tore the envelope up. As Li was about to leave the study, her voice stopped him. "Li, this wouldn't be the first time I stole."

Jody sat beside Li on the open carriage. Li had advised they go later, but Jody had insisted on the earlier hour, and now the fog was swirling around them. He reined the horse and peered through the heavy mist.

"We're lost, aren't we?"

"Have faith, Miss Stone. The waterfront district is not well-planned; the roads are poor, but I have been here many times."

"You and I know who I am, Li. Please continue to call me Jody."

"As you please, Miss Jody."

"It was you who saved me."

"Technically, Gibbons did the saving."

She was comforted by his smile, the only person in San Francisco who knew the secret of who she really was. "Mr. Powell is expecting me."

"Life holds many challenges for you. Finding the Settlement House is the least of them. You must increase your strength."

"What is that supposed to mean?"

"In time," Li said, "I will show you. It was a request from Professor Stone. I am a student of the martial arts and the Invisible World." Soon enough, despite the swirling fog, Li found the Settlement House.

Mr. Gordon Powell, the Settlement House Administrator, once again, led Jody through the gloomy institution. "It test's one's faith, really. What chance have they, one wonders. It's a terrible situation. In less than twenty years the population of this city has tripled. Most of those who've come are poor laborers from the railroads or dreamers from the gold mines who've lost their stake and haven't a penny. Their children go hungry in the streets or turn to crime."

A Cross hung above each door. Decrepit rooms were filled with unruly children from five to fifteen, more like warehousing lost souls than nurturing young bodies and minds. Powell stopped his tour, realizing he was alone. He looked back. Jody had remained behind, her gaze focused on a boy, about five, playing alone.

"Miss Stone... Miss Stone..."

Jody turned and caught up to Powell. "Has that boy been here long, Mr. Powell?"

"He came to us six months ago, off a ship from Canada. Once the mother arrived here, she abandoned him."

"Oh..." A trace of disappointment shaded Jody's face. She followed the Administrator into his cramped office.

"Anything you could do to help, Miss Stone, would be gratefully appreciated. Please, sit down."

Powell surveyed the stack of books he'd just removed from a canvas bag. Jody listened to his unexpected, disappointing reaction. "The books are well meant, Miss Stone. But who's to read then to the children who, themselves, can't make out a sentence of simple words?"

"I'll read them."

The Administrator shook his head. "I'm sorry, but I can't allow you to do that. Many of these children are very sick and contagious."

"I'm not eating their dinner, Mr. Powell; I'm feeding their soul."

Powell raised his brows and shook his head, again. "They're not like normal children. They're bitter, angry, tough. They haven't had your kind of comfort and upbringing. You're hardly prepared to engage this kind of conduct."

"I'll take my chances. As for their daily bread, I've brought you this." Jody took a few steps to his desk and removed a drawstring sack from her purse. As she emptied it, a dozen gold coins clattered across Powell's desk.

Chapter 22

Her eyes were closed. Her body still, but he knew she wasn't asleep. They had made love because she wanted to. She had told Billy: "My body needs ye. We dinnae know how the journey will end."

He knew so little about lovemaking, only what he had seen in films and what guys had told him in coarse, locker room language. But he had read once that girls liked to savor the moment, enjoying the waves of pleasure that coursed through their body. Or is she thinking about how she's going to feel when she has her son in her arms again? Or how far we'll travel before we find Bran?

Billy finished dressing and peered down at the cuarans binding his feet. He dipped his hand into his jacket pocket, removed his father's dog tag, and clasped the necklace around his neck. It was his talisman, the gift of sacred protection and of his return ticket to the Twenty-first Century. In the quest for El's son, Billy was assuming, like his father had in Iraq, the mantle of the warrior.

Ciaran was still asleep on the straw bed behind the table when Billy entered the room. It was the same bed Ciaran had made for Billy when he first arrived. El had put clean sheets on the cabinet bed. She had sprinkled herbs over the sheets, said prayers and told her brother he could not sleep in his own bed for seven nights. The shade of Adelard's death would then be gone.

Billy walked over to the fire, stoked it, and added a few pieces of peat. He looked over to the small square window. The slightest feeling of nostalgia crept into his heart for the place he was about to leave. I'll miss this cottage. *I'll miss everything that is here.* The morning light cast its thin silver rays across the table, the unlit lantern, and the memory of a boy making love to a Scottish girl across those polished wooden boards. El came out of the bedroom. She wore a pale-yellow tunic that fell to her knees. A belt cinched at her waist carried the sheath and dirk. She had on what looked like white leggings tied at the ankles. Several times she called Ciaran until he awoke. Her voice snapped and made it clear that she had taken command. He rubbed his eyes, threw on a padded waistcoat, and left the cottage.

"Billy," she said, "Ciaran is bringin' Aedan tae the front o' the house. Tak the pot an fill it wi' snow."

A blanket of fresh snow covered the ground and coated the branches with a thin, bright icing. Billy had witnessed mornings like this in Cederburgh but never so quiet, so haunted by a silence that seemed like hands hushing the mountains of the world. Then he heard the jangle of reins and Ciaran coming around the cottage with Aedan. Ciaran hadn't asked about the iPhone since Adelard's arrival. Billy thought that maybe Adelard's death had affected the boy more deeply than Billy had imagined. Maybe he wasn't racing me when we were digging Adelard's grave. Maybe every shovelful of dirt was a cruel reminder of digging his own father's grave.

Something I never had to do. Billy scooped up the snow with the pot and went back inside.

"How long do you think we'll be gone?" he asked.

El busied herself adding the pot of snow to another pot that hung on a fire hook. "Hand me the bowl on the kist."

Billy walked over to the chest and handed her a clay bowl. The commanding tone was back in her voice.

"A'm usin` special herbs in the porridge," she said. "They'll give ye strength an' stamina. Do ye know whit stamina is?"

"Do you know what a high performance-energy drink is? Huh?" Billy didn't wait for her answer. He told her that in his wrestling regimen he takes lots of vitamins and protein drinks.

"Maybe they're the same," she said. "Ma mither taught me special preparations. Ye can put the plates tae the table an' call in Ciaran."

"You never answered my question about how long we'll be gone. And what about food? Where will we eat?"

"Where does anybody eat on the road, Billy? Inns. Besides, we will take some food with us."

He shook his head, muttering to himself. "Do I know what stamina is?" Then he raised his voice. "I'm going back outside to pee."

"Write ma name in the snow!"

He walked over to a stand of white birch and made El's initials in the snow. He started the outline of a heart when the rattling scream of a bird startled him. He stepped back and shoved his penis into his pants. A huge raven spread its wings on a nearby branch. Again, the black bird screamed.

"What do you want?" Billy shouted.

"Your soul!"

"My soul? What are you talking about? What soul?"

"Your father loves you."

He knew the voice was in his head. Still, he wanted to believe that in this mythic world, someone in the universe, even if it were a bird, knew who he was. And where he was. He looked at the sky, crosshatched with dark branches behind the bird,

" You kept me up half the night with your cawing. Just now, you scared the shit out of me," he yelled. "Do you have anything more to say?"

The raven spread its wings, lifting-off in a single flutter. It circled the trees again, tilted its body upwards and was lost in a bank of dark clouds. Billy remembered seeing a nature show that described a small group of animals, ravens among them, that recognize and even mourn their dead. Was the raven here to mourn Adelard? he wondered. He looked back at the letters E and L in the snow, circled by half of a heart. The raven had returned to the branch. "Half is written," he whispered, "and the other half is five hundred years in your future."

El slung two satchels packed with provisions over Aedan's back. Billy looked past her shoulder to the cottage window. He thought he glimpsed Ciaran's face, watching them and then ducking away into darkness. "Should I say goodbye to him now?"

"He's no gonna like that, Billy. He says 'choppers' now an' he thinks ye're his friend. He doesn't want us to gae, but he also wants very much for me tae find ma son."

El mounted Aedan. Billy climbed on and wrapped his arms around her. "You packed the gold coins?"

"Aye," she said

She turned the horse to the road they had traveled once before. Her solemn mood offered no sense of excitement or expectation, but Billy read nothing into this. His experience with El, more intense and profound than any he had ever imagined with another person, had brought him to the understanding that the Highland girl was different, even mysterious and thrilling in the depth of her passions, and that he was better off accepting this mystery than trying to understand it.

"Look!" Billy pointed to the raven circling overhead. "'Tis the soul o' Adelard," she said, "protectin' us."

Sunlight stripped the sky of threatening clouds. Still, the day felt bitterly cold. Cederburgh-cold, Billy thought to himself, but in Cederburgh, he was dressed for the weather when it dipped below zero, not in tie-up tuews, a cotton tunic and leather wrappings on his feet. Even his parka seemed flimsy against the wind that blew off the sea, as, again, they passed Eilean a' Cheo, Isle of Skye. Digging his knees into the flanks of Aedan, Billy strained to unzip the back of his collar, releasing his rolled-up hood. He slipped it over his head, keeping his neck and ears warm.

"Loch Carron!" he shouted out, looking over to the river, giving its name his best Gaelic accent.

"Ye remember," she shouted back. "Guid Gaelic, laddie!"

He imagined her smiling, laughing to herself. Even at his expense, he preferred her laughter to her gray morning grumble. El reined Aedan to a trot and turned him down a rocky slope to the Loch. The earth was wet and brown and scattered with stones. The riders dismounted and led the stallion to the shore.

"Do you think we'll see those men again?"

"It doesnae matter. A know where tae gae." El raised her hand to his jacket hood. "Where did ye git this?"

"It's rolled-up in the back of my collar. There's a zipper back there." Billy turned, showing off the back of his parka.

"A like this better than the iPhone."

"That's because you have nobody to call on the iPhone," he laughed. "You have no idea how amazing it is. I can talk to anybody anywhere in the entire world."

"Can ye talk tae the man who has ma son?"

"You don't even know the name of the man." Billy squinted his eyes against the wind. "Besides, he has to have a phone and nobody in Scotland has a phone!"

"Kiss me."

"You don't get it, El. I'm talking about one of the greatest inventions in history, an invention that is totally changing our world!"

"How much more love is thare in that world o' yours with a phone than in ma heart fur ye? Th' kiss isn't an invention, Billy. Tis a promise an' a need."

The sound of water crashing over rocks and wind tearing through branches couldn't fill the hollow of emptiness he felt inside. No one had ever talked to him like this. "Why do you even love me?"

"Ye love me, dinnae ye?"

"Yes."

"Dae ye know why?"

"Not really. You're more than my imagination ever dreamed." The questions were making him uncomfortable. The sound of the river rushing past was unnerving him.

"Ye'll never find the reason, ye'll never know the reason.

Love is written somewhere far away. Ye had tae travel five hundred years to find that," she cried above the wind, "'An' A had tae lose a faither and ma son fur us tae find each other. That's the way 'twas written. Is that so bad? I'm not juist a pan o' barley cakes. Didn't ye feel ma heart when ye slept wi' me? It's got all the loneliness o' the world inside." She stared at him. "It's not a game, Billy. Now, kiss me."

He brought her into his arms and kissed her. "In our hearts," she said, "its love."

They passed through the burned-out village they had visited days before. A woman, bundled in a long black dress and a torn, gray coat, was rummaging through charred timbers, broken furniture, and piles of stone. With her back to Billy, she reminded him of the lone survivor of a terrible disaster, just as he had seen so many times on TV, picking over the remnants of a decimated life. El reined up the horse and called over to the woman. "A bheil thu eòlach air fear à oighreachd Morair a' Chinn Àird a tha a' falbh air each dubh?"

The woman answered with puzzled look in her eyes. "A bheil taigh-òsta mun cuairt far am faigh sinn biadh?" She told El that she didn't know any man with a black horse, but there was an inn past the hill with the flat top, where they could eat.

They rode past fields of grazing sheep, nibbling on patches of grass the sun had stripped of snow. Waves of pristine white hills rose to summits scattered with rust-stained boulders and steep cliffs.

"That's it!" El was pointing to a hill whose peak resembled the flat plane of a landing field. "That must be it. It shouldn't be long now."

The dimly lit room they stepped into had a low ceiling that seemed to squeeze out any sign of good-will and warmth. Tables ran along one wall ending at a wooden counter on their left. Lanterns burned to still the darkness. Three pairs of eyes looked up, surveying the unexpected visitors. Billy forced a smile, but only mute faces stared back. He followed El to a brown bearded, heavy-set man that Billy guessed was in his forties. He smoked a pipe and leaned his back against the wooden counter with no apparent interest in greeting his visitors. El handed the man a few silver coins. He pulled himself up, in what seemed a great, heaving annoyance, and moved behind the counter.

El grabbed Billy's arm and led him to a corner table. A lantern burned on a hook against the wall. "A told him we were lookin' for a tenant with a black horse an then I ordered some bread, some cheese, and ale. He isn't very friendly."

"Did he know the man we're looking for?"

"Na, but he said that by the time we reached Laird Kinnaird's estate, it would be nightfall."

Billy looked across the room at the two men clutching pewter cups and wrapped in shabby winter clothes. Both men had crinkly gray beards, and each wore a dark blue, knit wool cap that rimmed their gray brows. The men, he thought, were at least as old as his grandpa. He recalled a painting he'd seen on a field trip his high school class had made to the Art Institute in Chicago. It showed gritty old men huddled together like this in a cramped, lantern-lit

room, but never did he think he'd be in their midst, with a
Scottish girl he loved.

The corpulent innkeeper brought over the food on a
wooden tray. He set plates of bread and cheese, along with
two pewter mugs of ale, on the table. Billy thought the man
was going to leave, but he just stood over them as if he expected a tip.

Finally, the innkeeper turned to El. "Cò às tha e?"

"Spain," she answered. She turned to Billy. "Say somethin' tae th' man in Spanish."

"Hola. Como esta usted?" Billy returned a friendly smile.
It amused him that he was saying, "Hello, How are you?,"
the very first phrase he had learned in his beginning Spanish
class, to a stranger, in a land five hundred years ago, where
no one spoke Spanish.

The man nodded. "Dè thug thusa an-seo?"

Billy understood some of what El was telling the innkeeper, but he got lost once she passed mother and horse.

The man looked back at Billy. "Spain?" His dark eyes
shifted between Billy's hands and his face. "Tha a craiceann
ro bhàn."

"His skin is too light." She repeated his snide remark.
She looked up. "When were ye iver in Spain? He's from the
north. Bha a mhã thair nas bã ine na fiaclan do leinbh."

The innkeeper's face turned red. He slapped El hard
across her scar.

Before his hand had fallen to his side, Billy jumped to
his feet and slammed his dirk into the table. Blood rushed
to his forehead. "Tell him the next strike is to his heart."

El repeated the threat in Gaelic. The heavy-set man
wiped his hands on his apron and stepped back. "Thilg i

tàthag orm!" he roared. Billy's eyes flashed to the old men who had gotten up from their table and scrambled to retrieve swords hanging on the counter post.

El got to her feet, stuffed the bread and cheese in her pockets and grabbed Billy's arm, as he raised the dirk to its sheath. "We are leavin'!"

In four quick steps they were out of the inn.

El galloped Aedan down a deserted forest road. Reaching a river crossing, she slowed the horse's gait. Billy leaned to her ear. "Why did the inn keeper get so mad?"

"He said that I'd offended him whan A told him yer mither was whiter than his baby's teeth."

"We say it all the time in Cederburgh." Billy laughed, but his next thought quickly stilled the laughter: *I was ready to kill that man to protect El. That's probably a part of love, too.*

"We'll find a place soon tae rest. Look for a cave."

"Did you see that castle back there?" Billy asked, excitedly. "Maybe we could sleep there!"

"That wasnae a castle. 'It was an abbey. Monks live thare."

"It looked like a castle."

El laughed. "Dinnae argue with me, Billy. Ye showed me a picture ye told me was a car. A didnae tell ye it didnae look like a car. A know ma world an' ye know yours."

The sun had slipped far behind them. Light had run off the hills.

"Look, Billy," she said. "Look hard. Night will soon be with us." The wind shook the trees, throwing a ragged blanket of shadows across the snow.

Everything drew together in the darkness. A glow of light caught Billy's eye. "Look over there." He pointed El's arm to her right.

Coming down through the rocks on the hillside, they saw petals of light glimmering through trees. A dozen or so men and women were chanting, some holding lanterns. El reined in Aedan. She and Billy spotted a man, in the midst of the procession, carrying a large cross, illuminated by the lanterns. "They're celebratin' the birth o' Christ," El explained. "Listen." From across the wooded hillside, they heard the chanting voices of the worshippers.

"They found one helluva place to celebrate," Billy whispered. "Why don't they find a church or a cozy inn?"

"Now is the time o' Yultid."

"Yuletide," Billy repeated, correcting El's pronunciation. "When we go over to my grandma's house for Christmas, she plays CD's and one of the songs is about a yuletide."

"Well, Billy," El whispered back, "maybe yer grandma knows more about fifteen hundreds Scotland an' our festivals than A do, but until we meet up with her on the road, ye believe whit A'm tellin' ye." The lantern lights slowly disappeared.

El waited a moment longer and then headed Aedan up the snowy hillside. "In the past, folk begin their prayer ceremonies in caves. Let's hope they did this time."

Billy slipped off the back of the horse. "Wait here. I'm going to scope things out."

Quickly, he scrambled higher along the steep terrain. He moved from tree to tree, hoping no one from the procession would have turned back to spot him. The sense of exploring, of drawing on a secret mission, revived in him the excitement of searching through columns of tires for his father's enemy.

Billy noticed the stones to his left were gradually turning into what looked like crude steps. He climbed the stones and followed a path that ringed a narrow moonlit ridge. He stopped and peered into the mouth of a huge cave.

"Bats, rats, and snakes get your asses out of here!" he shouted. He took a step back and waved his arms. "El!"

She led Aedan into the cave and removed the leather pouches she had tied like saddlebags to his backside. Then she gave him a pat and sent him out of the cave. Billy came back with branches and handfuls of sticks. He had been camping enough times with Cash and Justin to know that setting the sticks up like a teepee was the best way to get a fire going. Then he set a ring of stones around the fire pit. He jabbed his hands into his jacket pockets in search of matches. Even before his fingers curled around the empty space, he knew it was pointless. Cash's silver lighter, stamped in red with "Hell Fire" on one side, sat on Billy's dresser in front of his father's picture.

"Dae ye know how tae start a fire like this?" El removed a piece of flint and a small ball that looked like rolled up brown yarn from one of the leather pouches.

Billy watched El pull apart some of the ball. "'Tis hemp," she said. "Dae ye know what hemp is?" She fluffed the strands of hemp into a small nest. Then she struck her knife repeatedly against the flint. Billy saw sparks in the darkness, and the tendrils of hemp caught fire. El slid the burning nest under the tepee of sticks. Flames budded and leapt through the teepee. Flashes of light burst across the cave walls. Billy smiled, praising her magical effort and quickly adding larger sticks. "You did it," he said, as he snapped branches across his knee.

"We did it." She looked at him as if her eyes could drill the words through his heart. "Niver forget that. In whatev'r universe we're in, tis always 'we'"

El spread a cloth on the ground, took the cheese and bread from her pockets and placed them on the cloth. They ate in silence, grateful for the warmth of the fire. The only sound was the howling of the wind. El went outside and brought Aedan into the cave. The stallion made no effort to go back out. Billy stared at the unprotected cave opening. Were soldiers to come, searching the area for the two of them, having heard of their whereabouts from the angry Innkeeper, or if thieves were to see the fire burning on the hillside cave, Billy knew that, despite their dirks, they were powerless to defend themselves. Even were Aedan to sound an alarm, as he did on the arrival of Adelard, they would be at the mercy of more lethal power.

El took the cold blanket off Aedan's back and unfolded it across the ground.

"The Yultid folk made me think o' somethin'. It comes from the Norse people. Dae ye know who they are?"

"Vikings."

She looked up with a skeptical gaze. "How dae ye know these things?"

He told her about his schoolbooks and movies. "If my iPhone could get a signal here, I could show you."

"Well, anyway," she said, ignoring his cheeky smile, "Odin wis a Viking god. His twelfth name wis Yultid." She explained how he would come to Earth in the twelfth month, disguised in a hooded cloak. He would sit with the people at the fire and then he would leave a gift of bread or coins.

"Do you think he'll come to visit us in this cave?"

"He has already come." A smile leapt into her eyes. "He gave me four gold coins."

"Adelard?"

"Aye! A know ma father in Heaven sent him. He, tae, wis a Viking."

Billy leaned away from the fire. He thought to himself, *So I must be a Viking, too.* He was beginning to believe in El's mystical world, the world of a mother's voice rising from the flames of a hearth and of a dog-tag flaring light in a faraway meadow. And staring into the flames she had just created, it struck him that with wormholes and expanding universes, TV transmission and trips to the moon, was his world any less mystical? Yes, there were formulas and statistics, but were they any different then the mumbo-jumbo, indecipherable words of an ancient world as passionately connected to the universe?

They lay down on the blanket, huddled together in their jackets. "Thank ye for savin' me from the innkeeper," she whispered. "Ye are a brave man, Billy Blackwell. Ye are the one tae find ma son. A knew it."

"You called me a coward once."

"A'v made more than one mistake in ma life." Her words brought a smile to his lips, worth far more than any high school match he might have forfeited. They fell asleep in the warmth of the fire. Aedan stood at the mouth of the cave guarding his keepers.

Chapter 23

The Palace Hotel ballroom glittered with the jeweled gowns, rings and necklaces of SanFrancisco's rich and famous gathered to attend the poor children's charity ball. Jody, dressed in a stunning, sky-blue gown, watched the attendees on the dance floor. Everyone shimmered with excess.

"J.D."

Jody turned to look at Aidan Campbell walking towards her. "You didn't think I wouldn't attend? You did get my letter, didn't you?"

"Yes."

"I'm not a writer, but I hope my words conveyed how sorry I was for my attitude and insensitivity the weekend you visited."

"Of course." She was embarrassed to tell him she'd torn the letter up. "I've thought about you ever since."

Like giddy vultures, Abigale and Emma, seated at a reserved table, watched Jody and Aidan. "Look, Emma, they're going on to the dance floor."

"Indeed, J.D. can't keep this a secret any longer."

More eyes than Abigail and Emma's turned to watch the young woman in the sky-blue gown and the tall, handsome bachelor gracefully moving to the dance floor music.

Light of a half-moon crossed the Stone townhouse. In the dim candlelight of Li's chambers, the Houseman, dressed in his familiar black robe and pants, led Jody through a series of accelerated and elaborate martial arts moves.

Jody's awkwardness was a thing of the past. With deft, skillful moves, she was a blur of motion.

Less than a week after the Charity Ball, Abigail and Emma hurried down the Stone's townhouse hallway, where Li ushered them into the parlor.

"It's in Ambrose Bierce's column in the San Francisco Newsletter! The town is talking about you and Aidan!" The banker's wife bubbled with excitement.

"We are so very happy for you," Emma exclaimed. "Will any of your family back East be making the journey here for the wedding? Or will it be in the East?"

Jody turned to Abigail. "Wedding?"

"Your wedding or the engagement."

Li, waiting patiently, raised his voice. "Do you want tea served in here, Miss Stone?"

"Thank you, Li." She turned to Abigail and Emma. "Please, sit down." Jody was quick to dismiss any chatter about an engagement and clearly more interested in finding out the financial results of the dance. She watched them take a seat together on the settee. "Have you made a final tally on our profits?"

Abigail and Emma exchanged a look. "We must talk about that. Emma has a record of the finances."

Jody watched Emma remove a small red ledger from a leather tote bag. "We have complete and detailed financial records," Emma explained, leafing through the ledger. "Here it is." She ran her hand down the page. "We sold sixty-five tickets. Ten of those were single tickets; the rest were as a couple. One hundred and forty people attended."

"How much money did we make?"

Emma paused slightly. "We don't show any excess revenue."

Stunned, Jody turned to Abigail, who quickly, firmly added, before Jody could voice her shock. "That sometimes happens."

"You told me to research the charities. I saw the children; I talked to the directors. I counted on being able to give them money." Her words mounted with anger. "They've counted on it!"

"Be calm, J.D." Abigail was shocked and affronted by Jody's tone. "They can't count entirely on us."

"We were going to build a new Settlement House!"

Emma came quickly to Abigail's defense. "Perhaps we gave out a few more complimentary tickets than we should have. But, in order to attract the cream of society, you've got to sometimes invite those notables that people are going to want to be seen with."

"Those 'notables' should have paid. They're the ones that can afford to!"

"In their eyes, their presence is their payment," Abigail insisted.

"And when I look in the eyes of the children, what should I say? We had a lovely night, we ate well, drank well, thank you for letting us use your name, your plight, your utter misfortune." Jody's words were twisting out of the heat in her voice and the unknown fate of her son. "I would have brought you the flowers but they died overnight!"

"I think you're taking this all too seriously. My husband administrates the second largest bank in San Francisco, yet even they miscalculate at times. We're only human."

"If only we were."

"What's that supposed to mean?" Abigail raised her chin. Li entered with a trey of cups, saucers and a pot of tea.

"Tea is served."

"At another time." Abigail got to her feet and turned to Emma. "Come along, Emma. We have a concert to ready ourselves for."

Li, somewhat bemused, kept to his duties. "Shall I show you to the door?"

"We'll have no trouble finding it," Abigail barked.

Jody watched them march out of the parlor. A moment later she heard the front door slam. She looked over to Li. "They'll pay for those tickets."

From off the ocean, a strong wind howled through the city.

Shutters banged against the townhouse windows. Moonlight scattered through the trees.

In the hallway of the Stone townhouse, the clock struck ten. Li turned down the kerosene lamps and retired for the night.

In her bedroom, Jody set down a book and got up from her chair. She stepped over to the dresser mirror, removed a ribbon from her hair and pulled her hair back into a tight bun.

She opened a dresser drawer and removed a leather case, placed it on the dresser and opened it to a pair of pearl-handle pistols. Then, she reached back into the drawer, removed a black mask and carefully slipped it over her eyes.

In his bedroom, Li, half asleep in his bed, lifted an eye to the window, listening to the wind rattle the shutters.

A shadowy figure, dressed in black and cloaked in a black cape, moved swiftly down the hallway, past the servant's quarters and exited the townhouse through a rear door.

A light mist surrounded the stables in the back of the townhouse. Jody led the sleek, black stallion out of his stall. The horse and rider disappeared into the fog.

At the crest of the hill, a dark figure riding a stallion emerged from the forest, bathed in swirling mist and moon-light. Below them, a carriage made its way along a winding trail. Abigail and her husband, Thomas Ralston, a bit drowsy from food and drink, sat together in the carriage, chatting over the affair they had just attended. They agreed that the music was "sublime" and the food was excellent.

Suddenly, the carriage stopped.

"Perhaps the wind blew down a tree," Thomas started to open the carriage door, but halfway out he stopped. A black gun was pointed at him in the hand of a rider cloaked in black. The gunman's black mask covered his eyes and a black kerchief was wrapped across the lower part of his face. Leather gloves hid the robber's hands. The Carriage Driver leaned to his passenger and handed him a note and an empty sack.

"What does the note say," Abigail asked, growing more frightened.

"The words have been clipped from newspapers and pasted together: 'REMOVE JEWELRY. PLACE IN SACK.' It says, ' NO ONE WILL BE HURT. OBEY OR…'"

Abigail put her hand to her lips. "Oh, lord! I'm going to faint." Her eyes glazed as she crumpled to the side of the carriage.

In the Stone residence, morning light streamed through the study windows. Li was straightening books and dusting the shelves. "Would that be the same Ralstons that troubled you with the charities?" he asked.

Jody was sitting in Professor Stone's favorite leather chair. She looked up from the newspaper she was reading. The headline read: "Masked Bandit Robs Banker and His Wife in the Corrigan Pass."

"I believe it is," she said, without a trace of irony. She got up and crossed to a walnut side table, where she opened a drawer and removed a large, red velvet purse. "Li, I have some jewelry I want you to sell."

"I see you found another cache," the Houseman smiled, without revealing a trace of complicity.

Two weeks had passed before Jody visited the Settlement House again. It was, indeed, a cause for celebration, and Mr. Powell was rummaging through his cabinet for two clean glasses. "Of course, as in the past, I will observe your wishes for strict anonymity," he said.

"But we couldn't keep our doors open without your kindness." Powell poured two glasses of sherry. He handed one to Jody and lifted his glass. "God save your soul."

"I'll need His grace," she said.

He set down his glass and took his seat behind his cluttered desk. "May I be personal, Miss Stone? Is it guilt because of the privileged life you've led or merely family tradition that engages your pursuit of charitable deeds?"

"Perhaps I simply enjoy children, Mr. Powell." Jody set her glass down on his desk. "I should have some more money for you very soon. We mustn't abandon the building fund. Good day."

Before Jody had taken two steps, Powell's voice stopped her. "Miss Stone, from what I've read in the papers, it might not be too far in the future before you have children of your own to worry about. A Scottish lad or lassie."

Jody's quizzical look was answered by two words from Powell. "Mr. Campbell." He raised his brows.

"You mustn't believe everything you read in the papers, either. Besides, why, in heavens, lad or lassie?"

"The Campbells came from Scotland. I'm told there's even a Campbell Castle somewhere in Scotland."

"That must have been hundreds of years ago."

"I believe it was. I've never been there."

"He's a rancher now, not some sort of knight. Good day," she said and left.

Powell's eyes turned from her quick departure to the pile of gold coins on his desk.

Rain threatened the evening sky. In the Stone parlor, Jody paced with the same restless energy as the visiting storm clouds. She looked over to Li tending the fire.

"I've begged for more than one scrap of bread in my life. And I came back from the dead, didn't I? I can out-ride most men and shoot the rain off a duck's back."

"You are a very good rider."

"It's been eight years since I ran away and six years since…" She stopped and turned to the windows.

"Since?"

"Nothing."

"Since the boy died..?"

"He didn't die." Jody watched the rain begin to streak the windows. "What do you know?" She turned back to Li. "Did Professor Stone…"

"No, Madame. But I carried you in from the street and cared for you when you were near death. I heard you mumble the name, 'Daniel'. It could have been your husband or your lover. But then I saw how much you wanted to help the children, and I knew the name was someone from your own flesh and blood."

"He was... He was my Danny. He is my son." Jody turned back to the windows, trying to grasp her emotions and forestall her tears.

Li, giving respect to her feelings, announced he would prepare a special Chinese dinner, Schezwan chicken. "It was among the Professor's favorites."

He started to leave, but before he reached the door, a strong, firm voice stopped him.

"I want the city papers, listing all the social events for the month," she said.

Days later, Jody sat in a garden café, sipping black tea, and reading a newspaper. Her eyes were focused on the Society Page. With a pen, she circled various upcoming social events, and occasionally she would glance up, watching the wealthy ladies lunching with friends. Two tables over, close to the garden entry, her eye caught the arrival of Abigail Ralston and Emma Tinsdale.

Whatever nervousness they held, in approaching Jody, was washed away by their ingratiating smiles.

"J.D, what a pleasant surprise. We haven't seen you in months," Abigail chimed. "We were so worried about you."

"Ever since we heard the very disheartening news that you and Mr. Campbell were no longer seeing each other. Or are you?" Emma asked.

"Emma, we mustn't pry." Abigail offered an apologetic smile. "J.D, I hope you're not offended you weren't invited to the Spring Ball. We tried to keep it small. After all, it was you who felt our expenses were too great last year."

"And," Emma added, "We gave the money to a very worthy cause. The city is planning an art museum."

"And then, of course, I suffered a frightful experience," Abigail confessed. "You probably read about the robbery in the papers. Mr. Ralston and I were nearly murdered by a ruthless horse bandit."

Jody raised her brows "Really?"

"Abigail couldn't speak for days."

"Weeks," her associate corrected her. "And they still haven't caught the miscreant."

"You must be very careful," Jody cautioned.

"And so must you, my dear. As my good husband, Mr. Ralston, has said so often, the burden of wealth is that those without it are constantly trying to unburden you of it."

"Which is not fair, at all," Emma added.

"But we are taking up your time. You seem preoccupied with your papers and reading, which I know you so much like to do. Come along, Emma."

Jody watched a waiter lead the two women to a table near a group of potted palms. Her gaze fell back to the "Calendar of Social Events."

The following night a black stallion galloped onto a country road and reared majestically into the path of an oncoming carriage. The driver abruptly reined his horse and reached for his rifle. The masked rider quickly shot the rifle from driver's hand. Jody motioned him to get down from his seat.

Mr. Tinsdale, round-faced with a handlebar moustache, stuck his head out of the carriage window.

Jody took aim above the window, driving Tinsdale's head back into the carriage. She threw a satchel to the driver, motioning him to open the carriage door.

Tinsdale and Emma scrambled out of the carriage. Emma, looking up at the masked rider, fainted into her husband's arms.

Late night robberies occurred almost weekly. On one occasion, a Security Guard, hidden on the roof of the carriage, leapt down, knocking Jody off her horse. She scrambled to her feet and released a devastating martial arts assault of whirling kicks, and devastating blows, overwhelming her attacker. Then, in a dazzling display of speed and balance, she spun towards the driver, pistol firing, and shot the gun from his hand.

The following week, for the first time Jody attempted a daylight robbery. Her horse raced the carriage across a swarm of hills. A man in the carriage threw open his door and fired back as Jody brilliantly wove through the path of bullets.

The heavy-set man ducked back into the carriage and looked over to his fellow traveler, who had turned to the oval window in the rear of the carriage. Aidan Campbell turned back. "There's only one person I've ever seen ride that well. And it wasn't a man."

"Then it must have been the devil in a cape!"

Above them, on the roof of the carriage, the man riding shotgun, hoping to appease the bandit, threw a large, heavy sack onto the dusty road. Jody reigned her horse and dismounted. She raced over to the canvas sack. Inside were at least twenty books on art, history, philosophy, and science. She reached for an envelope stuck between the pages of one of the books. The paper inside was an invoice, listing the title and price of each book, with the purchaser's name at the bottom: "Aidan Campbell".

Mr. Powell could hardly believe his good fortune. He surveyed the pile of currency and golden coins on his desk. "You really shouldn't be traveling alone with this much money. Every person of your social status is at risk now."

"My driver, Li, is very protective. I assure you; you needn't worry."

"May I ask how you raise these sums? Mind you, I don't mean to pry and sound ungrateful, but the talk among the clergy is that, since our previous benefactors are no longer contributing as generously nor were they ever as effective..." Powell rose from his chair. "I thought perhaps we could have a meeting in which you'd share your expertise."

"I'm flattered, Mr. Powell, but, really, I have no special secrets and my donors prefer to remain anonymous."

"Well, you're doing an excellent job of keeping their identities secret. It's almost as if you've taken a lesson or two from the Masked Rider," he chuckled. "Once, legend had a Zorro. Now, we have a *Zorrita*! I'm told that even with a cape, the body seems to have a feminine form." Again, he chuckled and led Jody to the door.

Li waited patiently on the carriage bench. He looked up as a man in a passing carriage caught his eye.

The man leaned back and looked at the newspaper on his lap. He studied the headline: "Reign of Terror Strikes High Society Again." Philo Storm set the paper aside and puffed thoughtfully on his cigar.

The last rays of sunlight were setting on the Stone townhouse.

Jody was standing in the middle of the parlor, practicing the musical scale, her voice loud, vibrant and unselfconscious, until she noticed Li, standing in the doorway. "Don't look at me like that; I'm not deranged. I'm practicing for a songfest with the children. I was a singer once." She paused. "Of course, it wasn't children I sang to."

Li set a vase of flowers he'd been holding on the table. "Miss Jody has a beautiful voice. These flowers came an hour ago, while you were resting. Along with this." He handed her a familiar embossed, white envelope.

Jody immediately opened the envelope. The handwriting, too, was familiar: "Darling, please be safe. The terror of robberies continues. Just last week, my carriage was chased by the Masked Rider. Fortunately, we escaped with only the loss of books, which I had purchased to distract me from thinking of you. Love, Aidan."

Before Jody looked up from the note, Li quietly asked, "Will you be going out tonight?"

"No."

The Houseman stood a moment longer, as if he wanted to or needed to say something more. "Forgive my boldness, Madame, but…"

"But what, Li?"

"From what I am told, among the household servants, he's considered a very decent man."

She looked down at the note, but she knew who Li was referring to.

"You've been very fortunate. Those opposing you will be more watchful, more cunning, and employ greater force."

"I serve a greater good."

"Then preserve it; do not risk it. Goodnight… Zorrita."

Philo Storm walked briskly down the street, stopping only once to read a poster nailed to a lamppost: "Reward – The Masked Rider - Zorrita - $1000.00."

Within the hour, Storm was sitting in the Ralston mansion parlor, conversing with Abigail and Emma. The two women had been anticipating his arrival, but hadn't quite expected the shrewd, smartly dressed, formidable man sitting across from them.

"Your husband hired me because of my reputation in the banking community. Any information you can give me may prove extraordinarily useful."

"I've already told the police exactly what happened," Emma said.

"Please, remember, I'm not a police officer; I'm an investigator. I use clues and information in a different way than the everyday copper."

The women were visibly impressed, wrapped in the excitement of their participation in catching a notorious criminal. "The bandit seems to know our way of life quite well,"

Abigail observed. "He always knows when we're having an event of some kind."

"He probably gets his information from the social calendar in your local paper."

"But he knows where we live. He stops our carriages always at the most isolated places on the route home. Isn't that so, Abigail?"

"Exactly."

Storm stopped to refill his teacup. "Have you a good whiskey for this?"

"Yes, of course." Abigail got up and went to a cabinet.

"Do you think he's one of your own?"

"What do you mean?" Abigail gave Storm's tea a splash of whiskey.

"A confidant."

The two women exchanged a perplexing look. Emma finally answered, "We don't know anyone who steals."

"Put on your thinking caps, ladies. Scrutinize your friends, your servants, social contacts. The evil, like decay, is sometimes among us. As you say, whomever it is, seems to know a good deal about you."

"Yes, indeed," Abigail concurred. "That would make perfect sense."

"We should be more secretive, like J.D."

"She only talks to children, Emma." Storm leaned forward. "J.D. whom?"

"Just a friend from back East. But..." Emma quickly added, "We had a slight falling out. She's marrying one of the richest men in Northern California... We think."

"The point is," Abigail emphasized, "she doesn't need to steal."

"It's just that we know so little about her. Only that she's the deceased Professor Jeremiah Stone's niece."

Abigail turned to Philo Storm. "He was one of our eminent historians."

"I, too, am a student of history. Specifically, of people's lives. One's past is always a map to one's present." Storm raised his cup. "Delicious tea, ladies."

In the Stone library that night, Jody sat at the Professor's desk. She set down her teacup and picked up a pen. "I think of you often, as well," she wrote. "Perhaps the distance between us isn't as great as I once thought."

Chapter 24

Billy stretched his arms and looked around. The fire smoldered. Aedan was gone. A veil of gray light covered the cave entry. He leapt to his feet and raced to the mouth of the cave, shouting into the heavy mist, "El! El!" He looked back to the burnt-out fire. The leather pouches were still beside the stones. The blanket they had slept on was still on the ground.

He raced outside, moving deeper into the mist and forest. Stumbling over rocks, he wished he were wearing his old hiking boots. A few, thin branches scratched his face and mounted his anger. "Damnit!" he shouted, "Where are you, El?"

A small, thin voice traveled uphill towards him. "A'm comin'." The smile on her face was all he needed to see. She was out of breath the last few arduous steps. "Aedan wanted tae eat. Thare wis more on the downhill side he could graze."

"You should have told me!"

"Ye were sleepin'. Dinnae argue. Give me a mornin' kiss." She dropped the reins and eagerly hugged Billy. "Ye have scrapes on yer face." She traced her finger across a thin, red line beneath his eye. "Thare's blood," she said and licked her finger. "Now, high school laddie, we are one."

"Don't leave me again without telling me where you're going. Even if I'm sleeping."

"A'm no going anywhere without ye." She kissed him again.

Aedan pawed the earth and moved ahead of them, as if he had heard enough of their adolescent drivel. The sun broke through the passing clouds but only briefly. It added no warmth to the frigid day, but it gave a special beauty to the surrounding hills, draped in gleaming sheets of snow and ridged, like the sunlit scales of dinosaurs, with great, rose-veined rocks. Billy held the reins. His whole physical being was immersed in this awesome, radiant spectacle of earth and sky. It reached his heart.

"Rein Aedan!" El yelled. "Leuk ahead! Take the road tae the woman with the basket."

The woman, about one hundred yards ahead, was wrapped in a heavy blue shawl. Her dark gray dress reached her ankles, and a white kerchief held back her brown hair. She turned at the approach of hoof beats and shouted in Gaelic.

El shouted back. "She's fearin' we're gonna steal her basket."

Billy stared at the woman's small, frightened eyes. "Tell her we'll pay for the food. We're starving!"

The woman lifted the yellow cloth that covered her goods. El leaned down and threw some coins into the basket, and the woman handed El a thick slice of oatcake. A few more words passed between them and then a smile appeared on the woman's gaunt, wary face. She continued down her muddy path, the braid of her long, brown hair bouncing against the back of her blue shawl.

"What did you tell her that made her smile?"

"We were married in an island kirk this mornin' an' ma great-great-grandmither from China joined the celebration."

"You're getting the hang of high school humor." Billy smiled to himself, as if he had achieved something, and turned Aedan back to the road.

He greedily scarfed down his portion of the oatcake, while El repeated more of what the woman had told her. Laird Kinnaird's estate was the next road on the left. "She said he's got a terrible temper, but the feuar is worse. That's the jimmy who collects the rents. 'Na one goes thare who doesn't have to. But none o' us are welcome anyway. Ye won't see any barns or cottages from the road,' she said."

Billy knew why they were on this road, but he had no idea how this vast, contentious, beautiful land was going to point them to a nine-month-old, stolen child.

He turned onto a muddy, rutted lane and scanned the wind- swept fields for any sign of life, any structure, any smoke curling into the gray sky.

"Where do the people live?"

"Keep going," she insisted, without bothering to answer. Only a few minutes had passed when he stopped the horse.

"Over there," he said, pointing to tracks in the snow-crusted field. "Those look like footprints."

"Follow thaim, Billy." Her voice rushed with excitement. "Take Aedan off the road."

They followed the prints for half the distance of a field that reached to the foot of steep, shale-colored hills. Hoof prints appeared alongside the human markings. "How could the horse just appear? His hooves were pointed in the same direction as the footprints."

El didn't have an answer. "Juist follow," she said. "It's ma world."

At times, where the snow had melted, they worried that they had lost their course. Twice they had to switch back and capture the trail again.

"Billy!" El nearly hopped over him. She was pointing towards a stream of smoke curling alongside a towering pine. A raven soared through the smoke.

"I see it!" Billy abruptly turned from the tracks and kicked Aedan into a full gallop. They passed a barn with a caved-in wall and a flock of sheep nuzzling patches of grass. A dog with brown and white markings chased them. "Cairo," he shouted, as if the dog were an ancestor of his own deceased pet.

There was no house, no castle, or several-storied manor of the kind Billy had seen in history books or on game screens. A man they came upon was tending a huge fire, stoking the flames with pitchforks of rubbish. El called over to him. "The sinn an toir gabhaltach aig a bheil each dubh agus leanabh-gille. Chuala mi gun robh e airson am balach a reic is bha mi ag iarraidh bruidhinn ris."

The man shook his head and turned back to the blazing fire.

"He knows nothin' aboot a tenant wi' a black horse or a laddie. He's juist hired fer the day," she told Billy. "He lives near the water. Thare's a house, he said, past the grove o' white birch. He told me tae talk tae the feuar."

"The feuar? The man with the terrible temper?" "Ay, the man who collects the tenants' rents."

As they came upon the grove, activity around them increased. A tall man, in black trews and jacket, was walking beside a black horse and cart of hay.

Making their way through the grove, Billy saw two men, with pipes in their mouths, herding a half dozen huge, horned, brown cows with hair on their necks.

"Really, are they cows?"

"It's no a sheep, Billy."

Less than a hundred yards ahead they saw a long, white house. To Billy's eye it looked as if three small cottages had been pushed together, like an old motel. The same pitched roof, that hung down to nearly the height of the door, sheltered the dwellings in a continuous line. Three windows faced the dirt road. Smoke rose from one of the two chimneys. A young man, armed with a sword, stepped forward and raised his hand. The stranger's straight blond hair framed an angular face, high cheekbones, and a square jaw. He reminded Billy of a Robin Hood character from a cartoon. But the demanding ring to his voice and the sword at his side kept Billy on guard.

El nudged Billy. "We should get aff Aedan."

She never stopped talking in Gaelic as she dismounted. Billy kept his eyes on the young man, about twenty, Billy's height, but ten or fifteen pounds heavier, Billy guessed, too chunky to be quick enough in a fight. His wrestling instincts were always measuring a foe or stranger. The lad wore a short gray, wool jacket that showed the puffy sleeves of his saffron shirt. His plaid skirt, cinched with a wide black belt, hung to his knees. He walked with a jerky, bow-legged gate, barelegged to his feet, and even they were bare.

"We are tae follow him," El said.

The young man stopped several yards from the house. He said something to El. Then he entered the house and closed the door behind him. For the first time since they began their journey, Billy noticed a hint of anxiety in El's eyes.

"He doesn't know anythin' aboot a black horse or someone sellin` a child."

"Who lives in the house?"

"The feuar."

"Kinnaird?"

"Na. He owns the estate. He lives in a castle. A dinnae know where. The land is given tae him by the Baron, an' the Baron is beholden tae King James the Fifth."

"So the Baron is in the house?"

"Billy, ah juist told ye, according tae the laddie, the feuar lives thare. Are ye this foolish in yer fancy brick school?"

Billy's gaze kept shifting between the house and El. He had never seen her this anxious. "Don't worry," he said. "If no one in the house knows anything about Bran, maybe they can direct us to someone who does. That's what brought us here. You've got to believe that."

For the first time since they began their journey together, it was Billy's voice that carried a comforting assurance. The young man stepped out of the house and waved them forward. Billy hesitated. "What about Aedan?"

"Move on. A stranger would be a fool tae come near Aedan."

Two men, Billy guessed to be in their fifties, were sitting at the corner of a long table. One wore a red and blue shawl draped across his shoulder. The more neatly groomed man had on a heavy, brown vest over a collarless shirt and a saffron scarf tied at his neck. That must be the feuar, Billy thought. Plates of food sat in front of the men. Lanterns were lit against the walls and still another glowed on the table beside the platters. Neither man offered a welcoming word. The glint in their eyes was hard, their mouths turned down into their thick gray beards. The man with the shawl wiped his mouth on a rag, grumbled something and looked over to the young attendant with the sword.

Before El could take a step back, the attendant grabbed El's arms. "Billy," she shouted, "they want tae kill us!"

In one blinding motion Billy drew the attendant's sword from its sheath and ran it up against the side of the young man's head, against his straight blond locks.

"Tell those men I'll kill him if he doesn't let you go. I killed a dozen men in El Paso!"

El blinked and repeated Billy's warning in Gaelic.

Both men seemed perplexed. Their conversation flared into some kind of argument, as they got to their feet.

El turned to Billy, her face drawn with fear. "The feuar is accusin' the other o' sellin` the child an' bringin' this trouble on thaim."

Billy kept the sword steady at the attendant's head.

Instead of tension corroding his nerves, in every particle of his being he felt possessed with a sense of recognition. He was the central, pivotal player in a quest adventure. Everything he had read, every game he had played coalesced in this moment of action and personality. "Ask them who he sold the child to."

El shouted in Gaelic, but before she could finish a sentence, the feuar picked up a knife and stabbed the other man through his vest. As he pulled the knife from the man's chest, his victim spun backwards, tumbling against the chairs, shattering the lantern. The feuar turned to the frightened attendant and shouted an order.

The attendant immediately released El's arms. Still, the Cederburgh boy didn't lower the sword. With its steel blade at the young man's temple, Billy looked over to El. "Ask him again what happened to the child."

El listened to the man in the brown vest spew out his allegations, angrily pounding the table and pointing to his victim.

"This is what he told me." El's voice started to break. "The child wis a boy. He wis abandoned by drunken soldiers near the water. One o' the tenant farmers found him." She reached for Billy's arm. "The man he stabbed at the table had taken the boy from the tenant fer payment. He didnae know what tae do with the laddie. His wife didnae want the trouble of another mouth to feed, so he sold the laddie."

"To who? To who did he sell the boy?" El turned back to the feuar.

He looked to his half-dead victim, who by now had grasped the edge of the table. Before he could upright himself, he stumbled back against the bench.

"Thàinig mallachd air an fhearrann seo ha cheann." The feuar pointed to Billy. "Innis dha an claidheamh ìsleachadh. Ś e mo mhac-sa a tha ha sheasamh an-sin. Èistidh e rium"

El quickly translated. "The man he stabbed has brought a curse upon the land. He wants ye tae put down the sword." She looked over to the terrified boy with the sword at his head. "That laddie is his son."

"First, let the man he stabbed speak, if he can."

"A speak." The wounded man pulled himself up to the bench. "A read the Holy Bible in English. Now A talk."

Despite his heavy accent, Billy caught enough of what the wounded man had said. "Tell us who you sold the baby to."

"An old woman. She lives over the river." He gasped for air and clutched the edge of the table. "God will punish me." His words spilled into a dark, anguished cry.

The feuar turned sharply and thrust his knife into the back of the penitent. A horrible, frightening groan, that seemed to climb the whitewashed walls, rose from the dying man's throat. A woman in a long, brown and straw yellow dress peeked out from a doorway.

"Till thusa," the feuar shouted, pointing his bloody hand at the woman. "Till thusa!" She turned in horror and closed the door behind her.

Billy seemed to merge with the energy of unfolding events. "Tell the guy to go over to the other side of the table." Billy lowered the sword. The young man followed El's instruction and hurried to his father's side.

"Tha e ag innse breugan," the killer screamed. "Chan eil clan aig a' bhoireannach a chionn 's gu bheil i ns bana-bhuidseach! Agus bidh daor-cheannachd again air. Laigh e mallachd air an taigh seo. Mallachd! Agus chan eil again ach a chorp mar dhìol air." He looked to his son. "Innis dhaibh cò am boireannach seo. Innis dhaibh an fhìrinn!"

Billy had no idea what the feuar was shouting, but on the face of the young man he could see that neither did he understand what was being asked of him or what he should say. His mouth was half open. Fear passed through him between his father's crazed eyes and the sword in Billy's hand.

He bumbled the beginning words. Then his voice picked up speed and he talked with his hands tossing about, as if what he was saying needed the urgency of his whole body. El turned to Billy with a look that told him she had just heard an even more unsettling story.

"Since he wis thirteen or fourteen years, the feuar's son has known aboot the old lady who bought the child. She has a beautiful lady friend. Some villagers say it's the daughter o' the witch's sister. Boys would gae to her an' they would bring her gifts, but some boys would leave, an' after, they started to say stupid things or not listen to thair mithers or faithers. Sometimes they would complain o' hearin' noises at night, and cry. That's what the faither wanted his son tae tell me." El took a deep breath. "Men still gae to her house, he said, but sometimes she isn't thare. The old lady is thare. Wrinkled an' bent over. She would tell the visitor she doesn't know where Maeve went."

She turned to the young man. "DÃ¨ an t-ainm a th'oirre, Maeve?"

The young man nodded.

"That's her name," El repeated. "Maeve. He said 'She will know whit's in yer mind. She will put a mallach, a curse, on ye.'"

Billy looked over to the dead man. "Is there anything we can do for him?"

"He sold ma son!" The words, like a shriek, jumped from El's lips, aghast at what Billy was suggesting. "He deserves his death!"

"He's dead but..."

"But whit? Is it any different than the men who stabbed Adelard?" El cried. "They haed no pity on him!"

"But that's not who we are. That's not who I want to become." Billy turned his defiant look from El to the young man. "Tell him to pick up the old man and lay him on the table."

The feuar bent down and helped the boy pick up the corpse and lay it on the table. It was the second time Billy had watched a man die.

"I will make them a trade." Billy glanced over to the closed door at one end of the room.

"Tell that woman we saw to bring us enough food for two days. Put it in a sack. And I'll give back his son the sword."

The feuar listened to El. He nodded and sent his son into the far room.

"The man on the table sold your son to an old witch, El. Take the bloody scarf from around his neck."

Blood was still seeping through the vest and from the back of the corpse's head. El drew back. "Ah canae touch him."

"Tell the feuar to untie the scarf. That white cloth on the table, tell him to wrap the scarf in the cloth and hand it to you."

The old man's hand was still shaking as he handed the bundled scarf to El. The door to the far room opened. Billy raised the sword. The son was carrying a woven sack. The woman in the brown and straw yellow dress peered from a crack in the doorway.

"Put the sack on the table," Billy commanded.

The terrified young man still didn't understand, but El made it clear to him. Once the sack was on the table, she snatched it up. "We're leaving now. Don't open the door until Aedan's tracks are lost in the wind! When we reach the woods, I will leave the sword at the rocks. And remember, I killed a dozen men in El Paso. Let no one follow us!"

For the last time, El translated Billy's words.

They rode past the man loading his cart with hay, past the barn and the men herding the cows. The sky was darkening again, as if the winter sun in Scotland never stayed longer than the time between clouds.

At the edge of the birch grove, Billy raised his arm. He thrust the sword into a mound of snow between the rocks. "May you remain bloodless!" he shouted. "And the snow never melt around you!"

"Ye'r getting guid at oaths 'n' curses, Billy."

He gave Aedan the lead of the reins and crossed the snowy field. They entered the shadowy woods, the quickest way, they were told, to reach the river village. "We must find the woman, Maeve!" he shouted.

"Billy, are ye always this —?"

"This what El? We're looking for your son!" He didn't know if she could hear him or not, but he didn't see the point of her question. Then he felt her lean close to his side.

"No wonder ye win the wrestlin' matches."

The half December moon hadn't yet risen above the trees.

What were once willowy shadows had turned into long stretches of darkness. El raised her voice. "A know ye're doin' this fer me an I love ye fer yer loyalty, bit somethin' in ye has to let go, Billy. Ye fell from the clouds, Ciaran said, to help me. I, maybe, can help ye," she said, "even in the midst o' ma tragedy."

"You don't know me, El. I'm in a strange land and this is the most serious thing I've ever done!"

"Findin' ma son?"

"Yes, that, but..." He pulled his head back. "Even more than that."

"Ye can trust me, Billy. If thare's somethin' ye want tae say, then say it."

"I also need to do what I need to do in my life."

El couldn't see the pain in his eyes. He didn't want to tell her any more than he already had.

Through the branches, Billy glimpsed the slim arch of the moon lost in the trees. He inhaled the forest dampness and the breath of pines.

"Whit is it ye need tae do?"

"Nothing," he shouted. "I don't need to do anything!"

"Whit's it ye need tae do, Billy?" she persisted, clutching his chest, as if she were shaking an answer from a bottle or a drawer.

"I have to..." He caught himself. She was buried in the past, five hundred years ago. He knew he could tell her what he'd never told anyone in his life. The past was a fragment, a wavering piece of cloth, torn from someone's life he would never see again. His secret would be safe. "I have to show my father I'm not afraid of death."

"Because he died?" El couldn't see his face. She couldn't see the deep sadness and pain in his eyes, the tremor on his lips. All she felt was the young man against her fists, and all she wanted was his love. "Because he died, Billy? Was he thinkin' o' ye when he died? Let go, Billy. Let go of yer faither."

The wind swept clumps of snow off the branches, falling in pools of moonlight around them. He never heard the last of her words.

"Ye dinnae need that shadow in yer life."

From their vantage point on the ridge, Billy and El looked past the snow-covered plateau to a wide, moonlit river.

"That's the water we have tae cross, where the laddie said the woman Maeve bides."

"I don't see any sign of a village." No smoke rose above the trees or even a flicker of light along the riverbanks.

"Ay, in the mornin' we will cross," she said.

Billy still held the reins as Aedan guided them on their steep descent. He was feeling more and more confident as a rider, but he let the horse's instincts determine their path. The only signs of life were deep tracks of animals embedded in the vast, moonlit crust. They rode several miles against a bitter wind. Escape from death at the feuar's house had sapped their emotional strength. They were exhausted and hungry. Billy's eyes caught a faint image blending with the skyline. It was hardly visible through the wind driven, swirling snow. Closer, he yelled out, "There's some kind of building ahead!" He was looking at what appeared to be a part of a wall, looming above the pines.

"That's a kirk, Billy. Give Aedan a kick."

Billy remembered that El had told him a kirk was a church, but giving Aedan a kick didn't make the wily horse move any faster. He threaded his way through the trees, unperturbed by the riders' anxieties.

No one was there to greet them when they entered the church ruins, only the wind howling through gaping holes in the stone skeleton of three heavily damaged walls, the tallest of which faced away from the river. It was peaked and riven with lengthy cracks, creating a ghostly presence against the black sky. Piles of stones were strewn through the muddy grounds. Billy and El dismounted. "Look over thare," she said, pointing to low, crumbled walls shaped like a storage container. It was almost hidden, covered with a canopy of branches. "Folk were here afore us."

They walked over to the crude makeshift shelter. Billy pulled off the top branches.

El peered in and jumped back. "Spiders! A hate spiders."

"Just like my little sister," Billy laughed. "We can flush them out with fire." Then his smile faded into a thought that hadn't left his mind since they fled the estate. "First, we have to bury the dead man's scarf."

"Why?" El looked at him as if he had just told her they were going to eat the spiders.

"Who would do it, if not us? Blessing his soul will bring the baby back."

He could see in her eyes that the thought he was crazy hadn't left her. More than once, he'd heard it said, "Like his old man, he'll fuck up." None of the town elders thought Cash Blackwell's son would ever have the discipline to win a wrestling championship or save a child.

He took her hand and together they wandered into a small graveyard behind the church. Rain clouds overhead turned silver as they crossed the moon. Some of the grave crosses were cracked, broken off, or lying, like stark white bones, in the muddy grass. And some were hidden in the shadows of trees.

"El, come over here." Billy was on his knees, poking at the ground with a broken branch. With the stick and a sharp stone, he had already dug a rough, foot-square hole. His fingers clawed at the earth. He felt connected to something that posed as time, earth in his fingers that bent toward the beginnings of life. He didn't understand why the feeling came over him or how it so quickly disappeared when she approached, but he knew he had come to the center of something that was as real as it was ephemeral and had something to do with his own existence, with the boy he was and the man he would become.

"It's only a few inches deep, but, for a moment, I thought I was close to the center of the world." He looked up at his lover. The anger he saw before in her eyes had disappeared. "Drop the scarf into the hole."

El unfolded the white cloth and let the bloody scarf fall. It was clear to her that just as Adelard's burial was somehow attached to her spiritual rite of passage, this was Billy's deed to perform. He covered the scarf with the upturned earth. He got off his knees and stood over the tiny plot. "We bless the soul of the man whose scarf this is." Then, recalling El's prayer at Adelard's grave, he tried to repeat in Gaelic: "Beannachdan Dia dhuit."

He didn't cross himself as El had, but he closed his eyes and repeated the prayer in English. "Blessings of God be with you."

"Ye did well," she said, as they walked, hand in hand, back to the deserted remnants of the church. "Th' Gaelic wis a bit rough, bit the feelin' wis perfect, e'en though A will never forget the man sold ma son." She stopped. "Now, ye've got to gather some wood, while A take Aedan fer food an' water."

Billy gulped down pieces of roasted lamb, slices of cheese, and hunks of barley bread, food they had confiscated at the feuar's house. He and El sat at the blazing fire inside the crumbling walls of the shelter. She had found a pewter mug among the debris. On rocks by the fire, she heated the mug of snow water, flavored with crumbs of barley cake and broken twigs.

"Are you sure this is tea?" he said, lifting the mug to his lips.

"A've no point in killin' ye now, Billy." El leaned her head against his shoulder. "Ye are ma sole protector. One scar on ma face is enough in this life." She cozied herself against him. "Ye're juist what A'm needing, a twenty-first century high school wrestler."

The last word was still on her lips when Aedan let out a wrenching neigh. He crashed his hooves against a stone post, sending sparks flying across the shelter.

It was the same horse's wild neigh Billy had heard the night Adelard came out of the woods. He pushed away from El, drew his dirk, and crawled into the corner of the hovel.

El peered over his shoulder. From behind the short wall, they had a clear view of Aedan and the moonlit grounds. Restlessly, the horse pawed the earth. The trail they had come in on was empty. Billy turned to the stand of Scotch pines that bordered the church grounds.

El whispered, "Look thare."

His eyes fell upon a vision more magnificent, more compelling than any he had seen in any computer game he'd ever played. The white stag stood motionless, silent, between the pines. His coat glowed like a white mast in the moonlight. His branched antlers curved upward and seemed to embrace the world above him and all of its stars. The deer didn't blink.

"What does it mean?"

"It means we can gae ahead."

"Will it stay here all night?"

"Likely no. He is a messenger an' has more folk tae see."

"What should we do?"

"Wait. Ma mither taught me that every animal has a message tae give us. Th' deer is well- known in our stories. It represents knowledge an' victory, but it also means ye must trust yer instincts." She looked into his eyes. "Dae ye know whit instincts are?"

"I fight with my instincts."

"Aye, but dinnae tell the deer. He knows who ye are. The deer is tellin' us somethin' else, somethin' more important than yer rough pride."

Billy turned to the moonlit animal. He could see the unrelenting alertness and deep foretelling in his black, shining eyes. He and El crawled back to the fire. "I hope you heard what he had to say. I was never good at Gaelic deer talk."

"Dae ye think that's funny? Have ye any idea how important this is tae me?" she snapped. "Dae ye have any notion o' how dangerous our journey is?"

"I know what this means to you! How many times do I have to tell you I love you? Doesn't that mean something?" Billy got to his knees and waved off the fire smoke and his teenage bravado. "Doesn't that count in why I'm here? We nearly got killed at the feuar's house. I know how dangerous our journey is! But we don't even know that the child we're chasing is Bran! I don't even know if this is a dream. If you're in my dream, that's all this is!"

"No!" she answered sharply. "A stood in the meadow an' prayed bi the pond. Ye appeared. It's real. Ma baby is alive an' that's real." Tears wet her eyes and she looked away towards the one standing wall. "Dinnae destroy ma belief, Billy. Dinnae take hope from a lassie with nothing tae lose."

He didn't want to reveal all of his doubts about their journey, based on her brother's scrambled report, a murder victim's confession, and a scared, panicked son's crazy talk about a witch and her whore friend. He stepped around the fire and kneeled at her side. "I'm sorry, El." He put his arm around her. "I don't want to ever see you cry. Not here, not anywhere, not even in my dreams."

The fire crackled and sparks jumped into the darkness with his words. Billy raised his eyes past the flames. In the distance, he could see the luminous deer still there.

He awoke to a sky the color of ash. He looked out towards the stand of Scotch pines. El was right. The white deer was gone. Billy kindled the fire and awakened El. They ate quickly. El packed what little food they had left into the woven sack. Billy stamped out the fire with stones. He guided the horse down a steep, rugged hillside. Aedan had gotten used to the boy's touch and his voice urging him on or slowing his gait. In the distance, beyond a wide, muddy expanse of peat bogs and still frozen pools of water, Billy could see the river. Picking his way across the watery terrain, Aedan, too, had no desire to gallop.

"In all o' Scotland," El said, "ye are niver far from water."

A harsh wind howled and blew against their faces, turning lips, cheeks, and eyelids into a frozen mask. El had the protection of Billy as a shield. He could feel her pressing her head against his back. Aedan stopped several yards before the river's rocky shore.

"How do we cross the river?"

"We have tae go further doun, past the waterfall. Maybe then the current will slow an' the water won't be as deep. Tis the only chance we have of findin' the village, Billy."

The waterfall gushed across the rocks in four crystal streams. Gray clouds had turned puffy white, and a strong winter sun finally breached the late morning sky. Billy and El stared down at the riverbed. Rust colored, green, and gray stones showed their faces beneath the shimmering liquid surface and offered the promise of a shallow transit.

"It's not as deep here," El said. "Take Aedan down tae the broken tree, an' we will have a go thare."

Ahead of them, a huge pine tree, felled by lightning or northern winds, sprawled its green branches into the river. Out of the silence, a high-pitched male voice rose, shouted in Gaelic from behind what was left of the tree. A man, no taller than the standing trunk, stepped out from behind it. He was bundled in a padded brown coat and wore high leather-wrapped boots. In his left hand he held a catching net tied to a stick. El pointed across the river and told the man they were going to cross it to the village. In his excited screech, he told El he was trying to catch fish for the Hogmanay feast.

"It comes after Yultid. It's part o' the Yule celebration and the comin' o' the new year," she told Billy. She dismounted from Aedan and walked along the shore to the fallen tree where the man stood. His bearded face cast a bubbly smile that kept Billy at ease.

"Ask him if the river is safe to cross or if it drops off halfway in."

The little man dropped his net and listened intently to El. At times he nodded and sometimes he burst into her speech with his own emphatic voice.

"What's happening, El?"

When she turned back, her face was streaked with fear and despair. "He told me the village is very excited. It's not juist aboot Hogmanay. Thare is a woman in the village named Maeve. The Baron, who owns all o' this land, has vowed tae kill her friend, the witch, unless the old hag brings him a laddie less than a year old before Yule Eve."

Billy quickly got off Aedan and moved towards El. When she turned back, the gray scar on her face had turned violet. "The fisherman says the Baron has a son, an' the woman he is married to canae bear children. He is makin' the laddie a Yultid gift to the two o' them."

"Has anyone seen the boy? What does he look like?" Billy didn't wait for her answer. "He could get any boy less than a year old. He doesn't need the boy the witch has!"

"What mither is gonna give up her son? What woman is gonna take a child torn from his mither's arms an' not feel a curse will be placed on her?" El raised her hands. "But from a witch's arms, o' course she will, to save the child!"

"We don't know that the boy is Bran!"

Aedan neighed, lifting his hoofs high in the air. The little man grabbed his net off the ground and took a frightened step back.

"But if it's Bran," El wailed, as loud as the horse's neigh, "what power dae we have against a witch?"

"We've got to cross the river first. Then we'll know. Follow me." Billy was in full command.

El's voice rang out. "Are ye gonna kiss me before we cross the water?" She was standing with her shoulders down and her fists clenched. "Our kiss will mak' the river safe."

Billy turned around and rushed into her arms. "Safety first, of course!"

"Stay close," she whispered. "The evil is near."

Chapter 25

Except for a series of garish paintings by local artists, the hotel lobby retained its modesty with stuffed furniture and dusty plants.

"Your newspaper, Mr. Storm." The Bell Captain, an eager young man, a few years from twenty, handed the investigator the daily paper.

"Thank you." Philo set down his morning whiskey, leaned back in the stuffed armchair and opened the paper to the "Social-Society" section. Soon, his eye caught the names he had most recently heard in his meeting with Abigail and Emma. "Rich, handsome, Mr. Aidan Campbell of the Campbell Ranch Enterprise has again been seen with Miss J.D. Stone. Is he the mysterious, Scottish angel supplying funds for her new Settlement House project or is cupid simply coming back for more horseplay?" Storm turned to the Bell Captain, "Boy!"

"Yes, sir."

"I've a quarter for you in exchange for the resident address of Miss J.D. Stone. I need it immediately."

Jody sat in a low chair, surrounded by five to seven-year- old children. She sang and led them in a familiar song: "Mary had a little lamb, little lamb, little lamb, Mary had a little lamb whose fleece was white…" The Settlement House children sang along, some with more enthusiasm than those who merely stared out the window or pinched their neighbor's arm. Nearby, in the river waterfront district, a woman in a tight-fitting, revealing dress and cheap, shiny jewelry stopped a man with her smile. Her rouged cheeks and scarlet lips broadcast her trade. She had added several inches to her waist and her facial lined had deepened. But the years hadn't obscured her likeness. Claire Woods, Jody's old friend from her brothel past, approached the man with the briefcase.

"Can I interest you in a cup of ale and a bit of joy?" The man, ignoring her solicitation, continued walking. "You wouldn't know what to do anyway!" she shouted after him.

A moment later, a rough-looking, white man, about thirty- five, stepped out of a doorway. A scar ran down his cheek and his tone was gruff. "Come on; we're wasting our time. There's better pickings in Chinatown."

Clare suddenly stopped. "Trey, wait!" Her eyes were riveted on a woman across the street.

Jody had just stepped out of the Settlement House and was about to get into a waiting Hansom Cab. Claire watched the Cab leave with Jodie. "What's wrong?"

"Nothing, Trey."

"You look like you'e seen a ghost."

"A ghost she was. Wait here."

Trey watched her walk to the Settlement House.

Claire, taking in her surroundings, immediately recognized the need for a more respectable, less aggressive demeanor. As Mr. Powell approached, she forced a congenial smile.

"Can I help you?"

"Yes, thank you. The woman who just left is a dear, old friend. We haven't seen each other in years."

Powell sized up Claire. The Settlement House was in the waterfront district. From Claire's dress and style, he knew full-well her unsavory occupation.

"You've probably mistaken her for someone else. The woman who just left is fairly recent to San Francisco."

"So am I. Jody and I traveled together years ago."

"Miss J.D. Stone is one of our most prominent benefactors.

Her uncle, Jeremiah Stone, was an eminent historian. The family is from Boston."

"You don't say?"

Mr. Powell firmed up his voice. "I've said it clearly enough."

Just as combative, the false sweetness faded from Claire's lips. "Now you listen. I may have more in common with the brats you shelter than them that pays the bills, but you don't nurse a dying tart without remembering her face!"

"I'm afraid you're badly mistaken, on top of which, you're badly mannered. You must leave!" Powell took her arm brusquely, ushering her back to the door.

"You ain't heard the last of me, sir. I've come to this city, too, to make my fortune; and I'll put up a bright, shiny brothel right next store!" She left, slamming the door in his face.

"I've dealt with swindlers and extortionists before!" he shouted, to the empty room.

A warm, summer day merged the colors of green, gold, and brown across the Campbell ranch. Jody stood at the corral fence, feeding a handful of hay to a beautiful, black colt.

"She's been waiting for you almost as long as I have." Aidan Campbell approached and put his arm around Jody. "I've named her *La Regresa*. It means, 'Return' in Spanish."

Together they watched the colt prance around the corral. Jody leaned in against Aidan, feeling his warmth and protection. "So you're Spanish; you're not Scottish like some people say."

"Darling, I work with a lot of Mexican laborers on the ranch. Naturally, I pick up a few Spanish words. Besides, I can't speak Gaelic."

"Not one word?"

"A loue ye."

Jody smiled. "I think I know what that means."

That night a soft breeze rustled the bedroom curtains. Candlelight flickered in a corner of the room as Jody and Aidan made love.

Days later, at the Stone residence, beautiful streaks of metallic silver and gold colored the evening sky. In the Townhouse study, Jody was lighting candles.

"He asked me to marry him, Li." She turned to her Houseman who had become her friend and confidant. "I never allowed myself to be happy. I've felt such regret. But that won't bring my son back, will it? I'm sure the church placed him well."

"As well as you would have done it yourself in your condition." Li spoke confidently, as he moved a chair closer to the table.

"And you believe that?"

"Yes."

Jody smiled, grateful for Li's support, and, at the same time, allowing her to feel the emotional room of a wished-for happiness with Aidan. "

"I can still have a family. Mr. Campbell wants an heir."

Li nodded. "I believe it's time to burn the mask and cape. Zorrita has had her say."

"And this, too. Mr. Campbell went on about his family roots in Scotland. There's a big green tapestry hanging on his dining room wall, with a picture in the center. He told me it was like a family, heraldic crest. Saying *heraldic* is hard enough. so I thought maybe I should know my family roots, like were we always just poor, without a voice in anything? I found a book in Professor Stone's library on ancestors. I looked up McDee, my father's last name and all I found were names like McGee. But then…" She noticed Li's eyes wander towards the windows. "Are you interested in this, at all?"

Li cleared his throat. "Very, Miss Jody." He cleared his throat again. "Ancestry is always interesting. I was sent here as an orphan child and scrambled my way from those settlement houses you visit to the streets of this city to Professor Stone finding me trying to steal his briefcase at a restaurant. He said, if you're that bad at stealing, let me give you a job you can do. I've been in this Townhouse ever since. My roots were washed away in the China Sea."

Jody was humbled by Li's remarks. "I'm so glad Professor Stone recognized your spirit and light." She walked away from the windows. "I'll finish quickly, I promise. It's my mother's maiden name, Morrison, like my uncle, that leads back to Scotland. Not to any castles, mind you, but from the Vikings. It's a Viking name, *Maurice*. And they came to Scotland and then to some island where they were judges." She paused a moment. "I'm a Scottish Viking. If only Danny would someday know he comes from Vikings."

"None of us really know where we come from, except from the stars. We only know where we are and that mystery that includes where we came from." The door chimed, interrupting Li's thoughts. He looked away. "Were you expecting someone, Miss Jody?"

"No."

"Is there anyone you don't want to see?"

"I don't think so. But who could it be towards evening?"

As Li left the study to answer the door, Jody quickly crossed the room to a small oval mirror and primped her hair. Before she had turned from the mirror, Li had returned, announcing the guest. She's an old friend, she says. Her name is Claire."

"Claire…" Jody hadn't gotten the name out of her mouth, when her old friend burst into the room, dressed-up in gaudy finery and bursting with affected charm.

"Well, as I live and breathe, if it isn't my little darling, Jody. You do remember, don't you?"

"Claire…"

Claire opened her arms and stepped forward. "Give us a hug for old times sake." She wrapped her arms around Jody, still totally stunned by the appearance of her old friend.

Just as quickly, Claire stepped back, admiring her one-time brothel mate. "Don't you look lovely. It's as if you died and came back an angel. And brought Heaven down with you, by the looks of things." She cast her envious gaze around the study. Jody's feelings were a confusion of happiness and a faint uneasiness. "Li, please bring a pot of tea for my friend."

"With something a little stronger on the side," Claire added. She turned back with the same swarmy admiration. "And look at you, with servants! Who would have thought the little whore they dumped in the road would one day be ruling as fine a mansion as this."

Claire tossed the word "whore" off casually, but it carried an edge that Jody alertly noted, re-enforcing her uneasiness.

"It's hardly a mansion, Claire. It was really a remarkable circumstance that put me here. Please, sit down."

"These feet could use a rest. You know what walking can do," she winked. Jody took a seat in one of the leather chairs, while Claire flounced herself down on the couch. "Whoever gave you this must have really enjoyed the bedroom banter."

"It wasn't like that, Claire. Professor Stone was like a father to me." She hesitated to say the next words from her mouth. "He taught me to be a lady."

"You can scrub the paint off a whore, Jody, but that don't change the calling. Of course, it's Miss J.D. Stone now, isn't it? No one in San Francisco knows the Jody I knew." She paused and smoothed a crease in her dress. "Not even the man you're going to marry, I expect."

Jody understood what Claire was getting at. Her years in saloons and whore houses had removed any traces of naiveté.

"What did you come here for, Claire? It wasn't to share our past."

"I helped deliver your Danny. I ran to the street and wiped your tears when they took that little boy away. I held your hand as we rode that rotten trail from brothel to brothel. And look what my good deeds got me!" Her voice rose with bitterness. "It's still a stranger's kindness I live on."

"I'm very grateful for what you did. I'll help you in any way I can."

"I'm sure that soothes your conscience. Helping the needy. I don't want charity like you give to those snotty-nosed brats at the Settlement House."

"Please don't speak like that."

"I deserve some of what you have. You'd have been dead or mad were it not for me!"

"I said I would help you, Claire."

The conversation abruptly stopped with the arrival of Li. "The tea is ready, Madame."

"Good enough, Li. Thank you, I'll pour the tea."

Chapter 26

"Pull!" El yelled. She leaned against the horse's mane. "Be a guid horse, Aedan, listen tae Billy."

Billy was trapped waist-high in the ice-cold river's current, pulling on a rope tied to the horse's neck. "He's afraid of something!" Billy shouted. "He keeps trying to turn. He wants to go back!" Billy pointed to the fisherman on the shore behind them. "He's trying to tell us something!"

The little man was shouting in Gaelic, with his fishing pole raised over his head. He was waving the net back and forth, like a mad signal corpsman on an aircraft carrier. El twisted her neck, craning her head against the river spray. When she turned back, Billy was gone. "Billy! Billy!"

In the wake of the waves, Billy's hidden face rose from the water. He was still hanging on to the rope, struggling to keep a semblance of balance.

"Dinnae drown on me!" she yelled.

"I stepped into some kind of sink-hole," he yelled back. "I'm okay!"

"The fisherman says tae turn yer back on Aedan 'n' face th' shore instead o' th' horse, 'n' he told me where tae leave his rope!"

"I was wondering about that just before I almost died!"

"Whit?"

"Nothing!" Billy battled the current, pivoting against the waves so that he was facing the far shore.

"Now pull!" she shouted. "Pull wi' aw yer might!"

The rope crested Billy's shoulder. The horse swished his giant head back and forth. "No, no, no," Aedan seemed to be saying, even as the momentum of his resistance stirred him forward. With each step closer to the riverbank, the current's raging muscle seemed to dissipate. The pressure against Billy's legs weakened. The freezing water level fell below his waist. He sloshed the last few yards, high stepping out of the water until his cuarans were ankle deep in snow.

"Let gae o' the rope," El cried out. She rode Aedan up the incline, dismounted, and set the horse to graze.

"I can't stay in these clothes," Billy chattered. "I'll freeze into ice."

"Then A could keep ye forever. It niver gets too warm in the summer here." She came up to him. "Kiss me," she said. "Ah new ma Billy wis strong enough tae fight a river an' win."

He kissed her, without putting his arms around her. "We're squishy." He grinned, flapping his arms, sending rainbow beads of water over their heads. "And I'll probably die of a cold before I freeze." He looked back across the river. "The little fisherman is gone."

"If he's behind a sprig o' heather, ye canae see him," El laughed. Her laughter was the first moment of lightness warming her face since they left the ruins of the kirk. "The fisherman told me that Aedan sensed an evil force. That's why he kept resistin' ye."

Billy took El's hand. He knew from living with Cairo that animals sense dangers and malevolent forces before they appear to the human eye.

Together, they walked past fallen branches poking through the snow, until they reached a huge boulder where Aedan was nuzzling the wet grass. El told Billy that the "wee man" mentioned he had a brother who lives in a hut not far from the village. "It has a door paintit green, he said, where we can stay."

"What if he doesn't want us?"

"He's no thare. He only uses it when he takes care o' a tenant's sheep i' the spring an' summer." The key, she told Billy, was behind the cottage, "under a broken chair."

"Exactly where my mom keeps our house key." Billy shivered out the last words, as if Gaelic had taken over his speech. His high school sense of humor was lost to the wind. El rode Aedan, following the river trail that led to the village. Billy sat behind, hugging her, hoping the wind would not freeze them together. They passed ramshackle cottages, mostly hidden by trees. The low hanging clouds seemed to be pushing down, crowding out what little sun was left, leaving in its wake a dark, menacing smear across the sky.

"Maybe all the cottages have green doors," Billy worried. "Maybe the fisherman was fooling us or trapping us."

El didn't answer. A minute later she raised her voice. "Can ye see the tree ahead, on yer right, with a stump beside it? Thare's a but-and-ben behind it."

"You mean a motel?" Billy shouted.

Everything the dwarf fisherman had told them rang true. Billy found the key under the broken chair, in back of the cottage with the green door.

Crossing the river, El had stored the leather supply pouch under the padding of her coat. With dry hemp and flint, she started a fire in the fire pit, a circle of stones in the middle of the single cottage room. Billy watched the stream of smoke curl through the fire hole in the thatched roof, feeling fortunate the fisherman's younger brother had left bricks of peat for his chilly spring return.

"His brother's name is Corc, the fisherman said. Blessit tae heaven, Corc." El tossed wood chips on the fire.

"And the fisherman?"

"Earnan," she said, and she blessed him, too. She got to her feet. "Now ye've got tae take off all yer clothes."

"Huh?"

"Dinna look like I took yer phone away. Ye want tae be dry an' warm, don't ye, Billy? Or do ye expect tae sleep like a sheep?" She moved closer to the fire and started stripping off her wet clothes. "How many times have we made love? Ye've seen every part o' ma body naked, juist not all together." She dropped her damp cotton shift to the floor. "It's only a matter o' puttin' all the naked bits intae a whole. Look." She smiled, showing off the curves of her body that caught the firelight's glow. "Ye dae the same," she said.

Billy looked around, as if a ghost or a small animal might be watching. He quickly shed his wet parka, shirt, and river-soaked trews. A feeling rose inside him. It was the expectancy of standing in their nakedness together, as he had never done before with anyone, in any time or place. Only in his teenage mind.

"This is how we came intae the world," she said, placing her hands above the flames.

"I can't believe I was this cold." He stared down. "My feet are blue."

"Be romantic, Billy. Feel the warmth o' the fire."

Their pale bodies glowed with a golden cast. The dog tag hanging at Billy's chest was the only thing he wore. "I have an idea," he said. He took the iPhone from the pocket inside his parka.

"Ye're no gonna try callin' someone now, are ye? A dinnae want ye invitin' a bunch o' folk over."

Billy tapped into an app and held up the phone. "Listen."

El's eyes widened hearing music flow from the tiny speaker.

"It's Neil Young, Harvest Moon."

"Tis beautiful."

"Would you care to dance?"

"Dance? Na? Here?"

"Aye," he said. Reaching out, he took her hand and brought her close so that their naked bodies almost touched. He tried his best, in the cramped space, to move to the music and keep her in step with him.

"A'v niver danced before," she said.

"I never loved before," he said.

Smoke rose through the fire hole. The wind ripped past the shuttered window. "Maybe ye could be romantic, Billy lad." And she kissed him.

They sat on the damp horse blanket eating their last bits of cheese and barley bread. Their clothes, spread out on a table and two chairs, dried at the fire.

"What else did the fisherman tell you?"

"Earnan said tae watch our pockets. Durin' the holidays, he said, some folk take advantage. No everybody has a good heart. He said tae use our instincts."

"Someone else told us that."

"The white deer."

Billy stopped at the sound of the bellicose wind, threatening to tear the shutters off or blow the roof into the sky. He looked around the cramped, shuddering space. "Where are we going to sleep?"

El shot a look to a pile of straw on boards in the dark corner.

"No chance, El. I'd sleep anywhere in the world with you, but that's a rat hotel and a spiders' crib. And who knows what else is in that straw?"

She turned back to Billy with the slightest glimmer of a smile on her face. "Na one knows we are here. Na one in the world."

"Every crawling creature in that straw knows we're here," he whispered. "And so does Earnan."

"Earnan doesnae know we stopped, Billy. Or that we found the key. Na one in the world knows we are here. Na one can hear us or knows we danced or knows how much we love each other. An all we kin hear is the wind."

"You're getting spooky on me."

"A'm feelin' like we are children at the beginning o' the world, like Adam an' Eve we are, an' we two are makin' the world again." She turned her gaze to the blazing fire. "Ye haven't seen the evil A have. Look again." She ran her fingers down the pink scar on her face. "Whan that happens, Billy, ye become a child again. Ye either let yourself die inside or ye open yourself up to all the beauty in the world, all the mysteries in the world, like Adelard comin' out o' the night or the white deer visitin' us. Or you comin' into ma life. For ye dinnae want to see the face o' that evil lurkin' again, even though ye know it's always in the world. So ye look fer whit nature gives us. Ye love the dancin' light on the rocks, the song of birds an' wind` an' the color of fields an' flowers openin' in springtime. Ay, ye prosper with these gifts. Because if ye dinnae open yourself up, ye become old very quickly an' bitter juist as quickly. A never want to see ye old or bitter." She looked up from the fire. "Ye'll promise me, won't ye?"

"Anything. I'll promise you anything."

"No juist anythin'. Ye'll promise me ye won't be bitter when ye get auld."

"Yes." He was mesmerized. He had never met anyone like her, who could put power into words and lead him to a belief he never had.

"Good." The smile that had faded from her gray eyes found its way back. "Mind the promise, Billy.

We won't always be in this cottage at the beginning o' the world an' ye won't always be in Scotland."

He sat naked, cross-legged, in front of the fire, with her head in his lap. She was asleep with her face turned towards the flames, her flowing reddish gold hair cushioned against his genitals. She didn't move.

He could not see her scar, but he knew it was there. She doesn't want me to see it, he thought. It was like an entry, a door for his heart to walk through, to a world of darkness and chaos, of betrayal, violence, and hate. The world his father had died in. Tears he never felt before fell down his cheeks into the strands of her golden hair. He had fought so hard in high school to be a man. He had never let his emotions show and had never let anyone beat him on the mat. With every victory he had proved to his father that he was a worthy son. Now his father was asking him to cry. The fire crackled and sparks of light flew up like a shower of gold around him and the woman asleep on his lap. "Not for me, Billy," he heard his father's voice. "Cry for the world that cannot find its way - and you, my Mighty Son, make it better. I have called you to this journey. I know you are brave and not afraid of death. In a world of darkness, it takes more courage to see and celebrate the grace and beauty of life."

Was it through the wind ripping at the shutters that he heard his father's voice, or did it come, he wondered, just as El's mother's voice had come, from the breath of the fire? His body jerked as he tried to hold back his tears.

El raised her head and opened her eyes. She stared at the flames. "The fire feels guid. Ye've done well keepin' it going. Now, it's yer turn tae sleep." She turned to him and saw his eyes filled with tears. "What's wrong?"

Billy wrapped his arms around her. "Thank you," he said, in a voice that rose above the wind. "Thank you for bringing us to the beginning of my world."

Billy rode Aedan along the river, following a road the width of a wagon's axle that led to the village. It was the kind of morning that reminded Billy of Cederburgh, of the hundreds of times he had crunched through snow to the waiting school bus that headed for Lincoln High. Instead of the bus's exhaust stinging the air, it was the woody scent of smoke from chimneys and fire holes. Cakes of snow clung to the leafless arms of the oaks and boughs of pines. The glistening white terrain was pitted with animal tracks, while hawks pirouetted in the sky above them.

I have called you to this journey. It wasn't his father's voice he heard as he rode the stallion towards the village, but the words still tumbled through his mind. They found a place to live in his heart. He knew that the beginning of the world he had felt at the fire with El was really the beginning of his new-born life. They passed a woman trailed by two children, like little ducks. She wore a long dress, a white bonnet and carried a covered basket. Closer to the village, Billy reigned the horse to let a man cross the road with a flock of sheep. A few fishermen were heading toward small boats resting on the rocks of an icy shore. Billy wasn't lulled into any notion that, in entering the village, they had reached the final resolution of their quest. He knew that the threat of a cunning witch was ahead of them. He understood that El would feel a heartbreaking loss if the child they were pursuing turned out not to be Bran.

He wasn't even sure that the witch had not already secretly given over the child to the Baron, in order to save her own life. No one knew the fate of the unknown child. The street was a vibrant picture of Sixteenth Century village commerce. People bustled in and out of shops, trading goods, chatting and shouting proclamations, none of which Billy understood. He and El passed an open market of canopied stalls. Billy glimpsed bins filled with fish, tubs of cheese, and vegetables. Slabs of meat hung from hooks, along with rabbits, still unskinned, chickens dangling by their feet, and whole hog heads displayed on greasy trays. "It's part o' the Hogmanay celebration," El explained.

The festive atmosphere reminded Billy of a Renaissance Faire he had gone to with his mother and Kaylee four summers ago. The velvety Faire dresses, swirling colors, and abounding music didn't match at all the mostly bearded men and plump women who filled the village lanes. Yet the celebratory Hogmanay mood gave Billy a trace of identification with his own personal history, and the fragrances of different foods were not unlike those that arose from his mother's and Grandma Hill's kitchens on holidays. They passed a blacksmith's shop, where golden flames blazed from a blackened forge harbored in its lean-to structure. A yellow inn, with white shuttered windows, stood out in a lane of cramped, stone-built shops and cottages. As the wide, plank door swung open to people entering and leaving the inn, Billy could hear voices and snatches of song.

"That's a carpenter shop, like ma faither had." El pointed away from the inn to a sign hanging in front of a building with a high- pitched roof.

Villagers cast curious and wary glances at the strange couple riding the sleek brown stallion. Billy managed a friendly smile and could only assume El was doing the same. On his right, he admired the intricate pattern of a stone wall that bordered the river. As they reached the outskirts of the village, heavily forested hills formed a valley passage with the river. Billy could make out a few cottages tucked between the trees, but he could see no trails to reach them. On a rise ahead of them stood an impressive stone building two stories high. A staircase, dusted with snow, curved up one of its sides.

"That's the kirk," El said. "The kirk gets its money from our King James. Now it's Catholic. Who knows whit the future will be?"

"Don't the people have a choice?"

"Ah told ye whit happened tae mah father an' ye saw whit happened to Adelard." In the same breath, she said, "Ride on, Billy," as if she had no patience with his worldly naivete.

The trail disappeared, giving way to vast snowdrift dunes and a desolate, forbidding plane, grayer still with the ebbing light. El hunched up against Billy. "Rein in the horse, Billy!" She shouted again, "Now, look up on that cliff."

He raised his eyes across the river to a formidable castle on the cliff.

"That's the Baron's castle, the man who swore tae murder the witch if she doesnae bring him a son by Yule Evenin'."

A triad of stone buildings, as high as three stories, rose into the twilight. From Billy's view, they seemed to be interconnected, with smoke rising from different chimneys.

In one of the myriad rooms of this towering edifice, Bran might now be crawling around, or sleeping, or cuddled in a barren woman's arms. But is it Bran? Billy wondered again. The question drummed through his mind, raising the stormy dust of doubts. He knew it was useless to tell El that the child the witch was holding might not be Bran. Because if it wasn't her son, then the continued unknown whereabouts of the boy would destroy her. And, in his own mind, without Bran's rescue into the safety of El's arms, Twenty-first Century Billy, the offspring of LuAnn and Cash, the high school- warrior holding the reins, would never be born.

"Mah baby's somewhere near here," El said, as if answering Billy's thoughts. "A can feel ma baby near."

"In the Baron's castle?"

"That ah dinnae know, bit A hear him screamin' ma name."

Chapter 27

C laire leaned back on the couch, making herself more comfortable. She felt she had the upper hand. "I like a bit of a kick in my tea," she said. "You must have some fine Irish whiskey."

Jody went to the cabinet, trying her best not to show any upset at Claire's startling arrival. "Are you living here now?" she asked.

"You might say. I've a man with me. Not the likes of Mr. Aidan Campbell, mind you. It would be a shame were he to find out how many men you've taken to bed." She paused, taking the bottle of whiskey from Jody. "Or that a teller was murdered at the bank you held up."

"It wasn't supposed to happen that way. I've told you before, the man who killed him paid with his own life."

She watched Claire pour a long shot of whiskey into her tea. "Still, no one likes to hear those things about their fiancé. It's all fair, Jody. Fair that you should have gotten this wonderful life. And fair that I should get a return on my good deeds. And my silence."

"I haven't got a great deal of money, Claire. This house was the bulk of the estate."

"Mr. Campbell has plenty of money." Claire got to her feet. "Castles in Scotland, they say, and ranches here. You won't be needing this house once you move to his ranch. Trey and I can live here just fine. It has plenty of rooms for all the girls we'll bring in."

Jody stood up. "I can't let you do that."

"Nonsense. I read the papers. Mr. Campbell is putting in a lot of money for your charities. In a way, he'd be doing the same for my girls. They're just a little older and wear a little less."

Jody had come back from the dead, had robbed the rich and suffered with the poor. She wasn't about to be intimidated. "You were a great friend to me once. I won't let you down, but I can't do more for you than I've offered."

"You will, if you want to save your marriage and the standing you have in this town. You've got until tomorrow to come up with a generous business proposition." She took a step towards the entry and turned. "I'm at the Golden Tides Hotel. I'm sure your stableboy can find it."

"Li is my Houseman and my teacher, not my stable boy."

"And there's more than just me that's looking for you."

"Li, Li!" Jody shouted angrily. "Show our visitor to the door."

The happiness Jody had felt moments before Claire's arrival had turned into a shattered peace. She walked over to the tall windows and pulled back the drape. She could see Clair climb into a carriage and saw in the moonlight the figure of Trey holding the horse's reigns. *Who else is looking for me*, she wondered. Turning back, her eyes met Li, standing in the entry. "That was a visit from my past."

The overcast day threatened rain, and the wind scattered debris across the road. Inside Mr. Powell's office at the Settlement House, the Administrator looked up from the bank note in his hand and across his desk to the man sitting in the chair.

"This is quite generous, Mr. Storm."

Philo Storm smiled agreeably. "The bankers I represent felt it was the least we could do. Of course, it in no way approaches the vast sums of your benefactor, Miss J.D. Stone." Storm leaned forward offering Powell a thin cigar.

"It isn't often I indulge myself like this," Powell said, taking the cigar.

"You must more often," the Investigator remarked, as he offered a light to the Administrator's cigar. "It eases the pressures and enhances the pleasures of the day."

"Yes, Miss Stone, as you suggested, is quite an extraordinary woman. She reads to the children, sings with them, risking her own health at every visit. She knew practically no one when she arrived here. Yet she's been able to raise a veritable fortune for us."

"From whom do you think this largess might have come?"

"We don't know."

"You've never been curious enough to ask?"

"I run a charity, not an investigative agency, Mr. Storm." Powell exhaled a stream of smoke. "If I were to believe everything said about her, I don't think I could take a cent of her money. Just the other day some lady came in off the street. Mind you, if I do say, a tramp, yet she claimed that Miss Stone was one of her own. Can you imagine that?"

"This woman hasn't come back?"

"No, thank Heavens. I had one of my little ones follow her to a hotel down the street. The Golden Tides Hotel. She was with a rough-looking man, the boy said. Of course, to these rascals, with the hard lives they've had, every adult looks suspect."

"Children are often closer to the truth."

Trey brought the match to his thin cigar. He watched Claire and Jody walking towards each other, under an arbor of trees.

"Was it too embarrassing to come to my hotel, dearie?" Claire offered a sarcastic smile. "I can assure you, we've been in worse together."

"I felt this was safer, Claire." Jody, anxious to resolve the awkward, uncomfortable meeting, quickly put forth her offer.

"I have a proposition. Three hundred dollars which I would pay you in two installments over a period of sixty days. I can't get the money faster than that."

"Surely, it doesn't take you sixty days to reach your future husband's ranch. Do you take me for a fool because I don't have a study shelved with books?"

"I can't go to Aidan."

"Why not? He loves you, doesn't he? Can't he forgive a few transgressions by a wayward girl."

"Shut up!" Jody was losing her patience. "I promised I'd help you, Claire, but I won't crawl for you."

"Oh, yes, you will. I want your house, Jody. Like I said, it will make a fine establishment for my business."

"I told you I can't do that. You won't get anything. The man who gave me my life back would never forgive me."

"He's dead."

"His memory isn't. I've got to live with that."

"You've too many memories to live with. Go back to your Settlement House, looking for your Danny in the eyes of all those little criminals." She took a step to leave and turned. "You're a fallen angel, Jody. One thousand dollars, the first of the week. Put it in my hands and you'll never see me again."

Li stood in the bedroom doorway, watching Jody frantically pack. She took a hairbrush, hand mirror, and perfume from the dresser. Then her gaze fell to the gold coin chain she had taken from her dying brother. For a moment, she touched it.

Then, quickly she turned. "Don't tell anyone where I've gone. I've hired a carriage."

"And if that woman comes back..? What should I tell her?"

"She won't come back."

Jody sat alone in a carriage, looking down at the sheaf of papers resting on her lap.

The horses galloped across a wooden bridge, rattling the carriage. The hills were covered with sage, and small purple flowers were beginning to blossom. She wasn't frightened, but anxiety crept through her nerves.

Chapter 28

Returning to the riverfront village, Billy and El led the horse to a dilapidated barn. For a few coins, the buxom woman, wrapped in a long, brown apron, agreed to feed Aedan and stall him until dark, less than an hour away. El refrained from asking the woman about "witches," even though, with an ominous, black patch covering her left eye, there was the chance she might know something about strange or mysterious events.

The two young lovers walked to the white-shuttered, yellow inn they had passed on their arrival. Above the door hung a great wood sign, embedded with a red and gold heraldic emblem, the kind Billy had seen on shields and castle gates in computer games. A babble of conversation, borne on the pungent aroma of ale and roasting meat, attacked his senses as he pulled open the door. They stepped into silence. Every eye at every table in the crowded room turned towards the two strangers.

"Keep walkin'." El grabbed Billy's arm. "They won't know anythin' ye say, so juist walk tae the back." She smiled to the people they passed, greeting them in Gaelic. "Nollaig Beag," she chimed, "Little Christmas."

A handful of men, smoking long pipes, leaned against the back wall. They wore brown vest-jackets over their long-sleeve, saffron shirts and skirts that came to their knees, or tight-fitting trews of the same chalky white Billy was wearing. They chatted and seemed to have no interest in finding a place to sit or, to Billy's relief, in striking up a conversation with him. Some of the men at the tables wore a plaid mantel, a *chlamy* El called it, draped over their shoulder, the kind, Billy recalled, that the feuar who murdered his tenant wore. The women were in long green and white dresses that brushed the plank floor. Wool shawls in reds, blues, and tans covered their shoulders. It was a spirited room of incessant chatter, spiked by loud bursts of gruff and high-pitched laughter.

Except for a boy about twelve, carrying trays of food and pewter mugs, Billy judged that he was the youngest person at the inn. He felt vaguely apprehensive, as if at any moment he might be challenged, or a curtain pulled back to expose his true, Twenty-first Century identity. At the same time, looking across the packed room, lit by more than a dozen lanterns, the boisterous holiday mood fired in him a genuine feeling of connection. *Who would have thought I'd be spending Christmas in Scotland?* He turned back to El. *Or with a Sixteenth Century girlfriend?*

"Now what do we do?"

"We wait until some folk leave an' then we tak their chairs an' order food." One of the men parked at the wall leaned to El. She answered quickly and turned to Billy. "He wanted tae know where we were from an' where ye got yer coat."

"Did you tell him I was trapped in a wormhole?"

"A told ye no to talk. Ye're no that funny," she whispered, "an' no one is gonna get yer silly high school humor.

SAVING MY ANCIENT LIFE

Look!" El pointed Billy towards a table against the far wall. Two women and a man were getting up and making their way toward the front door. A woman, at the same table, had her hand up, waving El and Billy to join her. "We've git a friend," El said, pulling Billy along.

Two men seated alongside the woman on the bench paid no attention until Billy and El reached the table. Finally, they looked up, grumbled a Gaelic greeting, and went back to their food.

"Cò às a tha sibh a' tighinn?" the woman asked, with a bright, engaging smile.

Without revealing the search for her son, El took a seat at the table across from the woman and pulled Billy down on the bench beside her. "An old fisherman telt us the' village has a witch." El looked around. "A hope she's no in the room."

The genial woman slapped the table with a hard laugh. "Everybody calls the old lady a witch. They e'en called me a witch!" She smiled and spoke in a brogue English Billy could understand. "A learned English from the soldiers. Many soldiers cross the river." She shifted her dark eyes to Billy. "Ye learn many things in bed." She leaned back, laughed again, and arched her body. "Dae A look like a witch?"

Her long black hair tied in a loose swirl fell across her shoulder. She was about forty, Billy thought, but could easily pass for several years younger had she been wearing clothes in the style his mother wore. Instead, her striped dress was much like that of the women who surrounded her. And like a few of them, her neckline plunged in a V, to a full, appealing bodice.

"The town is filled wi' gossip an' rumors." She seemed eager to talk, ignoring the two men who shared the table, neither of whom appeared to have any interest in joining the conversation. "The villagers dinnae know what a witch is.

They've niver seen this so-called witch do anythin' magic. All they want tae do is believe in superstitions." She paused and turned her head to the room.

"Look at them, drinkin' an' eatin', fillin' their stomachs an' their heads wi' gossip an' lies." She gave El a sharp look. "A know the old lady ye're lookin' to see if that's whit ye want."

Billy leaned to El's ear. "Ask her what her name is."

"Maeve. They call me Maeve."

El's eyes lit up. "Ye're Maeve?"

"Ay, A am," she answered proudly, leaning forward, pushing her bosom against the edge of the table, "A'm a woman men are attracted to, that's why the real whores in this toun - the pious woman who go tae that kirk on the hill, who bed a man an' marry him just tae have a pittance o' security an' a gaggle o' children under their feet – they call me a whore." She raised her hands and her red nails swooped through the smoky air. "Because their poor husbands, tired o' hearin' their nagging, come tae me in the middle o' the night, when the moon screams at the trees." In almost a whisper, she added, "'Hide their shadows,' the moon says."

"Ye talk tae the moon?"

"A hear the moon cry, ma dear." Maeve's dark eyes blazed with excitement. Again, she let out a vigorous laugh. She snapped her fingers, jeweled with rings, and waved the attendant boy to their table. "Let's eat an' drink! Tis a holiday!"

"A've heard stories o' witches," El said, "but Billy has niver seen one."

"We will see the old lady ye call a witch, but first it's better if we eat somethin'. The climb to her cottage is hard on the legs. Did ye see how steep the hills are?"

Billy nodded, uncertain what the woman wanted, if anything, and why they should listen to her, but he remembered the boy's admonition that Maeve could lead them to a witch who has a child promised to the Baron. Food was a welcome invitation. Neither traveler had eaten since they finished scraps of bread and cheese in the shepherd's shack. And though his lover, El, had her hand covering his own, he was not unmindful of Maeve's voluptuous body. Still his intention, his purpose in finding the witch's captive child, allowed for no diversion of thought.

"'An why is it ye want tae see the old crow," the dark-haired woman asked, casting her gaze directly at Billy.

"Why?" El nervously cleared her throat, not risking the chance for Billy to launch into his high school humor. "We were told she has somethin' we are interested in."

"She has very little, ma dear. She lives on greens an' porridge."

"She doesnae have any children?"

"Ha! A woman her age!" Maeve let out her throaty laugh that sounded more like a cackle. "She can barely hold a candle, let alone a child."

"But folk have said she has a child."

Though Maeve looked up at El with a steady, friendly smile, Billy could see a faint kind of suspicion growing in the whore's eyes. He leaned forward. "If not her, do you know of any child that doesn't have its mother?"

"The old crow told me she is keepin' a child for someone else. No for long. Ye see, it's no her child. She doesnae have a child, as A said, but the child is no well. He's acting crazy, she told me."

"He!" El blurted, grabbing the edge of the table. "Tis a laddie?"

"Ay, but he won't listen tae her."

"He's juist a baby. No e'en a year old."

Maeve held her visitor's imploring look. "A never said he wis no yet a year auld."

"It was the fisherman who told us!" Billy made a forceful effort to squelch Maeve's growing suspicion. "Maybe we didn't quite understand him."

"A've never seen the laddie," Maeve insisted, but she added that, according to the witch, the boy throws things at her, scratches himself, crawls in circles and screams like his foot is caught in a net. 'Somethin's wrong in his head,' the old crow says. 'The laddie will murder himself wi' anger'."

"Murder himself...?" Before the last word had left El's lips, the servant boy plunked down a tray of cheese, oatcakes, and three mugs of ale, putting an end to Maeve's alarming description.

Billy watched their new friend hand the servant boy some coins and brush her long hair to the side. On her neck, just below the ear, Billy caught a glimpse of thin, blue lines etched in her skin. He didn't know what they were or what they meant, but they reminded him of talons, the claw of a bird in pictures he'd seen of eagles and vultures.

"Please, let's enjoy the food," she said, handing mugs of ale to her guests. "Ye're gonna need the energy," she added, setting an oatcake and cheese on Billy's plate.

He took one sip of ale and nearly coughed up the mouthful of his drink. Maeve laughed.

El put her hand on his arm, "Are ye okay?"

"I'm fine," he croaked, blushing and clearing his throat.

El broke off a piece of oatcake, her anxiety reduced to tapping her finger on the crumbs. Her thoughts were no longer at the table, swirling in the fear and terror of seeing a child, her naked child, crawling around in circles, hissing, scratching himself, and screaming. Billy turned his eyes to Maeve who was drinking the ale and seemed not at all disturbed by the grief and anxiety that were slowly drawing the color from El's face. "Bran would niver behave like that," El mumbled to Billy.

"Unless he misses his real mother," he answered in a low voice. "Who wants to grow up with a witch?"

"Dae ye still want tae see the old hag?"

El lifted her head. "We want tae talk tae her."

"'Tis going tae get dark soon." Maeve pushed aside her plate and finished off the ale.

The incessant chatter of the holiday crowd and thick clouds of pipe smoke made Billy even more anxious to breathe in the fresh evening air, cold as it was. "Do you know the way?"

"Ay, A know the way."

Her answer seemed to host a hidden meaning. Billy eased his hand down to the sheath of his dirk.

Standing outside the inn, in the falling darkness, Maeve told her new friends to ride out of town "in the direction o' the kirk. I will have a fire burnin` in front o' the old crow's cottage. That is how ye will find her. A will tell her yer names so that she lets ye in." She pressed Billy's hand warmly and then was gone.

Billy remembered seeing the cottages sequestered in the forested hills they had passed on their way back to the village. "It's not an easy climb," he told El.

"A would climb through the flames o' hell fer ma son," she answered.

The lane was less crowded, as they made their way to Aedan's stall. "Do you trust her?" Billy kept his eyes straight ahead, averting any glances from the people closing their shops.

"She is aw there is tae trust. El's firm voice had lost its edge. She knows where the old lady bides, an' whit she told us aboot Bran is likely true."

"But, like you said, he was never that way with you."

"He wis only two months old when the soldiers took him. An' A'm not a witch."

"But Maeve is." Billy stopped in front of the stable. "I'm sure she's the witch, El. My instinct tells me she is. I told you once, I fight with my instincts."

It had started to snow again. Lanterns, hanging in the arch of the doorway, had been lit. The light fell across El's face. He could still see the strong will in her eyes, but sadness was the veil that surrounded them. "We will know soon enough."

"Wait." He reached out to her arm.

"Whit?"

"Don't you think it's a little weird, that among all those people, the only place we found to sit was next to woman named Maeve? If those guys hadn't gotten up, we might never have found her."

"But they did get up, Billy. Someone wants me tae find ma son." She raised her eyes. "Ma mither, ma fatiher, even God. An' me, Billy, so ye can be born an' A'll have someone from the meadow tae love."

"You're saying none of this has been an accident?"

"Nothin' between us has been an accident, Billy."

She walked over to the stall keeper, glaring at the strangers with her one good eye, waiting for the balance of her fee. El wished her *Nollaig Beag*, paid her, and went back to retrieve Aedan. Billy watched, as she walked down the narrow lane, lit by the glow of lanterns hooked to the stall posts. His eyes followed the frail body in which so often he had felt the storm of love. Now, through the bars of light and shadow, he felt, instead, her shattered nerves and heart bravely fighting off the torrent of fear and struggling for the will to stay intact. And he wondered if the Universe in some kind of mysterious way was maneuvering their lives on planet Earth. He thought back to his bike ride to Steve's. If the snowstorm hadn't hit, he would have arrived sooner. Everything would have synced up to a different time. Perhaps he wouldn't have felt the need to rush. He wouldn't have missed a step jumping on the tires, a step he had never missed. He wouldn't have fallen and would have missed his journey to a Scottish cottage five hundred years in the past. Everything in the Universe, he decided, was connected to a single moment. Or a single voice.

I called you to this journey, he remembered his father's words. And then another voice cracked through the silence.

"Let's gae," she said. "May God be with us."

He mounted Aedan and pulled El up to her perch behind him. They rode out of the village into a moonlit night, darkened by a galley of clouds moving swiftly across the sky from beyond the Baron's castle. But the child, they were certain, just as Maeve had told them, was still safe in the witch's cottage.

Chapter 29

It was late in the day that Jody finally stepped out of the carriage onto the Campbell ranch and into Aidan Campbell's waiting arms. The fading sunlight was not nearly as warm as Aidan's embrace. That evening, with papers spread across the dining room table, Aidan and Jody examined the blueprint plans for the new Settlement House. The mood sparkled with the excitement of a young couple designing their first home.

"Over here," Jody tapped her finger, "are the sleeping quarters. There'll be room enough for fifty children. And two bathrooms at the end of the hall, so the boys and girls each have their own. And five stalls in each of them."

Aidan pointed to a blocked-out area. "And this?"

"An infirmary. Looks small, doesn't it?"

"Let's hope it won't be needed that much." Aidan looked across the table to Jody. "I'm impressed. And did you bring the blueprints for our children, as well?

Jody raised her eyes. "Our children?"

"That's part of the marriage plan, isn't it?" He smiled. "This ranch has had the Campbell name for fifty years and I intend it will for a long time after this."

"Well, then," she said, walking to the end of the table. "We'll have to do something about that, won't we?"

He took her hand. "We're going to be very happy." But he couldn't ignore the faint reserve in her smile. "What are you thinking? Something's on your mind."

"I have something to ask of you. I need some money."

"For the Settlement House?"

"No, Aidan. I promised someone…"

"Who?"

"A friend. One thousand dollars." He let go of her hand, but his eyes never moved. "I understand if it's not forthcoming," she added quickly. "It's a great sum of money. But I have an income, and over time, I can…"

"When do you need it?"

"Now."

"Then you'll have it now."

She saw the deep trust and affection in his eyes, something she had never witnessed before in any man's eyes looking at her.

At nearly the same time, Philo Storm stood across the street and several houses down from the Stone townhouse. He waited behind a band of sycamores. Li, who had just stepped out of the townhouse, had no idea who Philo Storm was or what he looked like. Li's attention was focused on Gibbons who had started his early evening scamper half-way down the street.

Storm's own entry to the townhouse relied on his past investigative skills. He quickly rifled through papers and letters in the study desk and had peeked through four-bedroom doors before he discovered Jody's room. Opening the armoire, his eyes fell upon the long, black shirt, black pants and mask. He stuffed the mask in his jacket pocket. He turned to the dresser. He glossed over perfume bottles, a few ceramic figures, and a Bible. Part of a gold chain hung out of the Bible pages, the same gold chain Jody had taken from her dying brother.

In less than an hour Philo Storm's carriage pulled up in front of the Settlement House. The Administrator greeted him at the door, explaining that he hadn't seen Miss Stone in several days, since she picked up the Settlement plans to show Aidan Campbell.

"But the woman who said all those terrible things about her I did happen to see, unfortunately not under the best circumstances."

The Investigator's curiosity suddenly quickened. "What would you mean by that?"

"I found her drunken in the street, less than a block from here. She muttered the same foul accusations against Miss Stone. She even said she'd grow rich off Miss Stone. But she also seemed quite remorseful, in that drunken way people often express their regrets."

"You say this occurred in the street, outside?"

"Yes, I helped her to her hotel."

"Which hotel would that be?"

Storm knocked hard on the second-floor hotel room door. "Miss Woods! Miss Woods! Open up!" Twice, Storm smashed his shoulder against the door before it flew open. He drew his Colt 455 and entered. An unmade bed jutted out from one corner. A tall, armoire stood next to it. An empty whiskey bottle and two glasses sat on a table in front of the window. A sheet of paper showed a crudely drawn map with "Campbell Ranch" printed at a star. Then Storm's gaze fell to a spot on the floor at the foot of the armoire. There was no mistaking the blood on the floor. He opened the armoire door. Claire Woods was propped up against the back wall. Blood soaked the front of her dress. The empty stare of death was in her eyes.

"The Campbell Ranch!" he shouted to the Hotel Boy, as he raced through the lobby.

"On the old Holdenbrooke Road, past the mail stop!"

"And just between us," Storm shouted back as he pushed open the hotel door. "There's a dead body in room 26B!"

Two drivers sat on the carriage buckboard, ready to start the journey from the Campbell Ranch to San Francisco and Jody's townhouse. Aidan looked up to Jody smiling in the carriage window.

"The money is secure?"

"Don't worry. I'll see you midweek at my home... Our home." She touched her fingers to her lips, in a kiss.

Jody heaved a sigh and leaned back in her seat. "He loves me," she thought. "And I love him."

It was nearing mid-day and Trey was riding hard towards the Campbell ranch, while Philo Storm, on the same Holdenbrooke Road, was racing to thwart another murder. Jody gazed vacantly, lost in thought, and closed her eyes. Her hands rested peacefully on the black leather bag on her lap. The clatter of the carriage horses awakened her to their slower gait, coming to a halt in front of a small, country inn. The carriage door opened, and the driver peeked in. "We're picking up a passenger, Mam. You can come down for a stretch."

A tall woman carrying a valise came out of the inn. She set the valise down and called out, "Kalen! Kalen!" A moment later she saw Jody standing next to the carriage. "The Innkeeper told me we'd be riding with you," she said, approaching Jody. I'm Mrs. Hopper." Her blond hair fell past her shoulders and her smile was embracing.

Jody was pleased that another passenger would be accompanying her. "My pleasure meeting you. Company always makes the journey seem shorter."

"If you don't mind children," Mrs. Hopper said, with a bit of a laugh. "They can make you wish you were already there."

"How many children have you?"

"Just one. My son Kalen."

"Ma!" A boy's voice drew both their looks to the creek alongside the Inn.

The small, lithe boy, with a mop of dark brown hair, held up a wiggly tadpole. "I caught a frog!"

"Put him back, Kalen. The carriage is here!" The boy stood for a moment, not moving, his eyes briefly focused on Jody.

Then he turned back.

"You know how little boys are," Mrs. Hopper said. "They can't keep their hands off anything that moves."

Jody looked back at the empty space where the boy had been.

"Is something wrong, Miss Stone?"

"Nothing."

Back on the road. The carriage kept a brisk pace, as if making up for the lost time stopping at the Inn. Inside the carriage, Mrs. Hopper and Kalen sat together across from Jody. He shifted his brown eyes between her and the big black purse she kept beneath her crossed arms. Mrs. Hopper leaned to Kallen. "Don't stare. You're going to make Miss Stone feel uncomfortable."

"I don't mind the attention from a handsome young man," Jody said, with a smile. "Do you get to San Francisco very often?"

"I've been a few times with my husband. This is Kalen's first trip."

Kalen proudly added, "I'm going to get new boots."

The carriage charged down the forest road. Neither women were aware that ahead of them was a killer and a man trying desperately to prevent the murder.

Kalen had drifted off to sleep, his head resting against his mother, with her arm around him.

"They're worth all the trouble they put you through," Mrs. Hopper said, close to a sigh.

"I want a handful myself," Jody said. "Well, at least, enough to make the kitchen table look full. Does Kalen have brothers and sisters?"

"I can't have children. Kalen was a gift. He was brought to us just before his second birthday."

Stroking his dark, curly hair, as dark as Jody's, Mrs. Hopper drew back the boy's tangled locks. She noticed Jody staring at the red mark on the boy's forehead.

"That's not a sore.," she was quick to explain. "It's a birthmark. They say…"

"He was kissed by an angel."

They both smiled. And Jody took a deep breath. "How did Kalen come to you, if I may ask?"

"Through a patient of my husband. John's a doctor. The man told him a nearby church had taken in a small boy and was looking for a home for the child. We were the lucky ones." She glanced down, making sure Kalen was not awake to overhear the conversation. "He doesn't know he was adopted. You hear terrible stories of abandoned children, half-alive when they find them or ridden with disease. Kalen was perfectly healthy."

The boy stirred. Mrs. Hopper rocked him gently with the rumbling of the carriage. "The church people wouldn't tell us who the mother was. Sometimes, I think it's better I don't know. Then I'd have a picture of her in my head. I'd be thinking what she must be thinking or feeling over all these years." She looked up. "All's he's got is one foot just a little bigger than the other. That's why we're going to San Francisco. His first pair of boots I want specially made, just to fit the difference in his foot size." She glanced out the window. "I sometimes wonder if she knew about his foot."

Mrs. Hopper's words flowed across Jody's mind, but her heart was wrapped around the child an arm's length from her. She could only sit in stunned, heart-wrenching silence, staring at her son.

"I hope my prattling on didn't discomfort you."

"No. He's a beautiful boy... So beautiful." Jody looked out the carriage window, staring blankly at the blur of images that passed before her eyes.

The words hadn't even reached the air when the carriage came to a thunderous halt, jolting Mrs. Hopper, Jody, and Kalen. The carriage driver reined the horses before a pile of boulders blocking the road. Shots rang out. The shotgun driver, reaching for his gun, tumbled into the dusty trail. Inside the carriage, Mrs. Hopper, nearly hysterical, grabbed Kalen to her chest. Jody peered out the carriage window. She saw Trey riding out from behind the boulders. "I want J.D. Stone!" he shouted. The wounded driver on the ground raised his gun. Trey fired back, killing the man before he could return fire. In the turmoil, the driver on the buckboard, having fought through stage hold-ups before, sagely reined the horses around the boulders and whipped them off the road, through the brush.

Shots ripped through the carriage. Mrs. Hopper clung to Kalen. "We're going to die," she cried.

"Get down as low as you can!" Jody ordered. She pushed open the carriage door.

"Miss Stone! Don't!" Mrs. Hopper screamed, with a terrified look.

"Two things I can do quite well, Mrs. Hopper. One's ride; the other's shoot." She swung the door out, shielding herself against the gunfire.

Jody grabbed the carriage rail and pulled herself up and over the top of the carriage, as bullets scorched the air. Then she slid down to the bench, beside the driver, racing the horses through a stretch of curves. Jody grabbed the shotgun at his side. As she shot back at Trey, the driver lost control of the horses' momentum. They crashed through a covey of trees and barreled into the forest, smashing through branches and brush, finally stopping in a small clearing. Jody grabbed the reins and told the driver, "Take the harnesses off the horses!"

She swung down and threw open the carriage door. "Get out!

Hurry!" She reached out to help Mrs. Hopper and Kalen climb down from the carriage. "Follow me." She brought them around to the driver, holding the reins of one of the freed horses.

"Take the horse and follow the river."

"We can't leave you." Mrs. Hopper's terrified look reflected the imminent terror surrounding them and the terror Jody, left alone, was about to engage.

"Take Kalen and go! Please. It's me the bandit wants." "But—"

Jody cut her off. "If you save the boy, you're saving my heart!"

The driver helped Mrs. Hopper mount the horse. He lifted the boy into her arms.

Jody looked over to the boy. "Go. I love you."

As Mrs. Hopper started off towards the river, Kalen looked back. Jody raised a hand of love. Then the horse, the rider, and the boy disappeared into the forest.

Shots rang out, as Jody scrambled back to the carriage. The driver lay dead at the horse's hooves. Jody heard the rustle of leaves, the snap of a twig, a bird's caw.

Her eyes darted from one frightening sound to the next. She picked up the driver's side gun and drew back deeper into the forest. With each step, she heard a waterfall grow louder. A shot ripped past her. She fired back at a quick movement behind the trees. With the next pull of the trigger, she heard the hollow "click" of a spent gun. Jody took another step back and felt the hard, damp surface of the rocks against her back and the crashing sound of the waterfall.

Trey stepped into the clearing, his gun pointed at Jody. "Drop the gun." His lips curled in a grim smile as the gun fell from her hand. "Claire told me you came back from the dead. This time you won't be coming back. You can join her on the other side."

"What do you want?"

"The thousand dollars Claire told me you were getting from Mr. Campbell."

"He wouldn't give me the money."

"You're lying. Start walking back to the carriage. Keep your hands up. One foolish move and there's one less bullet in this chamber."

Jody wasn't sorry if her life was to end on the forest trail. She had seen her son. He was in the care of someone who loved him, and she knew he would grow up to a wonderful life. Flies had started to buzz around the dead driver on the ground. The carriage door hung open, Jody leaned-in to retrieve her black purse. As she turned back, with the purse in her extended hand, her right leg flew up, smashing her boot against the killer's hand, knocking the gun to the ground. She whirled and leg-kicked Trey backwards. "Li is my Master!" she shouted.

Trey scrambled to his feet and pulled a hunting knife from his belt sheath. "There's more than one way of dying." He lunged and swiped the air inches from Jody. She dodged his assault, at the same time, picking up a long branch. Using the branch like a martial-arts baton, with moves she had learned from Li, she sent a blow to Trey's stomach, doubling him up. Another lightning blow to his head knocked him to the ground. He crawled to his gun a few feet away. As he picked it up, a shot rang out. Trey's eyes widened. The gun dropped from his hand. His face hit the earth.

Jody looked into the eyes of Philo Storm. A whisp of smoke rose from the barrel of his gun. "I met a frightened woman with her son, on the road where it crosses the river. She said you saved their lives."

"Who are you?"

"I should be asking that question of you, Jody McDee. I see you fight like the devil, even without a mask." He reached in his pocket and tossed the black mask to her feet.

Jody rode the carriage horse. With Storm at her side, they headed back to town.

"Mr. Powell told me you've been the driving force behind the new Settlement House. He called you his angel. Of course, he doesn't have to know where the money came from."

"It came from those who promised it. I only thought it was fair." She looked over to the Bank Investigator. "What do you want me to do, Mr. Storm?"

As they reached the sunlit hills above the Bay area, they stopped. "I want you to finish the Settlement House. In all my years, I've never set a man or woman free. You know your way into town from here, and I know my way out of town.

Goodbye, Miss Stone." He started to turn and stopped.

He reached in his coat pocket. "I promised your uncle I'd return this when I saw you." He handed her a small brown envelope. Then, he rode off and descended the trail, disappearing into the mountain shadows.

Jody opened the envelope and removed the gold coin chain.

Chapter 30

Billy rode through the night across the frosted plain. He felt El's hands clasped around him, painfully distraught yet desperately hopeful. The pounding of the horse's hooves spoke to him, encouraged him, thrilled him with a life-giving force he'd never felt before. Finally, he was the elemental being he was. As many computer games as Billy had played, moving from one threatening obstacle, one frightening challenge to the next, finally confronting the maniacal nemesis, he knew this was different. This was real time and real lives at stake in a country he felt a kinship with, in a century he believed was his. It was his own life he was saving. He looked across the forested hills, lost in darkness to a moonlight that could not find its way through the chunky canopy of branches and boughs.

"Look ahead!" El shouted.

Far up the hill a faint gleam rose against a thin white column. Closer, Billy realized the flames were lighting the front wall of a cottage. He reined in Aedan and led him to the foot of the hillside.

Billy and El dismounted. "That must be the fire Maeve lit," he said.

El walked over to the horse and whispered to it. Then she took Billy's hand. "He will no gae far. He'll wait fer us."

Billy shifted his gaze to the distant plume of light. "The last time Aedan waited for us, a man was murdered in the feurar's house."

"That's no an omen, Billy, but if it's fer ma baby, A'm ready to do the killin'."

Less than one hundred feet up the hillside, Billy let go of El's hand. They both struggled, crawling under the low branches, around thickets of frosted brambles, over ice and rocks.

"Are you okay?"

"Keep going!" she gasped.

Maeve must know another way of getting up to the cottage she didn't tell us, he thought. *Probably on a broomstick.*

As the trees thinned out, he could see ahead of him a respite from the challenging climb. The dense ground-cover of brambles had been hacked away. The two seekers crawled into a clearing. Flames leapt from a large pit, surrounded by huge, white stones blackened with indecipherable script. Billy got to his feet and helped El up. She wiped tears from her eyes with her bloodied hands. He looked over to the cottage. It was larger than he had envisioned from his constricted, flatland view. The back end ballooned up, as if some kind of makeshift attic had been grafted on to the roof, with one small window looking out on the clearing. But smoke, instead of rising from the chimney, was drifting from the attic window.

"El, something's wrong. Look at that window. Something in that house is on fire."

"Bran, we've got tae get Bran out!" The words rushed in a breath. Billy grabbed her hand. Together, they raced past the raging fire pit to the rounded oak door.

"Maeve!" Billy pounded on the door. "Maeve, there's a fire in your house! Open the door!"

El's eyes fixed on the blue and white silk crescent tacked to a plank. "Billy, look. It's the seal o' the Baron. His soldiers have been here!"

Billy rattled the rusted iron latch. With a blunt, shoulder thrust, he forced the door open.

They entered a small, dark room. Red tapestries, threaded with gold, hung from the walls. A candle burned on a corner table. "Maeve! Witch! Whatever your name, please answ–." His voice stopped short, arrested by the sight of a clothed body in the corner. Billy rushed over to an old woman slumped against the wall. Even in the mask of death, he had never seen a face as menacing. "Maeve… Are you Maeve…? Is Maeve here?" He turned to El. "Bring the candle here?"

"Where's ma son? Is he alive? Ask her where Bran is." The words spilled out in fear.

"Of course, I will. Get the candle!" He looked over to the stairwell. Smoke was pouring into the room and flames scorched the sides of the velvet tapestries.

Billy took the candle and held it near the witch's face. Tendrils of knotted, gray hair hung down her wrinkled cheeks from a skullcap of tangled, snake-like braids. Then he saw the dark lines of the claw etched in her skin, in the same place he had seen them on Maeve's neck.

"The key," she muttered.

"She's saying something, Billy!"

"What key, Maeve?"

Her hand moved slightly against the ripped folds of her dress. Billy pried the bony, ringed fingers back.

"Whit is it, Billy?"

"A key." He drew a silver key from the palm of the witch's bloody hand.

Her eyes stayed closed, but her lips moved slightly. "The Baron's soldiers took the laddie," she gasped, trying to raise her head. "He'll die at the Battle o' Solway, drown in the water Esk."

Billy looked up at El. "Do you know the Battle she's talking about?"

"Na." El shook her head. "A have heard of the River Esk, that is all. Put this on her lips." She scraped snow from her jacket sleeve and handed it to Billy.

"Thay murdered me," Maeve mumbled. "A gave them the laddie and still, they murdered me."

Thick waves of smoke were choking the room. Billy looked over to the rush of flames climbing the tapestries.

"We can't stay here, El. We've got to get out." He turned back to the witch and bathed her lips in the handful of snow. "Should we take you outside?"

"A lived wi' the fire; A will die wi' the flames."

He thought of the feuar's son screaming about her, yet seeing her bloody and disheveled body, as if she were tangled up with death, he felt sad. "Find the laddie or he will die," she gasped, "in an English water twenty years from now."

"We will. We will find him." He stared at her a moment longer. "Bless you, too," he whispered. He got to his feet and took El's hand. "We must go to the Baron's castle."

"Dae ye have the key, Billy? The silver key?"

Billy pulled open the door. "I have it," he said, rushing into the night. "But the Baron's castle probably has a hundred doors."

"It's a witch's key. It will open the door we need."

Aedan stamped and whinnied when he heard El and Billy approach the foot of the hillside. Quickly the pair mounted the great horse, with Billy at the reigns. As they raced across the valley plain, the witch's words drummed through Billy's mind: "Find the laddie or he will die in an English water twenty years from now. That's it! That's what Maeve is telling us. If Bran stays in the Baron's family, he will drown someday at the Battle of Solway, drown in the River Esk, and I and my father will never be born a Blackwell!"

The boy, the girl and the horse, a triumvirate of hope, sped towards the bridge that crossed the river to the cliffs and the Baron's castle.

The thick, iron-studded gate that secured the castle was closed, locked-down to a scruff of grass. At the sound of the hoofbeats, the Gatehouse keeper, dressed in proper, ceremonial Guard attire, emerged from a door beside the gate, with his hand raised.

El quickly explained that she and her rider had rode in great haste from the nearby village to assist the woman caring for a newly arrived child. She introduced Billy as the son of Cairistiona, the famous healer from the village who had been called upon to subdue the distemper and hysteria the child was suffering. El told the Guard that her rider was mute but that she carried with her medication, as well as herbs and healing potions for the child. Billy and El looked up to the candle-lit chambers and halls on the higher floors beyond the gatehouse. They could hear the music and laughter that celebrated the arrival of the child, gifted, as the Guard explained, to the Baron's son and wife by Baron MacanUidhir, himself, to assure the order of succession for many years to come.

From his manner, it was clear that the young gatekeeper had already indulged in some elements of the celebration. He was vastly accommodating and excited to assist in the comforting of the newly arrived child who, it seemed, was taken earlier from the celebration. The child, accompanied by a woman, was resting in one of the tower apartments. El drew one of Alderad's gold coins from a pocket she had sewn inside her jacket. She leaned forward with her arm outstretched. "This is a Yultid present from the healer Cairistiona."

For a moment, the wobbly gatekeeper stared at the gold coin on his palm, having never seen such wealth in his own hand. He told El to thank the healer Cairistiona, although, under the influence of holiday cheer, he made several attempts at pronouncing her name correctly. He stepped aside and allowed them passage through the tall, plank doorway, abutting the heavily fortified gate. "The tower is juist past the courtyard," he told them.

Billy and El rode Aedan across the castle grounds. Passing the moonlit courtyard, they quickly came upon the tower, rising high above the adjacent stone wall. The two riders dismounted. Except for El's quick reassurance and commands to Aedan, they moved in silence to the tower door. With the turn of one silver key, El was about to rest her eyes on her child, the boy who had been abducted by drunken soldiers, sold by a man now dead, imprisoned by a bitter witch and taken, through the act of a violent murder, into the privileged arms of royalty. A Bloody transit to his mother's arms.

The door opened at the turn of the silver key. The hollow sound of a dark, spiral staircase rose in front of them. Billy led the way up the twisting stairwell, lit by burning candles in polished copper sconces. The steps of death were up, he remembered El telling him. They passed a half-opened door. Light spilled into the stairwell, but there was no sound of a screaming baby. Within seconds, a man with shaggy black hair and a black beard came to the door and questioned their presence. El quickly retold the story she had told the gatekeeper. Fortunately, the man had heard of the famous village healer Cairistiona, which freed them to continue their ascent. The Guard shouted to El, "Ceithir oidhirpean eile den staidhre!"

The apartment, she told Billy, was only "Four more turns o' the stairwell."

The door was arched and scarred with the fierce struggles of the castle's history. With more bravado than trepidation, Billy turned the witch's key again. The door opened to a stout woman in a long, blue dressing gown standing straight up, beside her cushioned chair. Her straw-blond hair was half-hidden by a white lace cap, and her guarded look shielded her surprise.

"CÃ² th 'annad?"

El relayed the same story she had told the gatekeeper and had repeated to the Guard, one hundred steps below. Her voice was halting, her eyes constantly darting towards the moaning and crying she knew rose from the heart of her son, hidden from her view by the corner darkness and a silk curtain shielding his bed.

The woman, with what seemed to be genuine maternal concern, nodded and explained in a soft, apologetic voice that she had tried all kinds of cooing, singing, dancing with the boy, already newly christened Toag, but none of her comforting efforts seemed to still the child's unrest. Billy, unable to comprehend any of what the two women were saying, stared at an arrow-slit, a narrow opening in the stone wall across the room. It was wider than most he had seen in castle pictures, and several of the stones around the slit were broken away. He was almost certain he could angle his body through the aperture if trouble arose.

He watched El breathe deeply as she walked into the darkness to retrieve her son. He did not understand what she was saying, but he could hear the love and tears in her voice as she lifted Bran from the bed. She emerged into the candlelit room with Bran secure in the folds of her padded coat. His moaning had stopped. The crying was silenced. His limbs seemed at ease in her arms. In some kind of memory, hidden deep in the metaphysical biology of life, the soul knew he was home.

El explained, with urgency in her voice, that, at the Baron's request, she had to take the baby to the celebration for, once again, all to see, adore and offer a final toast to the good fortune of his son and daughter -in-law. It was the ultimate Yultid gift. When the woman mentioned that she had heard about a murder involved in securing the child, El responded with ignorance, knowing nothing of the circumstances which brought the child to the castle. Instead, she apologized for taking another blanket to keep the child warm. Throughout the conversation, she could not bring herself to iterating Toag, the boy's newly christened name.

It was impossible to know what if any of El's story the attendant nanny believed, but, judging from the look on her face, the moment El picked up Bran and stilled his tantrums, the older woman's instincts told her that Toag was a fiction and that the child was in the arms of its natural mother. Before Billy could open the door, the Guard, from one hundred steps below, stepped in. He was uniformed in crimson and gold and armed with a long sword. And in the same gruff voice Billy had heard him bello only minutes before, the Guard demanded to know Billy's name.

"Go!" Billy exhorted El. "Wait with Aedan under the arrow- slit that's behind the woman. The one with the broken stones. I'll be there soon."

El told the Guard that she was ordered to appear immediately at the Baron's party, but that Billy would explain everything. With Bran bundled against her, she rushed out of the open door.

The Guard turned to Billy and continued shouting in Gaelic. The attendant woman turned to Billy. Judging by the look of concern on her face, narrowing to fear, it was clear that Billy needed to answer the Guard quickly or do something extraordinary in the next few seconds to save his life. Billy assumed the Guard was asking him who he was and how they entered the castle.

"I'm from Cederburgh, Illinois. I came all the way through a wormhole just to meet Elspeth and help her find her son. I should be in school now."

The Guard looked to the woman. "Do you understand what he's saying?" he demanded in Gaelic, as Billy moved closer to the broken arrow-slit.

The woman answered in a stern Gaelic voice.

The Guard nodded, keeping one eye on her, and shooting threatening glances towards Billy, who, by now, had one hand on the broken arrow-slit. "Stop!" the Guard drew his sword and shouted in Gaelic.

At the same time, Billy swung one leg over the casement. "I must return to the people I love." He lifted himself up, shimmying himself through the narrow opening, as the Guard, screaming more Gaelic threats and curses, charged across the room.

From below, El waited, with Bran cradled against her. She sat astride Aedan and watched Billy grab one of the thick vines that clung to the tower wall. She heard the clash of the Guard's sword futilely striking the stone aperture, as Billy, hand over hand, shimmied down the frozen vine.

"Stop, on orders of King James and the Baron MacanUidhir!" The Gaelic roar crossed the frozen night.

Billy swiftly mounted Aedan and turned the horse back, galloping across the royal grounds, past the corral and the courtyard to the gate house. El clutched the sides of Billy's parka with her fists, with Bran snuggled in her padded coat. Abruptly awakened from sleep as Aedan and his passengers thundered to a stop, the gatekeeper jumped to attention and greeted the silent rider and the village healer's assistant.

"Aye," she said to the Gatekeeper in Gaelic. "We are finishit here. The Baron is very happy with the herbs an' medication."

Sleepy-eyed, the Gatekeeper yawned and opened the gatehouse door.

Snow filled the night sky, as bells rang from the castle towers. El wasn't sure whether the bells were an urgent signal of alarm or the still jubilant celebration of the Baron's

Yuletide gift. She glanced back to see the Castle Gate opening, and she knew it wasn't a gift the horsemen were bringing her. Still, she knew in her heart that all the Baron's horses would never catch up to the speed of Aedan and the direction, into the darkness, the horse had chosen.

Chapter 31

Aidan stared at the two gold coin necklaces in his hand. He was deeply grateful that Jody had survived the near fatal encounter with Trey and just as astounded by the story of her life she had just recounted.

"Now you know everything," she said. "from a Viking whore with a half-breed son." A doorbell chimed. Jody looked up at Aidan with a "who could that be?" look. She stepped out of the study into the entry hall.

Li stood at the open doorway. He turned to Jody. "Mrs. Hopper. She says she knows you."

Two conflicting feelings grabbed at Jody's heart: the longing to see her son once more and the resulting loss that again was inevitable. "Please, let her in."

"She's with a boy."

"Yes."

"I understand." In Li's look, in his downward glance, it was clear that Jody's mumbling words when the Houseman had brought her back from death had something to do with the boy standing with Mrs. Hopper. Li turned back and welcomed them in.

"We're on our way home; the carriage is waiting." Mrs. Hopper spoke quickly. "But I couldn't leave without thanking you a thousand times over. You saved our lives." She glanced downward. "And Kalen wanted to show you his new boots. He insisted."

Jody's eyes turned to the boy, to his shiny, brown leather boots. Then she met his gaze, holding his look as if it were an embrace shadowed by time but never forgotten. "They're so beautiful," she said.

"We'll never forget you," Mrs. Hopper said.

"Nor I you."

Mrs. Hopper took Kalen's hand and started down the path. Jody called out, "Mrs. Hopper! Someday... you'll come back."

Mrs. Hopper answered with a nod, as if the meaning of the request and all its underlying history were somehow understood. Watching the carriage ride off, a song from Jody's past rose to her lips. Softly, she hummed: "In many of the worlds I've searched for you... Many are the nights I think of you... Many are the days you fill my heart... In many of my dreams you are the starring part..." The carriage disappeared at the curve of the tree-shaded road.

Jody turned back to Li, standing in the hallway. "You saved my life that I might see him again."

"Nothing in life is accidental, Miss Jody. The past will always be a part of you."

Chapter 32

Billy had done what he swore he would do. His youthful bravado, "I have never lost a match," showed itself to be true. The lost child was back in the arms of the teenage mother. Billy mindlessly tapped his fingers on the wood table and his boot on the slate floor. He felt a creeping loss, a hollowness, inside him. "It's over, isn't it?"

She didn't answer. El got up from the table and walked over to the hearth. There, in a little bed, beside the stones, she put down Bran. She looked over to Billy. "Ciaran will take ye tae the place where ye fell from the clouds."

Billy understood, even though his heart was shaking with a loneliness he couldn't control, with a voice louder than the winds through the Highland trees.

"Ye gave me a gift," she said, "ma son. This is ma gift tae ye, Billy Blackwell. Many times ye told me ye were a wrestler. Bit yer greatest challenge won't be who ye fight."

In the hazy shaft of morning light, El walked toward him and took his hand.

"Everything ye've done with me is real in ye. What ye felt in ma arms. What ye felt fightin' the forces of evil. Everything," she said. "Dinnae let anybody ever take the feelings away from ye. That is yer greatest challenge. The feeling to believe who ye are. Ye are the dream an' the dreamer. A never want to see ye old or bitter. Billy saved Bran so Billy could have a life in five hundred years." El put her hands on his arms. "Dae ye hear me?"

He wrapped her in his arms. He kissed her with the passion of a boy who had found his manhood on a mythical journey in the snowbound hills of centuries past. "Everything lastin'," she whispered, "is written on the heart."

Ciaran led him down the road. Billy looked back only once.

Puffs of smoke rose from the chimney of the little cottage, half hidden by trees and overshadowed by the great boulder on its side. "Billy!" Ciaran called out. Billy turned. Above him, a great black raven circled in the white sky. "Adelard, protect her!" Billy shouted.

Step by step, Billy walked in Aedan's hoof prints. He felt the sun on his face, but his body felt colder. They were walking into a wind that brought with it a mist. The shadows of clouds covered him. He shoved his hands into his pockets. "Ciaran!" He looked to his side. "Ciaran?" The Scottish boy waved an arm and heaved a snowball into the air.

Billy smiled. He watched the white sphere scale the air, finally reaching a branch of the tallest tree, where it broke apart, scattering a veil of silver flakes. Billy looked around. Ciaran was gone. The glittering light of the snowflakes vanished. The Cederburgh boy touched the metal dog tag and walked into the clouds of an eternal silence.

Chapter 33

The Bay fog had lifted, leaving the noon day sun to shine on the beautiful, new Settlement House that sprawled across a city lot, far enough from the waterfront bars, seedy hotels and criminal designs. On the dais, in the reception hall, Jody and Aidan sat together with a few members of the church. Mr. Gordon Powell waited a moment for the invited guests to settle before he stood up and walked to the lectern. He looked out on the modest gathering, clearly, by their dress, suggesting an abundance of wealth. The Settlement Director began with a great, embracing smile.

"It is my great honor to introduce to you the two people most responsible for this remarkable new facility, Miss J.D. Stone and Mr. Aidan Campbell."

As Jody and Aidan stepped up to the podium, the audience applause, loudly enthusiastic, was mixed with a dabble of respectful clapping from Abigail and Emma, seated together.

"I wish to thank all of you for your generous support and contributions," Jody said, with a deeply felt care. "And we do mean all of you, even in ways you'll never know." She let her smile linger, offering a bit of mystery.

Led by Mr. Powell, the audience stood and applauded. The children's choir, to the right of the lectern, began singing "Amazing Grace."

Jody sat in the shaman's room, slowly opening her eyes. The crescendo of applause and children's voices lingered through her mind, as she looked over to the burning candle and incense streaming from the marble figure of Our Lady of Guadalupe. Her eyes slowly focused on the shaman's smile, her red lips, coal black eyes and the wrinkles that surrounded them, until her figure came to life.

"You're back; you have come back."

"Where was I?"

"Only you can answer that." The shaman lifted her head. Her straight, black hair fell back against her shoulders. "Are you who you think you are?"

LuAnn hesitated. "That was me. I think it was me."

"You're certain? I don't want you to be confused."

"It wasn't my name. And my hair isn't that dark. Not as dark as Jody's. That's it!" Her face lit with a smile. "That was her name, Jody. She was beautiful." LuAnn brought her hand to her heart. "Here, in her heart. That's where she was beautiful."

"Have you ever been told that?"

"No." She hesitated. "I think that I'm loved. My kids love me. But because I'm their mother. Cash, that was my husband, never told me I was beautiful. Not until he went away. He fought in Iraq. Then he wrote me letters and said he loved me and I was beautiful, but he died before we could live our lives together again."

"Never wait for someone to say you are beautiful. You are. I see it in your soul."

"And I remember a boy, a little boy... and an old man reaching out to help me. He had books."

"He is your wisdom guide."

"And the boy must be love."

"They will be your guides, love and wisdom, in your lifetime."

"Are we making this up? Does everyone who comes here get the same gun-fight-whore-house journey?"

"You only get one journey, and it is always into your soul, my dear. Everyone has a different journey." Tia Luisa leaned forward. "That is why you were brought here. To know that you are la luz, the light. You met a part of yourself you never knew existed. She was noble. She grabbed her destiny. She gave up her love, her son, that he might go on to find his own destiny, just as Billy, the lost boy who is not lost, is finding his soul. Jody is a part of you - in your heart and every nerve - you must never forget that. As the poet Hafiz said, "You are the light."

Chapter 34

Billy crawled out of the tire hole. A security light cast a thin ray in the warehouse darkness. His head felt muddled, but he knew where he was and what he had to do. Not wanting to set off the alarm, he found the key to a small, wooden side door. He left the warehouse. The showroom was dark. He started walking in the direction of home. It took him a few blocks to realize that the reason he was walking was because he didn't have his bike. "Maybe it's in the showroom. I'll get it tomorrow."

It was cold, but it wasn't snowing. Signs and storefronts that at first appeared blurry were coming into sharper focus. Headlights of passing cars seemed to be saying, "Wake up, Billy, wake up," prying his mind from a misty past. Christmas window decorations and store window displays grounded him in the familiar present. Each token of the material world tumbled like ocean waves into his awareness. Seeing his reflection in a storefront window, he cupped a handful of snow and wiped away smudges of tire marks from his forehead. His pace quickened. He turned off the busy thoroughfare onto the silence of residential streets. He recognized every house, every bus stop, every corner mailbox. He was hoping he would see someone he knew or had talked to once or twice in his past, but no one sat on their porch in freezing weather or strolled the icy sidewalks.

Holiday lights, glowing around windows and trimmed rooftops, were like bells in his head, joining the metallic sound of wind-swept silver bells that decorated some of the porches and gates. He had no idea how much time had passed, but he knew he'd never gotten home this late from work.

He texted LuAnn: "Be home in less than..." The phone went dead. *Ciaran wouldn't have been happy about that. The journey is over.*

Driving back from Aunt Luisa's house, LuAnn was singing, "I am the light. I got the chops. I got me some lovin' and love never stops..." Her jaw dropped. The music from her lips stopped. Ahead of her she saw a boy's figure walking along a path between the snowbanks. The team jacket was his. Slowly she drove up alongside her son. She buttoned down the window. "Billy! Billy!"

He looked over. Before he even saw her face, he recognized the car. "Mom!"

He pulled open the car door and got in.

"Billy, thank God you're coming home. Where've you been?" "A long story, Mom. I can't start talking about it now but someday I will. What day is it?"

"Wednesday. You've been missing for two nights."

LuAnn drove away from the curb. "Steve called, He said you left your bike at the store and the door left open."

"I'll get back to him, get the bike and I'll think of something." Billy picked up the paper bag at his feet. "What's in the bag?"

"Oh, just a candle and some tissues."

"You drove out in a snowstorm to buy a candle?"

"Sometimes you need the light." Tears wet her eyes. "Someone told me you were on a sacred journey."

"Well... I did meet a wonderful girl, a woman really. She was your age..."

LuAnn glanced over. "Billy I'm thirty-three years old."

"I mean, the same age, when you had me."

"And so, you've been with her all this time, and you didn't call?"

"I couldn't, Mom. Like I said, someday I'll explain." He leaned his head back. "But maybe some things are unexplainable."

LuAnn kept her eyes on the road. "A sacred journey with a girl." The glimmer of a smile lit her eyes. "Some things are like that... unexplainable." She steered the Chevy up the Blackwell driveway. "You're back for Christmas. Kaylee will be out of her mind to see you. She was so worried."

"It's Yuletide, Mom. I learned that. All the way back to the Vikings."

"Vikings, of course." LuAnn parked and set the brake. "We're definitely Vikings, Billy."

Billy slept deeper and longer than he had ever slept. It wasn't the snowplow that awakened him or Kaylee's periodic peeking into his room. It was the quiet knock on his bedroom door. "Billy, it's going on eleven," LuAnn said.

He rolled over. "I'm almost there, Mom. I'll be up in a minute." He clasped his hands under his head and leaned back on the pillow. He thought of calling Justin and getting together with his wrestling team later in the day. He had no idea what he would say to them or to Coach Anderson. He knew he had to say something, and it had to make sense. Or did it? Could he mention wormholes, or Scotland, or saving his own life five hundred years ago? Or tell them that he fell, dazed and disoriented, and wandered about in the winter storm? And he would enrich the story in each retelling. "Oh yeah, now I remember this," he would say.

And they would stare wide-eyed and believe him, because he was the best wrestler in the school.

He saw the snow falling outside his window and he thought of the snow falling outside the small, square cottage window where he first saw the silver threads of a Scottish dawn and darkness fall into a Highland night. He heard Kaylee's footsteps running down the hallway, and through that same hallway, he smelled the fragrance of toast and coffee from the kitchen. And like a channel to his past, he smiled at the thought of rabbit stew and the grainy soup he had learned to love. His gaze wandered for a moment to the dresser across from him, where the trophies he had won stood like small golden statues guarding the picture of his father. And then he heard his voice.

"I have called you to this journey."

Billy answered softly, "And so I went."

Nothing was left of the world he had visited. But everything, the icy rivers, the luminous deer, the raven's cry, the horse's eyes, the dirk's point, and El's kiss would always be there, just as she had told him, written across his heart.

LuAnn lit the candle in the living room window and thanked Tia Luisa. And she wondered, is time any different for any of us, going back and forth through the worlds in our minds and in our hearts, searching for the truth of who we really are? Of where we have been and where we are going? And aren't we all entrusted to save our own lives...

The End

Acknowledgments

Kathy Luber – My wife and soulmate, for
her divine patience and support

My sisters, Rochelle and Sandra, for
their loving encouragement

Aaron Brewer and the Support Staff at
Palmetto Publishing, with a special thanks
to my Project Manager, Sophia Pike.

Natalie Bates – Author, playwright, for her timeless
encouragement

Sharon Paice MacLeod – who gave
the book its Scottish flair.

About the Author

Ken Luber attended the renowned Writers Workshop at the University of Iowa, after having graduated from Ripon College. In his early years, he travelled around the world, mostly hitchhiking and studying the world cultures. Ken received a Writer/Director Fellowship at the American Film Institute and has written and directed for film, television, and theatre. His feature film "Howzer" was shown at the New American Director Series at the Whitney Museum in New York City and distributed by Warner Bros. Ken's recent young-adult time-travel novel, "The Sun Jumpers," won the publisher's Award of Literary Excellence, and has been optioned by a major animation studio for a TV series. "Esperanza: the Musical of Hope," for which he wrote the book and lyrics, music composed by Saverio Rapezzi, had its full-production, world premiere at Mt. San Jacinto College. For several years he wrote, directed, and produced On-Air promotional material for CBS-TV and directed the "Tony Randall Show." Born in Wisconsin, Ken has worked as a house painter, pizza maker, door-to-door vacuum cleaner salesman, and ESL teacher. He has a son and daughter, and now lives with his artist-writer wife Kathleen, in Southern California.

CHECK OUT KEN LUBER'S OTHER BOOKS!

Milton Keynes UK
Ingram Content Group UK Ltd.
UKHW010643020624
443357UK00002B/14